Somebody's Baby

Somebody's Baby

◇   ◇   ◇   ◇   ◇   ◇   ◇

Claire Harrison

 Doubleday

NEW YORK   LONDON   TORONTO   SYDNEY   AUCKLAND

All of the characters in this book are fictitious,
and any resemblance to actual persons, living or dead,
is purely coincidental.

PUBLISHED BY DOUBLEDAY
a division of Bantam Doubleday Dell Publishing Group, Inc.
666 Fifth Avenue, New York, New York 10103

DOUBLEDAY and the portrayal of an anchor with a dolphin
are trademarks of Doubleday, a division of
Bantam Doubleday Dell Publishing Group, Inc.

Library of Congress Cataloging-in-Publication Data

Harrison, Claire.
  Somebody's baby / Claire Harrison. — 1st ed.
    p.   cm.
  ISBN 0-385-26087-3
  I. Title.
PR9199.3.H3467S65   1989
813'.54—dc19   88-31467
                                            CIP

Canadian Cataloguing in Publication Data

Harrison, Claire.
  Somebody's baby

ISBN 0-385-26087-3

I. Title.

PS3558.A797S65   1989   813'.54   C89-093780-X

Designed by Ann Gold

To Dinah, who listened; to Roy, who advised
To Lisa and Becky, who made it possible
And especially to John, who cared most of all

"When you yourself had borne a child, Kristin, methought you would understand," her mother had said once. Now she understood that her mother's heart had been scored deep with memories of her daughter, memories of thoughts for her child from the time it was unborn and from all the years a child remembers nothing of, memories of fear and hope and dreams that children never know have been dreamed for them, until their own time comes to fear and hope and dream in secret. . . .
 —Sigrid Undset,
  Kristin Lavransdatter:
  Volume III, The Cross

Somebody's
Baby

1

◇ ◇ ◇ The nail-biting should have been the first sign to Nora Beeme that something was wrong. Her daughter Christine had given up that nervous habit when she'd discovered the wonders of Revlon nail shades. But Nora didn't notice, because she wasn't thinking about Christine. Nor was she able to keep her attention on her husband Marty's careful laying out of the week's events for the benefit of their children. Recently, she had found that the weekly Family Management Sessions made her lustful. Her mind strayed into secret sexual fantasies. Sometimes Marty was in them; sometimes he wasn't. Some had black men in them; some had women. Nora enjoyed them all.

"Nora, are you with us?"

Nora dragged herself out of the clutches of a male dancer who was wearing nothing more than a red G-string and a black mask, his skin oiled, his muscles hard. "I'm sorry. What were you saying?"

"I was saying," Marty said patiently, "that Danny is going to have to figure out how he's getting from Scouts to choir practice on Thursday night. We have a concert then, don't we?"

Marty could never have been a male dancer. Nora mentally auditioned him, encasing his heavy genitals in a G-string. She pranced him around the living room and flexed the muscles in his narrow shoulders. He looked absurd. He was too tall, too thin and too hairy, covered in a mat of dark curls that blanketed his chest, the backs of his hands and long fingers, his legs from ankle to groin. But then perfect bodies were for fantasies. Marty's was a warm and fuzzy reality that was as familiar to Nora in all its curves and crevices as her own. Besides, he couldn't dance worth a damn. His size thirteen feet had tripped over Nora's toes so many times that she had given up trying to teach him.

"Yes," she said. "The Mozart."

"I thought so."

Marty, she saw, was in his pompous mode. Nora had decided on her twentieth wedding anniversary that she found this an endearing quality rather than an irritating one. This gentle pomposity was a new development, acquired since he'd gone from research into management at Devlin Electronics, and layered on top of an already calm and rational temperament. He now made pronouncements, and spoke with his fingers pressed together and held just below his chin. Sometimes the fingers pushed his square chin into a deep, professorial wrinkle. When he also furrowed his wide brow, Nora thought she could see the man he'd be at eighty: still handsome because of the good bones, but totally bald then instead of with thinning, salt-sprinkled curls. Long cheeks with lines etched deeply down them. Eyes still dark and intent below the arched eyebrows that gave him a look of always being faintly surprised.

"Well, Danny?"

Nora knew that the children hated these sessions. They constantly shifted position on the couch. They spoke only when spoken to. They looked everywhere except at their parents. Christine, who was fifteen, rubbed her shoes against the pile of the carpet and looked extremely bored, a configuration of facial muscles that she had honed to a fine art. Danny, eleven, wiggled, put his sneakered feet on the glass coffee table, remembered that he wasn't supposed to, and lifted them again. Then, for no particular reason, he pressed his face into a throw pillow and blew a drum roll of rude noises.

"You're so disgusting," Christine said, while Nora sighed and added, "Danny, stop that."

"Well," Marty said patiently.

Danny lifted his head. In looks he resembled Nora. He had her blond, unruly, straight hair and a small duplicate of her straight nose. His face, like hers, was a round smoothness that brought itself to a point at the chin. Although he was a slob and a terrible whiner, he was, in the secret recesses of her heart, Nora's favorite child. She loved his freckles, his skinny, flaky knees and his dirty fingernails. She wasn't sure why she loved him best. Was it the resemblance? The ease with which he'd been born? Or was it because he had been such a placid baby, riding solemnly on her hip, smiling serenely at the world? As compared to Christine, that is, whose birth had been long and painful and who had walked early, her pudgy fingers quickly finding their way into every forbidden corner of the house.

"I think there might not be any choir practice."

"You don't remember?"

"Well, Billy wasn't sure. He said he thought there was, but he wasn't sure."

"Why are we depending on Billy for this vital bit of information? Why don't you have the facts?"

"Uh, I guess I wasn't listening."

"I guess not."

"Could Mom call the church tomorrow?"

Her son, the choirboy. Nora came from a Jewish background; Marty from a Protestant one. Neither of them attended any place of worship or considered themselves even faintly religious, but Danny had wanted to go to church ever since his friend, Billy, had joined the Fairfax Presbyterian Church Choir. The minister, Reverend Bracken, hadn't seemed to mind that the rest of the family weren't churchgoers or that Danny had no particular interest in anything ecclesiastical other than the music. "A nice boy," he'd told Nora when she'd come to pick him up from a practice, "with a very nice voice." From which Nora had deduced that entry into the choir had very little to do with religious fervour and a great deal to do with the high turnover in boy sopranos.

"You're going to do the phoning, young man."

Danny squirmed harder. "Can't Mom do it?"

"No, it's your responsibility."

Danny threw an imploring glance at Nora, who looked impassive and disinterested. Of course, she would end up phoning, but she and Marty were in full agreement concerning the benefits that could accrue from a brief stint of childhood misery.

"Please, Mom. Please."

"No."

"M-o-o-m. Please."

"The answer is no."

"She-it." This was supposed to be said under his breath but was clearly audible, a challenging verbal swagger.

"I beg your pardon," Marty said coldly.

"Sorry, Dad."

Marty now turned his attention to Christine. "I've noticed a small problem with your room again."

"Large," Nora said. "I had to wade through the debris to find her dresser."

"Yeah," Danny said, cheerful now that his moment in the spotlight was over. "Her room's a mess. A real garbage dump."

"Danny," Marty said warningly.

Christine ignored them all, studying the tips of her pink sneakers and chewing on her thumbnail, her braces glinting in the lamplight. She had the prettiness of the Beeme women; a narrow face with small, delicate features, hazel-brown eyes, and thick brown hair that had recently been permed and cut to chin level so that she had a vaguely exotic, Egyptian air. Nora tried to remember if she'd had, at fifteen, the same ability as her daughter to absorb words and deaden them so completely. Christine had once been a somber little girl with a sweet smile whose face displayed every emotion. Now, she was a murky pool with a deceptively calm surface. Words dropped in and left no ripples.

During the Family Management Sessions, her expression never deviated from that polite but oh-please-give-me-a-break look.

Christine was also fastidious, in a way Nora had never been and never would be. Her eyes were always carefully made up, her fingernails and toenails polished, her clothes neat and smooth. This was possibly the only miracle Nora would witness in her lifetime. Her daughter emerged every morning, like a phoenix rising, from the piles of books and papers, the half-filled cups and empty candy bar wrappers, the crumpled blouses, skirts and pants, the wads of soiled underpants and bras—as perfect as if she'd stepped out of one of the ads from the *Seventeen* magazines that she read so avidly.

"Don't you think," Marty said, "that your room had something to do with failing your French test?"

"Oh, Daddy."

"No, I mean it. If your surroundings are disorganized, your brain can't be far behind."

"Actually," Christine said. "I keep it on a leash so it's never too far away."

Nora and Danny laughed and Marty, who hated distractions, said, "All right. Very funny."

"Everybody failed that test. It was really hard."

Nora said, "Good grades are important. Think about college."

Marty said, "I don't care about everybody."

Christine gave Marty an annoyed look. "Why do you always say that? I bet you took a parents' training course before I was born and had to repeat it a million times."

"Only five hundred," Marty said, "but I'm a quick learner. Now, what are you going to do about your room? It seems to have reached a new depth of depravity this week."

Christine shrugged. "I guess I'll clean it."

When Marty had suggested the Family Management Sessions as an alternative to pitched battles and sibling rivalry, Nora hadn't been convinced that a family could be run like a corporate division. But the gatherings in the living room had a tone of surprising civility, and had proved to be a genteel and often humorous way to air grievances and differences. Maybe it was because the children knew Marty really meant business when he called them to order. Maybe it was because they hated the sessions and would agree to anything to end them. But Nora had an uneasy inkling that the sessions worked because she couldn't scream her lungs out while seated on one of the blue wing chairs, her feet comfortably raised on the ottoman, the family cat, Marzipan, curled warmly on her knees. Instead, she tended to mild smiles and hot fantasies.

"Now," Marty said, "let me sum this up. Nora, you have a dentist appointment on Friday afternoon, which means you'll be late coming home, and you'd like the children to have the table set and dinner started when you arrive."

"I hate the way Christine makes hamburgers," Danny said. "She puts in onions, and they're so gross."

Christine said, "Shut up, jerk."

Marty went on. "Danny will find out the schedule regarding choir practice. Christine will have her room cleaned by Tuesday. By the way, will that young love-struck gentleman—what was his name, Jay?—the one with the guitar permanently attached to his right hand, be hanging around here on Friday again?"

Christine made a face. "Come on, Daddy."

"Well, I have been tripping over him frequently."

"We're friends."

"She kissed him once," Danny said, looking triumphant. "I saw it."

Christine gave Danny a withering look. "It was on the cheek, you spying creep."

"Okay, okay," Marty said. "There, I think that's about everything. Nora?"

"I've got nothing to add."

"Okay. What about you, Christine?" Marty bestowed on his daughter his most tender smile. Nora knew that Christine was his favorite child, and he was her favorite parent. She had smiled at him first, had walked to him first, had said "Daddy" long before she'd verbally acknowledged Nora's existence. When Christine was little, she and Marty used to have whispering sessions together, secrets that they kept and giggled over. And even now, long after she had given up sitting on Nora's lap, she still liked to cuddle next to Marty when he was reading the newspaper or watching TV.

"Christine, are you with us? Is there anything you'd like to add or subtract?"

Christine had bitten her thumbnail down to a ragged edge and was now working on her left pinky, but once again Nora didn't notice. She was plotting the strategy of making love to Marty that evening before the eleven o'clock news. That was always the cutoff point, because she was too tired by then and Marty was addicted to the news at night. She was thinking along these lines: Danny will probably go to bed at nine, and when he's asleep, he's dead to the world. Then there was Christine. She had an unfortunate way of wandering around the house before she went to bed, coming into Nora and Marty's bedroom to chat and going into their bathroom where she fooled around with Nora's cosmetics and perfume. On the other hand, she did have an English test on Monday and might be convinced that she'd better stay in her room and study. That left Nora's mother, who called on Sunday nights regular as clockwork.

Nora was trying to remember the last time she and Marty had had spontaneous sex since that weekend they'd taken in New York, when Christine gave another sullen shrug of her shoulders and said, "I think I'm going to have a baby."

Nora might have sexual fantasies, but her business partner lived them. Joanne White had three children, ran a Girl Scout troop, fund-raised for the Women's Hospital Auxiliary and averaged, over the twenty-one years of her married life, .39 affairs per annum. She insisted that this rate was necessary to the survival of her marriage, which Nora envisioned as a rocky landscape frequented by tornadoes and hurricanes. Whereas she and Marty rarely argued, Joanne and Grant were rarely at peace. They fought over the children, house-decorating, money, vacations, and sexual positions. They screamed at one another and slammed doors so that their huge mock-Tudor house shook. When a fight grew to unmanageable proportions, Grant would withdraw into his law practice and his stamp collection, while Joanne would spend secret afternoons at the Aurora Motel, ten miles south on Highway 312.

("That silent treatment gets to me," Joanne had once explained. "Grant looks so triumphant when he's pulling it off. He has this horrible smirk on his face, as if he's knows something I don't, as if he's won a big point somewhere. It drives me crazy. I just have to get back at him."

"But what," Nora had wanted to know, "is the point of revenge if Grant doesn't know about it?"

"I know about it. That's good enough.")

Joanne did not, on first glance, look like an adulteress. Second glance either. She had the anonymity of a grocery store shopper. She was a big, solid woman, taller than Nora, with a heavy bone structure and flesh to go with it. Her features were broad and Slavic, and her hair was a gray-streaked brown that she parted on the side and wore straight to her chin. She was the sort of woman who required longer association for her beauty to become obvious. Over the years, Nora had slowly become aware of the intriguing way in which Joanne's blue eyes drooped at the outer edges, and the seductive quality of her smooth, creamy skin.

She had met Joanne at college, where they'd both been studying early childhood education. They hadn't been particular friends in school, but had, coincidentally, each landed their first job in the Fairfax school system. Joanne was already married then to Grant, who was in his first year at a law firm, and they lived in a small, cramped apartment, where Nora met Marty after a noisy, smoky, marijuana-scented party in 1968. In those days, Joanne wore wide headbands and long caftans. She had just had Matthew and nursed him in public, defiantly unzipping her caftan and releasing a large, creamy breast that was bigger than the baby's head. To Nora, who had suffered if her nipples showed despite the layers of sweater and bra, Joanne had been both shocking and exhilarating.

In time, each of them had come to the separate discovery

that, although they liked children, they hated teaching. Joanne quit after Nina, her second child, was born; Nora a year later when she was pregnant with Christine. Wailing babies and squabbling two-year-olds brought them together with the sort of bonding that is usually only acquired by soldiers under fire. They carpooled, babysat for one another, had the same pediatrician, and shared a chicken pox epidemic. As their friendship grew stronger, they began to talk about opening a store together, an enterprise that wasn't entirely pie-in-the-sky, because the village of Fairfax itself was really nothing more than a crossroads surrounded by suburban tracts. It had only an Exxon gas station, a post office housed in a joke of a drugstore and a fly-infested corner grocery which they patronized only in emergencies—when they ran out of beer, for example, or Pampers or Tampax.

Opportunity presented itself through a combination of circumstances. A speculator, smelling the scent of suburban dollars with nowhere to go, decided to build a shopping mall between Fairfax and the nearby town of Burtonville; Nora's aunt, forgotten in a nursing home, died and surprised her with a bequest; and the youngest child of the two families, Patrick, Joanne's third and unplanned baby, entered first grade. Grant, whose law firm was in on the land sale for the shopping mall, brought the idea up at a dinner, and all of a sudden the hours spent speculating over innumerable coffees, the idle talk while children napped, and the wishful thinking between washerloads of diapers became a sudden reality. Nora and Joanne opened a modestly successful store that reflected what they knew best: The Kids' Place, filled with well-designed toys, charming books, educational games and adorable clothing.

"So that's what happened," Nora was saying as she and Joanne sipped coffee in the back room of The Kids' Place, waiting for 10 A.M. when the shopping mall opened. They sat on folding chairs surrounded by unopened boxes and crates, piles of invoices and sales slips, and rolls of ribbon, gift wrap and corrugated cardboard.

Joanne took a deep breath. "Jesus."

"She dropped it on us, just like a bomb."

"But—Christine. She's such a sensible kid."

"Since when?"

"Since she was born. Remember how she used to make Matthew look both ways before he crossed the street? When he was five and she was only three?"

"We were so stunned that we just sat there, all of us, and then—you won't believe this—Danny sat up and said in a horrified whisper, 'You mean you did it with a boy?' "

"Oh, God, leave it to Danny. He always did like to have everything down pat."

"At least I now know we're getting our money's worth out of Grade Six Sex Ed."

Joanne touched Nora's hand. "Oh, Nora."

"I just wish she hadn't told us when Danny was there."

"Well, why did she? I'd have thought she'd wait and tell you in private."

Nora gave an unhappy sigh. "I suppose she felt safer telling us that way. You see, no one's allowed to get angry at one of the sessions. It's one of Marty's cardinal rules."

"Well, if it's any comfort, I think you should consider it a compliment she told you at all."

"Meaning there's a bright side to this?"

"Meaning the kid could have kept her mouth shut and had an abortion and you'd never know a thing. Isn't it better that you're talking to one another?"

Nora tried to envision Christine making that lonely decision and going through an abortion on her own. "She couldn't have done it," she said with a little shudder. "She always ends up telling us things. Sometimes in her own sweet time. Sometimes we have to pry it out of her. But we usually find out. But still— Danny. He's upset now, and the whole neighborhood's going to know."

"Can't you swear him to secrecy?"

"Danny? He's got the biggest mouth on Cedarview Crescent."

Danny's notoriety had begun at age five, when he'd been

unable to keep to himself the recently learned truth about Santa Claus. He had divulged the secret at a neighborhood Christmas party when a hired Saint Nick had arrived with three elves to hand out presents. Nora would never forget the way in which he'd stood up before the assembled crowd of excited children, and fired with revelatory zeal, had announced in a high, piping voice that Santa Claus was really a daddy with a pillow for a stomach and a make-believe beard. A dead silence had followed; then a sob had been heard as little Katie Hough broke down. Parents had rushed in to save the moment, and Danny had been quickly whisked away, but his reputation had been cemented for all time.

"What about Marty?" Joanne asked. "How did he take it?"

Nora thought of Marty and the way his body had stiffened and rocked backward at Christine's words, as if he'd been hit. Nora herself hadn't budged; she'd just felt an odd lightness that was almost immediately overtaken by a thick, heavy sensation that seeped painfully into her head.

"You know Marty, he's taking the rational approach. That she may just be late. That we need all the facts first. She's going in for a urine test today."

"How late is she?"

"Three weeks, but she's irregular anyway."

"What about the boy? What's his name—Jay?"

"It isn't Jay."

"Uh-oh, the plot thickens."

"It's someone that she met at a party—a college boy who crashed with some friends."

Information on the party had slowly been released in the days following the Family Management Session. There had been no parents present, a fact fuzzily concealed by Christine when she'd told Nora of the invitation. There had also been beer in the refrigerator and whiskey in the cupboard. These details had been leaked to the older sister of one of the invitees, who'd arrived with several friends and a lot more beer. The friends, college boys, had made use of their seniority to cut a swath through the high school girls, and Christine, who'd drunk the first gin and tonic of her life, had been willingly seduced by one of them.

Joanne's watch beeped ten, and they both stood up. "Well, thank heavens," Joanne said, "that we're not living in the fifties and sixties any more. Remember what that was like? Remember the fear? The Fate Worse Than Death? Oh God, did I ever tell you about the time my period was six days late—my first year in college? Those were six of the most awful days of my life. Nothing has quite surpassed them since." She shook her head at the memory. "At least, if Christine's pregnant, you can get her an abortion and be done with it."

"Yes," Nora said, and as she followed Joanne out of the drab back office and into the bright, fluorescent-lit showroom, she suddenly understood what that odd lightness had been: the release of her adult self, a dizzying slip back in time, a hovering over the image of herself at fifteen. 1961. That had been the year that she and her best friend, Stacey Epstein, had intensely discussed sex and every ramification of it that their limited imaginations could envision. Although neither of them had yet been French-kissed, both had thrilled and shuddered at the image of themselves as fallen women.

("You mustn't let anyone get inside. Not for even one second."

"You can't get pregnant from just one second."

"Yes, you can. Suppose he couldn't control himself."

"He'd have to get out real quick."

"But if there was one little drop . . ."

"I don't believe it."

"It's true!"

"Suppose it happened, how would you tell your parents?"

A dramatic trying out of the words: "Mom . . . Dad . . . I think I'm going to have a baby."

"My father would kill me."

"Mine wouldn't have to—I'd just die anyway."

"Oh, God, wouldn't it be awful?")

That odd, dizzy lightness. Déjà vu.

It wasn't every mother, Nora was thinking, who would have the experience of taking her daughter to the orthodontist and obstetrician all in the same afternoon. Since both Dr. Miller and Dr. Roya had offices in the Burtonville Medical Center, she found herself sitting next to several pre- and barely post-pubescent teenagers with glittering mouths one minute, and several fully-blown pregnant women the next. Dr. Miller had in his waiting room a glass case of orthodontic trophies: anonymous plaster casts of before and after occlusions. Dr. Roya had a large bulletin board with photographs of babies she'd delivered, colored snapshots of bald heads and tiny pear-shaped faces, with notes attached: "With many thanks from Sasha, 8 lbs. 15 oz., and her happy parents."

Dr. Roya also had a table covered with booklets about pregnancy and delivery. There was one on nutrition, with a photo of a smiling mother-to-be. There was another on stages of pregnancy, with delicate drawings of open-sesame abdomens and upside-down fetuses. Neither Nora nor Christine picked up any of these. Christine was sitting very still, her ankles crossed, her hands clasped together. She was a vision in innocent pink, dressed in pale pink stirrup pants and a too-large pink blouse, clasped at the waist by a pink belt. Her hoop earrings were a shade of hot pink exactly matched by her lipstick and the laces in her sneakers. Her nails, needless to say, coordinated.

On the other hand, the mother of the pregnant teenager had not been able to coordinate anything that morning. She had forgotten to put on lipstick; she had been unable to find the blue heels that matched her blue suit. Ever since Christine's blood test had come back positive, Nora had had the feeling that her sense of being in control was an illusion—as if the solid rock on which she were sitting, queen-of-the-mountain-style, was in reality covered with a cobweb of cracks and about to fall into rubble. The rock, of course, was her family, and from her mother-perch Nora had always carefully surveyed its nooks and crannies, checking for unexpected scratches, wear and tear, erosion. As long as she could see in every direction, she had thought she and Marty and the children would be safe. She hadn't realized that the rock was subject to silent, internal movements that would make her perch tremble so she had to hold on for dear life.

The door to Dr. Roya's office opened, and another pregnant

woman walked in, her abdomen ballooned out in front of her. Nora glanced at her and then quickly looked away. That sense of precarious hold was ridiculous—wasn't it? Nothing had actually changed in the Beeme household. This morning, for instance, Marty had kissed her good-bye, picked up his briefcase and gone off to work. She had sipped at her coffee while reading the New York *Times*. Christine and Danny had argued over who could read the back of the Cheerios box while they ate their cereal. And nothing *would* change, because she and Marty were in firm agreement over what they considered best for Christine. She was young, she had her whole future ahead of her, in this modern day and age there was no need for any girl to have to bear a baby she didn't want. They said these things to one another, and just in case their daughter had some foolish, romantic notion about babies, Nora said them to Christine.

At first Nora had been reassured by the fact that Christine appeared to be disinterested in any aspect of the abortion other than the physical. She had said, "Will it hurt?" and made the screwed-up face of her childhood when she'd had to take a dose of medicine ("Will it taste bad?") and "When will I be able to go home?" ("When can I go out and play?"). But after that Nora noticed that Christine was in a state of sullen and heavy anger. This state was no longer unusual for her. The serious little girl with the flashing, sweet smile had yielded to an adolescent of erratic mood swings. This change had arrived like unwanted luggage along with her breasts and menstrual period, and like the latter was cyclical and frequently marked by an extreme irritability. The latest bout, however, seemed worse than usual, and Nora became convinced that Christine was brooding over the abortion.

"She's upset," Nora said to Marty the evening before the appointment with Dr. Roya. They were sitting in the living room, reading the newspaper. "I can tell."

"Uh-huh."

"She's not the type to come out and say it, you know. She's not articulate about stuff like that."

"Mmmm."

"But she's just been awful. She threw a fit today because

Danny borrowed her garbage pail. It was almost World War Three."

Mumble.

"Marty, are you listening?"

His head was still behind the newspaper. "I'm listening."

"Well, what do you think?"

He lowered the paper and looked at her over his glasses. "Am I supposed to come up with a definitive statement?"

"She's so unhappy."

"She'll get over it."

"Marty, these things aren't as simple as you make them out to be."

"So go talk to her."

"I was wondering if *you* wanted to go and talk to her." She gave him a pleading look. "She relates a lot better to you lately than she does to me."

"Good try, Nora." He lifted the paper again, and Nora acknowledged defeat. Marty had always shied away from talking to the children about issues that involved sex.

She found Christine in her bedroom, sitting on the floor in an oasis surrounded by strewn clothes with the cat, Marzipan, in her lap and Walkman headphones on her ears. Nora tried to ignore the crumpled clothing, but no matter where she looked there was a tangle of belongings, odd conjunctions of items that juxtaposed the past and present into an unholy mess. She glanced and then looked quickly away from the white-and-gold-streaked dresser, which she had laboriously hand-finished several years ago. It was covered with perfume bottles, lipstick rolls and pens scattered like pick-up sticks, a jumble of bracelets, mismatched earrings, a miniature family of china collies, a lariat Christine had made in camp five summers before and a picture of herself at one year of age, naked except for a diaper and grinning like a maniac as she lifted an ice cream cone to her already smeared mouth.

Nora repressed an overwhelming urge to nag, sat down on the edge of the unmade bed as Christine pulled the earphones off, and concentrated on her daughter's face, which was dotted with a brown, slightly green-tinted cream.

"What is that stuff?"

"Zit medicine."

"Honey, you hardly have any."

"Mom, I have thousands." Christine lifted up her bangs. "I'm crawling with them."

"All right, you have thousands. Maybe even a million."

Christine sighed and gave Marzipan a long stroke down his gray and white back. "Okay," she said. "Lay the trip on me."

"The trip?"

"The 'how come you have to resort to two-year-old behavior when your brother's around?' trip."

It was hard not to be angry at that perfect mimicking of her own irritable voice, but Nora tried. "It's not just the fight with Danny," she said evenly. "It's also the stamping around and the slamming of doors and the mean remarks and the general lack of friendly cooperation."

Christine didn't say anything, but leaned over and buried her face in Marzipan's ruff.

Nora proceeded carefully. "I'm willing to understand that some of this behavior may have to do with going to see Dr. Roya tomorrow and having to have an abortion. I'm sure you're scared. But you can't blame Daddy and me for wishing that you'd talk it out rather than expressing it in— What? Christine, you're mumbling. Maybe the cat can hear you, but I can't."

Christine lifted her head slightly. "It's not all that stuff."

"It isn't?"

The dark, curly hair shivered as Christine shook her head.

"Are you worried about how Daddy and I feel?"

"No."

Nora sat back and looked at the shelves of toys that Christine had outgrown but still refused to give away: two teddy bears and other stuffed animals, a collection of World Dolls, a complete and well-worn set of Laura Ingalls Wilder books. "So what is it then?" she said lightly, thinking that if it wasn't the abortion, then it had to be something manageable, easy, innocuous. "Just generally rotten teenage behavior?"

Christine raised her head, and there were tears in her eyes. "I saw him at the shopping mall."

"Saw who?" Nora asked in bewilderment.

"Him. He acted as if he didn't even know who I was." The tears were there, but Christine's back was straight and her chin very firm. "He just glanced at me. And then he looked away."

Nora suddenly understood and felt an unexpected rush of pain, as if Christine's words had tapped a reservoir of feelings she'd long ago forgotten. She remembered the agonies she'd endured the day she'd found out that Andrew Stone, her college lover, had secretly been going out with someone else. She remembered the agonizing aftermath of her only one-night stand, when the stranger whom she'd slept with on the last evening of a teachers' conference had not called her, despite sweeping post-coital promises that at twenty-one she'd been naive enough to believe.

It wasn't physically possible to have one's heart break, but as Nora looked at her daughter's vulnerable face with its freckles and braces and dots of cream, hers felt as if it had come close.

"Oh, honey," she said, "I know how you must feel."

"You'd think he'd remember me, wouldn't you? I mean he picked me out from all the other girls."

"Things can happen at parties that—"

"He said I was different."

"There was a lot of alcohol at that party."

"He said I was really pretty."

"He was drinking, Christine. He might not remember anything he said."

"Oh, Mom." The chin was trembling now. "It was so horrible, and I was . . . so . . . humiliated."

"Mom? Mom, I'm scared."

The whisper brought Nora back to the cheerful waiting room with its hum of muzak and the wall mosaic of baby faces. The controlled vision in pink that she'd brought with her had dissolved. Christine had gone very pale. Nora took one of Christine's hands; it was cold and clammy. "Dr. Roya isn't going to do the abortion now," she whispered back.

"I know."

"She's just going to check and make sure everything is all right before setting up an appointment for you."

"It's going to be horrible."

"She's very nice," Nora said. "You'll like her."

"I think I'm going to throw up."

Nora looked at her in alarm. "Really throw up, or just feeling like it?"

Christine gave an experimental swallow. "I think—just feeling like it. Maybe."

"Would it make you feel better if I went in with you?"

Christine nodded, so Nora later found herself perched on a stool by the examining table, making idle chatter with Dr. Roya, who was young and breezy, about the vagaries of the spring weather (". . . cooler than usual . . . so much rain . . .") while the doctor had two fingers up her daughter's vagina and a palm pressed on her abdomen. The casual atmosphere worked, because Christine slowly relaxed, her grip easing on Nora's hand. Nora should have relaxed, too. Dr. Roya acted as if she examined pregnant fifteen-year-olds every day, and maybe she did. She was gentle and explained everything to Christine before touching her.

Nora should have relaxed, but she couldn't. Even though she had the satisfaction of knowing that she was in the process of tidying things up, the tension remained. As she and Dr. Roya chatted across Christine's bent knees, Nora felt her smile grow ever more false, until her lips trembled from their effort to stay in place and the small muscles at the corner of her mouth began to ache.

Marty always paced when he was relating something to Nora that upset him. It didn't matter that he was stark naked and the curtain hadn't been drawn in the bedroom. He walked back and forth on a line in the pattern of the blue-and-white Chinese rug, the lenses of his glasses glinting in the light, his hands making angry stabs in the air.

"So, of course, Bariskofsky is trying his damndest to make sure that I have to report to him. It's a power play, only he has the subtlety of an elephant. He told McAllister that Marketing should have been involved right at the beginning. At the beginning! As if he knew the first thing about R & D. Well, I told McAllister what I thought about that—having those guys poking their noses in our business, telling us what to do. How the hell do they expect innovation with a system like that?"

Nora had never really understood what Marty did between the time that he left in the morning and came back at night. Oh, she understood the larger framework. Devlin Electronics was a defense contractor, and Marty was involved in the design of communications systems for satellites. But any details finer than that were lost to her in a willful act of ignorance. Marty had often explained the subtle intricacies of this technology or that, and Nora had nodded and smiled, the good and interested wife. But, in truth, her brain refused to absorb any of it. Of what use to her was information on the latest microchip or a new twist in computer language? On the other hand, she knew by heart all about Marty's anxiety, that tortuous circuitry of ambition and jealousy. Nora was an expert on turf battles, pecking orders, the tight bottleneck of promotion and the intense competition between the science/research types and the Harvard MBA bastards.

"Mmmm," she said soothingly. She was already in bed, and had been reading Sigrid Undset's *Kristin Lavransdatter,* a novel about marriage and motherhood in the fourteenth century, which she now reluctantly set aside.

Marty wandered over to the window and stared out at their darkened front yard. There were street lights on Cedarview Crescent, but they were few and far between.

"And then I told McAllister to give me two more engineers. Just two. Of course I'll have to go through all the administrative bullshit and rigmarole, but it'll make the different between sweating out the deadline or slipping in under the wire."

Kristin Lavransdatter had a husband who fought for the

King, God and Norway. The gap between her life and Nora's was immense, but Nora was feeling a strong connection. When Kristin's husband complained about the state of his armor, shifting military allegiances and battle strategies, Kristin felt just as helpless as Nora did when Marty complained about Devlin Electronics. She stifled a sigh, made more soothing sounds and then said, "If you don't close that curtain, the entire neighborhood will know why I married you."

Devlin Electronics was forgotten. The mention of sex always made Marty playful, as if it were capable of stripping off the crusted accretions of fatherhood, mortgage payments and career. He raised an eyebrow, gave Nora a grin and waggled his flaccid penis at her. "Is this why you married me?"

"I'm not telling," she said.

Marty pulled the curtains closed. "How come I thought it was for the power of my intellect?"

Nora leaned back against the pillow and clasped her hands behind her neck. "I fooled you," she said. The sheet and blankets only came to her waist so that her breasts were bare. They were smooth and pale, soft and round. They'd never been stylish, having been too small for the bosomy standards of the fifties and sixties and too big for the androgynous seventies and eighties. Nonetheless, she had learned to like them.

Marty sat down beside her and touched a nipple with a forefinger. His penis was no longer limp, but rising thickly from its nest of curly dark hair. She put her hand around it. Aroused, Marty's flesh was always burning hot.

"Is it possible," he said, "that we are about to have one of our 2.5 sexual interludes per week?"

"What do you mean, 2.5? I recall a passionate moment last Wednesday."

He leaned forward and nibbled on her neck. "That was Monday."

"Wednesday."

"Monday."

"Monday your allergies were bothering you."

"Wednesday you had a headache."

Nora sat up, bent over and reciprocally nibbled on the end of his penis. He was fresh from a shower and his skin smelled sweetly of Camay soap. "Okay, it was Tuesday."

"Mmmm," he said. "Are the kids asleep?"

"I think so, but maybe you should lock the door."

As Marty got up, Nora clicked off the light of her night table and lay back on the pillow, closing her eyes and dabbling luxuriously through her selection of fantasies. There was the boy brothel fantasy; no, she was bored with that one. The French Riviera lesbian fantasy; no, she didn't feel like that either. What about the medical school fantasy? Experimentally, she let her mind sink into that one—the hard bed, the draped sheets, the white lights. No. Ugh. It smacked too much of Christine on Dr. Roya's examining table. As Marty slipped between the covers, Nora felt a sudden nostalgia for the sweet southern belle and dildo fantasy, the one that involved layers upon layers of petticoats like mounds of whipped cream and the delicate eyelet bloomers below. But she hadn't been able to use that one since she'd told it to Marty years ago. Fantasies, she'd discovered, shriveled and died in the light of disclosure. Their power lay in the private way they could be played out in the darkness behind her eyelids.

Marty touched the anticipatory wetness between her legs. "That's nice," he said and began to stroke her clitoris.

Nora ran a hand through the tangle of hair on his belly and back around to his buttocks. "It's your lucky day," she said.

"Maybe it's your lucky day."

She pinched him. "Perversion is against the law."

"You going to report me?" he murmured into her ear as her knee slid between his legs.

"It depends," she murmured back.

"Depends on what?"

His fingers made a silky circle of her clitoris, and Nora sighed.

"I'm not telling."

But there was nothing different or perverse that two consenting adults could attempt without the stimulus of mechanical and visual aids that Marty and Nora hadn't tried in twenty-plus years of enthusiastic and imaginative lovemaking. Well, not always so enthusiastic and sometimes dull, Nora conceded, but then in twenty years there were bound to be slumps and doldrums. The pleasure to be found was in the knowledge they shared, the polite courtesies of longtime partners, the unspoken agreements that always resulted in mutual satisfaction. And when they were finished, and Marty had turned over on his side so she could lie belly to his warm back, Nora sleepily understood that this lovemaking was the core of her rock. Everything around it could shift and crack, the earth could tremble, the rains pour down in a deluge, but if this was steady, unchangeable and unmovable, then she was well and truly safe.

2

◇   ◇   ◇   Dr. Roya herself phoned Nora two days after Christine's examination. "I'm really sorry," she said, "but I'm not going to be able to perform Christine's abortion. The nurses at the hospital are refusing to assist at abortions any more."

"Oh," Nora said. "All of them?"

Dr. Roya sighed loudly. "Not all, but we have a very active, very disruptive 'Nurses for Life' group. At any rate, I'm sorry about Christine, but she'll have to go to the clinic in Syracuse."

"Syracuse," Nora echoed in surprise. Syracuse was a hundred miles away. "What about Laurel Springs General or Symington?"

"Laurel Springs never did abortions, and I'm afraid there might be trouble at Symington. Believe me, the clinic in Syracuse is your best bet. The staff there is very pleasant, and I know the doctor in charge. He's very good."

"Well," Nora said, "if we have to, we have to. Do we need a referral?"

"No, but I'll call and let them know that Christine's my patient."

After she hung up the phone, Nora wondered at her surprise. There had been small bits in the Fairfax–Burtonville *Leader* about trouble at the hospital: threatening letters, pickets, a nurse fired and then reinstated again. She hadn't bothered reading the articles, because the part of her life that had been once so intricately bound up with babies and pregnancies was over. Marty had had a vasectomy two years after Danny had been born.

That indifference had also casually propelled her past a display that the Fairfax Coalition for Life had set up in the shopping mall two weeks earlier—before Christine had told them that she might be pregnant. Nora had heard about the Coalition; they too had gotten their name into the newspaper, but she knew no one involved with them and had generally ignored their existence. Above their booth had been a large poster of a fetus and next to it a sign saying: ABORTION MEANS NO JUDGE, NO JURY, NO TRIAL, NO APPEAL, AND NO STAY OF EXECUTION. Nora had glanced at it and then at the women who were handing out leaflets. She'd been faintly surprised to find that she recognized one of them, Sylvia Allison, a woman who lived three blocks away and who had a son in Danny's class.

She'd quickened her step then, not wanting to be acknowledged or drawn into a discussion. Nora was pro-choice, an attitude that was part of a personal philosophy that embraced sixties liberalism and seventies feminism. But this philosophy was admittedly fuzzy at the edges. She had once been at a cocktail party at the Whites' where her belief that the country needed a better welfare system had been caustically attacked by a government lawyer. Nora, who had no studies to quote, no horror stories to tell, no statistics for ammunition, nothing but a gut feeling, had been easily cut to shreds. The lawyer's smugness had brought back an old sense of inadequacy. When her contemporaries had been marching in Washington with Martin Luther King, she'd been in college and far too busy with courses and young men to give much thought to civil rights. While women activists had burned their bras and their personal bridges, she'd been hard at work being a wife and mother. Nora had felt a tapestry of morality being woven all around her, but she had done nothing to be a part of it. Her sense of guilt had once driven her to make a contribution to NOW, but she'd then found herself on so many mailing lists—Save the Whales, Get Guns off the Streets of America, Boycott California Grapes—that she'd never contributed again.

But the argument with the lawyer had bothered her so much that she had talked it over with Marty when they'd gotten home from the Whites' party.

"God, that lawyer," she said. "He drowned me in statistics. I couldn't breathe."

Marty hung his tie over a chair and began to unbutton his shirt. "There are two kinds of liars, you know. Damn liars and statisticians."

Nora sat on the edge of the bed and began to pull off her stockings. "Arguments like that make me feel so helpless. So frustrated. It doesn't matter how many newspapers and magazines I read, I never seem to know enough."

"The guy was a jerk." Marty pulled off his shirt and looked at it. "Too damned tight in the collar. You think my neck is getting fat?" He walked to the mirror over Nora's dresser and studied his reflection, twisting his head this way and that.

Nora took the crumpled mass of her stockings and threw it into the dirty laundry basket in the closet. "If we were the kind of people who got involved in things, political things, I'd have been able to quote some statistics of my own."

"You mean join a political party? You know what that is? Meetings piled on meetings. Lots of bullshitting. People shooting off their mouths. I get enough of that at work."

"But don't you feel just a little bit guilty? I mean, look how you're enjoying the benefits of other people's labor."

"What labor?"

"The work people have done—are doing—to make sure we live in a democratic society."

Marty turned from his reflection. "Christ, Nora. It's two o'clock in the morning. I drank too much and ate too much for amateur political science." He looked down at the hairy flesh at the vicinity of his belt buckle. "You think I'm getting fat?"

"You know what I mean," she said stubbornly. "What if red-necks like that ran the country?"

He unzipped his pants. "This is the way I look at it: I have a mortgage, two kids and a job; I vote and pay my taxes; I'm doing my bit for the country."

"Okay, I know I'm going to sound like one of Danny's Superman comic books, but what about changing the system, fighting injustice, that sort of thing?"

Marty dropped his pants over a chair, stepped out of his jockey-shorts and, cleaning out his belly button with a forefinger, flicked the lint away. Then he ran a hand over his belly. "Not bad for forty-five, huh? Not bad."

Nora, who was naked by this time, went up to him and, putting her arms around him, cupped his buttocks in her hands. "Not bad," she confirmed.

Marty gave her a suspicious look. "I know what this is—all talk and no action."

"You want action at two o'clock in the morning?"

"Do you?"

"I'm just being friendly."

"Hmmph—that's what I thought." But he put his arms around her, so they stood hugging and swaying slightly.

"I mean, we're lucky, aren't we?" Nora asked. "To have enough food on the table and a roof over our heads?"

"You just want to tell that asshole where to shove it next time you meet him."

"There's that," Nora admitted and then stood back a bit. "Actually," she added, "you are getting a bit of a pot. You should lay off the beer."

Marty looked crestfallen. "You think so?" He pushed her away, examined his reflection in the mirror once more and then yawned. "The reason we're not out there acting like Superman," he said, "is because we're not joiners. We never have been."

Nora knew what he meant. She had once become a Brownie leader for Christine's sake, and it had been one of the more painful experiences of her life. There had been paperwork, meetings, phone calls and errands, but none of that had been as awful as the constant demand to be both diplomatic and persuasive at the same time. She hadn't done it well. She'd come to hate bratty children and their equally bratty parents. She'd wondered why, when the tenth parent had backed out of a commitment, she even bothered trying to give their daughters a meaningful experience for two hours a week. Over the year of her leadership she'd grown more and more tense, until the sound of little girls' voices, echoing in the church basement where the 32nd Brownie troop met, had given her such severe headaches that she'd had to spend the day after each meeting in bed.

Still, a part of her wanted to be the kind of person whose firm convictions led to firm and honorable actions. When she and Joanne had applied to the bank for a loan to start The Kids' Place, the manager hadn't regarded them as idiots, hadn't wondered what a couple of housewives thought they knew about retailing, hadn't insisted that their husbands co-sign the papers. Nora knew whom she had to thank for his respect: that faceless army of women who had organized, marched, made speeches and licked a million stamps. She had not been one of them, and Nora could not be as dismissive about her lack of action as Marty was about his.

She was lazy, she thought, and selfish. Too comfortable in her cocoon of family and home.

Too protected.

The Beemes' house was in a subdivision that had been built on one of the hills overlooking the Susquehanna River. It was neither the largest nor the smallest house on Cedarview Crescent, but an ordinary brick split-level with four bedrooms, surrounded by hedges, its backyard shaded by a sprawling dogwood tree that bloomed pink and white in the spring. Nora and Marty had bought the house ten years earlier, and it had several features that Nora liked. One was the view from the dining room window, a vista of lawns and rooftops sloping all the way down to the river, which from a distance appeared to be a glittering spill of silver thread. Another was the breakfast nook that faced south, allowing her to hang foliage—ferns and ivies and spider plants—in its large bay window. The third was the den, with its thick carpet and fireplace, a wintertime trysting place with Marty when the children weren't home. But the feature that had really sold the house to Nora and Marty was that the children's bedrooms were on the lower level of the split. This meant that she didn't pass their doorways on her daily rounds, a fact that minimized the shock and aggravation that she invariably felt at the chaos that could materialize in ten by thirteen feet of living space.

Nonetheless, there were times when she was forced to descend to the children's level: spring cleaning, for instance, when the winter clothes had to be put away, or when she felt called upon once again to solve the mystery of the disappearing kitchen scissors. Then there were those particularly unforgettable times when a strange smell or unexpected animal life forced an emergency search. Danny's room was especially prone to the latter. He had once brought home acorns that housed a variety of mealybug that liked to live under carpets. He had secretly tried to keep caterpillars alive in a corner of his closet. Nora had recently found a dead robin in his desk drawer.

"Oh, my God!" she'd exclaimed, gingerly lifting it by one clawed foot. "Where did you get this?"

"Now, Mom, don't get mega-upset."

"This is disgusting! It *stinks*. You don't put *dead* things in your drawers."

Danny had assumed an aggrieved expression. "Well, I wasn't going to keep it forever."

"Why keep it at all?"

"I dunno."

But usually Nora's anger was prompted by more mundane discoveries, like the dirty T-shirts shoved into a drawer, the moldy towel from three showers back under the bed, the discovery of her long-lost pincushion in a box of baseball cards.

"What were you doing with this?"

"I don't remember."

"But it's mine, Danny. I was wondering where it was."

"I would have told you if I remembered."

Nora sat down heavily on the chair by his desk. Somewhere below the mess was the little boy's room she'd created six years earlier. She had spent many pleasurable hours picking out the maple captain's bed and the spread with its blue-and-white rocket ships. She had herself painted the walls, sewn the blue curtains and hung the wooden letters that spelled DANNY over the door. Now every horizontal surface, including the bed, was littered with toys and comics, while the vertical ones were papered with posters of rock stars whose names she couldn't remember and whose songs she didn't understand.

"Your room really gets to me, Danny," she said. "I feel like bringing a huge garbage pail in here and emptying everything into it."

"Everything?"

"Everything."

Danny was organizing a pile of playing cards into their respective decks. "I'd be mad," he said, "if you did that."

"I'm mad now."

He looked up and studied her. "Not *that* mad," he said shrewdly.

It was always humiliating to discover how accurately your children could judge the rise and fall of your blood pressure. "Don't push me, Danny," she warned, wearily rubbing her eyes. "One day you'll come home and find that the Hulk has been taken out of action."

"Mom?"

"Mmmm?"

"Is Christine really going to get rid of the baby?"

"Yes."

"Isn't that against the law?"

"What law?"

"That law. The Commandment one—about killing."

The task of bringing up children was one that Nora had never taken lightly. She had understood that all children, even her lovely, smiling infants, were really savages who had to be tamed, shaped and molded. When Christine had tried to put her baby finger in a light plug, Nora had picked her up and taken her away. When Danny had crayoned his wall, he'd been firmly told that coloring was for paper only. Light plugs and crayons had led to toilet and table etiquette, which, in turn, had evolved into instruction in the higher, finer art of ethics.

Most of that instruction was simple ("You have to share," "No hitting even though you're angry," "Two wrongs don't make a right") even though the issues often were not. When she had said those things, her voice so positive and knowing, Nora had felt as if she were in a child's picture, the kind that both Christine and Danny had drawn in kindergarten, with a bright yellow sun, intense blue sky and impossibly green grass. The people in those drawings had balloon heads with big smiles and twig-like appendages. Nora had been one of them, striding through primary colors, her body free of the encumbrances of flesh and ambiguities and misgivings.

"It's not against the law of the United States," she said carefully, "for a girl or woman to have an abortion if she doesn't want to have a baby."

"But isn't that killing—like murder?"

"Who told you that?"

He shrugged. "Nobody."

"Danny, the baby isn't exactly a baby yet. It's just a bunch of cells. It doesn't even look like a baby."

"But it would be a baby when it got bigger."

"Uh-huh."

"Does that mean you could have gotten rid of me if you'd wanted to?"

Danny was the only member of the family who had blue eyes. They were neither a dark blue nor a pale blue but somewhere in the middle, and so clear and pure that Nora had always felt she could see right through them.

"Yes, but we wanted you."

Danny bent his head so that a fringe of straight blond hair fell forward; he studied the jack of spades he held in his hand. "But I thought killing was against the law," he muttered.

"It's not like killing a person," Nora said patiently. "The bunch of cells can't think."

"I wouldn't mind a baby," he said. "I'd like us to have one."

"It's not us that would be having the baby. It's Christine, and she's too young to be a mother. She has to finish her schooling."

"We could take care of it."

"Danny, Daddy and I have to go to work every day. We have to make money so that we can keep our house and have food to eat."

"We could hire a babysitter," he said stubbornly.

"It wouldn't work, Danny. It really wouldn't." Nora stood up. "By the way, if this room isn't clean by two o'clock, you lose this week's allowance."

"Mom! That's not fair!"

"Nobody said life was going to be fair."

"Why do you always tell me that?"

"Because it's true."

The day Nora drove Christine to the clinic in Syracuse, the March rains had finally stopped. There was little green on the hills surrounding the highway except for the occasional clump of conifers, but the temperature was almost balmy and the sun was shining between great, scudding white clouds. The brightness outside the car was in direct contrast to the gloom within. Christine was still moody and sulky, but then Nora supposed she had reasons: humiliation and apprehension, combined with a residue of anger from the battle they'd had the day before over her spring wardrobe. Nora had insisted that the Beeme budget could not be stretched to include Benetton sweaters, Ralph Lauren jackets, Esprit skirts and Calvin Klein jeans. Christine had accused her of deliberately attempting to sabotage her social existence. Nora had said that, as far as she was concerned, popularity had little to do with clothes and a lot to do with personality. Christine had said that Nora didn't understand a thing.

It wasn't as if Nora hadn't been warned. She read magazines; she had friends with teenaged daughters; she had once been an adolescent herself. She could distinctly remember hating her own mother, an overworked plump woman who hadn't had a single moment to worry about Nora's growing pains. Her father, Leo Felsher, had owned a bakery, and the family had lived right above it. Leo, who never trusted anyone who wasn't a blood relative not to steal from him, refused to hire help and worked from morning to night. Esther, her mother, not only worked beside him, but also took care of Nora and her brother Ben, making meals and cleaning the apartment. As soon as her head had reached the counter, Nora had also worked in the bakery.

What Nora had hated about her mother was the slavish way Esther yielded to Leo's whims and needs and angers. He was a yeller and a screamer, and Esther had cringed before the sound of his voice, had scurried to his commands, had accommodated him even when that accommodation went beyond the bounds of reason. Esther was sick with a flu and Leo wanted his dinner? The good wife, flushed with fever, crawled out of her sick bed and placed a meal before him. Esther wanted to go to temple on Yom Kippur, but Leo, the atheist, wanted to keep the bakery open? The obedient wife stood behind the counter and packaged bagels for gentiles.

Nora's hatred was ugly and unfair, she had known even then, but she hadn't been able to help herself. The hatred had spilled over until there were days when she couldn't stand even to look at her mother: the way her broad nose creased at the base, the bulge of her stomach beneath an apron, the corns on her toes. Her mother's stupidity had also known no bounds. She refused to comprehend the significance of a hem an inch too long. She actually believed that a pleasant smile could make a girl popular. In short, she was painfully un-cool and oblivious to her daughter's sufferings. Fifteen-year-old Nora had vowed that she would never in a million years be like Esther, and that if and when she ever had a daughter, she would be sympathetic, understanding, forgiving, generous and kind.

The ironies of history were not lost on her.

Of course, this recent battle with Christine was nothing new, merely part of the ebb and flow of a general turbulence that had started at puberty. Nora either found herself in the wrong or intensely disliked most of the time. She was mean, heartless, cruel, a daughter-torturer. She had the sensation, one she now realized her mother must have shared, that she was a despotic dictator in a miniature country with a bad track record in human rights. On some days, the only thing that kept the fragile thread of her tolerance from snapping was that she could look into Christine's narrow face and see the ghostly rounded cheeks and bright smile of the little girl she'd once been. Occasionally that little girl even reappeared, as if from behind a curtain, for brief and poignant moments. Nora was always hooked by those moments, softened by their sweetness, undone with love. She was always astonished to discover how far and wide and deep that river of love flowed. It seemed to have no bottom, no edges, no limit.

But more often than not Christine was frowning, as she was now, slumped in her seat, staring off into the passing landscape of skeletal trees and bare ground. She wasn't in pink today, but in denim: jeans, a jean jacket with sleeves too long, and scruffy Docksiders. Every once in a while she lifted her hands and nervously pushed her hair behind her ears. Nora had tried to alleviate some of the gloom by turning the car radio to WFCR, but the station was playing a loud, booming kind of music with no melodic line at all. She turned the radio off and tried for civilized conversation. "I saw the flowers Jessica gave you," she said. "Nice carnations."

Christine pulled herself up. "Jessica's the only one I told. April and Marilyn don't know yet."

Christine, Jessica, April and Marilyn had known each other since junior high and still hung out together, four seemingly giddy adolescents who screamed, shrieked, giggled and talked constantly. When the four of them were in one room the decibel level rose, and the activities were frenetic. They tried on one another's clothes, read to each other from *Seventeen* and *Mademoiselle,* experimented with cosmetics, dispensed advice and shared intimacies in conversations punctuated with "Ohmygod's" and "hesaidthat's!" When they weren't together, the telephone was their preferred means of communication. It rang first thing in the morning, stopped for a compulsory break during school hours, and continued as soon as Christine came home.

("Wasn't that one of the gruesome foursome?" Marty had once asked Christine after she had just finished a long and animated phone conversation.

"Uh-huh. April."

"Didn't you just see her on the bus?"

"Uh-huh."

"Could you be so kind as to tell me what precisely can happen between the time *she* got off the bus and *you* got here that requires a twenty-minute phone call?"

"Everything, Daddy," Christine had said, letting Marty know with just the right amount of wide-eyed astonishment just how ignorant he was.)

But below the surface of the friendship, allegiances among the four girls were shifting constantly, inspiring envy and rivalries. Sometimes Nora was privy to the various cabals and intrigues; sometimes she wasn't. But she found she had forgotten the intensity of such relationships. Christine could be unhappy for days over a slight, a blabbed secret, a suspected disloyalty.

"April would absolutely freak out if she knew," Christine went on. "And I can't tell Marilyn without her telling April. Besides, April is mad at me, because she thinks I told Philip that she thought he was good-looking."

No one dated in Christine's group of friends, at least not the way that Nora and her friends had done twenty-five years earlier. Instead, the girls formed a small nucleus with several boys in shifting, complex orbits. Some of the boys were steady companions like Jay, while others were more comet-like, dropping in at regular but infrequent interludes.

"And is Philip good-looking?"

"God, no. He's a doorknob."

Nora tasted the word. "A doorknob?"

"A nerd, a jerk. That's why I couldn't have told him that April thought he was good-looking. Because he isn't. But April is so hyper-crazy about things like that and she . . ."

As she drove, the dark ribbon of highway unwinding behind

her, and Christine talking beside her in that querulous, immature voice she had whenever she discussed trouble with her friends, Nora reflected with satisfaction on the rightness of the decision she and Marty had made. Christine was half-child/half-woman, caught in an adolescent limbo. Even her body was not yet fully formed: the breasts still slight, the hips boyish. Pregnancy had done little except to slightly darken the small aureoles of her breasts. Nora couldn't imagine that half-child/half-woman's body bearing an infant. It seemed wrong and reckless of nature to even make it possible. So she didn't think of the abortion as a taking away of a living thing. She saw it as restoration—like having a mole removed—and a way of turning the clock back. By the time this day was over, her daughter's body would have been returned to her in its pure and pristine state.

A road sign flashed by, SYRACUSE, NEXT 3 EXITS, and Nora maneuvered over to the right lane in preparation for the off-ramp. "Get the map from the glove compartment, will you?" she asked. "The clinic's on Fairmont Avenue, but I'm not sure where that is." But Christine didn't move as the car went down the ramp and onto South Salina Street. "Christine, did you hear me?"

"Mom?" The voice was low and uncertain. "Can I tell you something?"

The traffic was heavy, as South Salina was a main thoroughfare. Nora didn't even have time to glance at Christine as she was forced by a truck into the left lane.

"What?" she said impatiently.

"I—I don't think I want to have an abortion."

The car veered suddenly as Nora inadvertently slammed on the brake, and the truck beside them gave a sharp bark of its horn. The driver also rolled down his window and hollered, "Jesus fucking Christ, lady! Watch what you're doing!"

Nora managed to make a left turn into the crowded parking lot of a shopping plaza and finally found a spot in front of Kresge's Department Store. She turned off the ignition and then swiveled in her seat. "Now," she said carefully, "what are you trying to say?"

"Mom, I know everything you're going to tell me. I know

all the arguments, and I've thought about them, I really have. But I don't think I want to have an abortion."

"I know you're scared and that's—"

"It doesn't have anything to do with being scared. I mean, I am scared, but that's not the reason."

In fact, Nora could see that Christine had been far more scared of telling this to Nora than she'd been of anything else. Her skin was so pale that the freckles were dark across her nose, and she was nibbling again at her nails. Those nails. Nora realized that she should have been watching them closely. Gone were the smooth, filed edges and sharp little points. They were blunt and ragged, the work of hours of nail-biting.

Nora sighed. "You couldn't tell me this at home? You had to wait until we'd driven a hundred miles?"

"I'm sorry, Mom, but I still had to think about it."

Nora glanced down the storefronts of the plaza. There was a Quick Print, a Holiday Gift Shop, Dorothy's Ladies Fashions, and a Sammy's Subs. "Let's get something to drink," she said, "and we can talk about it."

Sammy's Subs was deserted, but Nora and Christine still sat in the very back booth. It wasn't the sort of place that Nora usually inhabited. She could feel the cracked vinyl of the seat beneath her skirt and the rough surface of the formica table beneath her fingers. Graffiti had been etched into its surface: *Andrea loves Billy . . . Screw the whole world.* Christine had ordered a Coke, while Nora sipped at a cup of bad coffee from a Styrofoam cup. They didn't speak until the man behind the counter had walked down to the front and a soda machine blocked his pointed white cap from view.

"Now," Nora said.

Christine reached into her purse and pulled out a booklet. "See, I got this about a week ago." She pushed it across the table at Nora. "And I didn't know anything about this stuff until I read it."

Like the booklets that had sat on Dr. Roya's table, this was an innocuous-looking, glossy-paged affair with the photograph of a woman in a maternity dress on the cover. She was neither beautiful nor homely, just pregnant and young and smiling slightly as she walked through a bucolic landscape of trees and dappled sunlight. Superimposed over her profiled, swelling abdomen was a photograph of an embryo in its fetal sac. The booklet's name, in delicate, flowing print, was *How You Grew.*

Nora flipped through the first few pages. They described the first days of pregnancy in pictures and text. On the first page the picture appeared to be a fuzzy peach in a raised circle. In the second, the peach had turned into a dozen or more irregularly shaped balls. Under the caption marked "14 Days" was a photograph that looked to be a blown-up section of the moon's pocked surface with a circular lump in the center. Below that photograph the caption read, "The new baby nesting in the warm, soft lining of the uterus."

Christine reached across and pointed to "28 Days." "That's what the baby looks like now. Isn't that neat?"

This photograph showed an amorphous, doughy-white, curled shape within a clear sac. Nora read, *The new baby is a small and self-contained entity. Each cell is controlled by a master genetic code that orders the formation of tissues and organs. This orchestration of cells is a true miracle.* She turned to the last page. It was entitled *Death—A Solution?* and had two photographs. One was of a dead fetus with placenta in a white bowl; the other was of a collection of tiny, white, but identifiable, human parts—arms, legs, hands, feet—strewn against a blue background.

"Who gave you this?" she asked.

"A Mrs. Allison. She came to the school to be in a debate with a woman from . . . uh, I don't remember, some national women's group. It was hosted by the Debating Club. She was really good, Mom. She had a way of talking about teenagers like me . . . well, that sounded like she knew what I was feeling."

"Such as?"

"Well, she talked about being confused. She really understood how confusing the whole thing is. The other woman talked about that, too, but you could see that she really thought a girl would be crazy not to want an abortion. Her big point was about women having control over their bodies, but Mrs. Allison talked about how families didn't always understand why a girl might not be certain of what she wanted to do. It was like she knew what I was thinking. Anyway, when it was over, she saw me and we talked a bit. See, her son knows Danny, and she'd heard I was pregnant. She wasn't pushy, Mom. I told her that I was going to have an abortion. She said, 'Is that your decision or your parents'?' I said I didn't really know. Then she asked me if I'd like to see this booklet. She was really nice about it."

Fate and the obvious. The Debating Club and Danny. The minute she had seen the booklet, Nora had understood one part of the circuitous connection that tied her house to that bunch of busy, officious-looking women at the Coalition for Life's booth. Danny had blabbed as she had been sure he would, and the spring breeze had picked up his words and wafted them into the waiting and wanting hands of those women. Nor was she surprised that Sylvia Allison had approached Christine. A woman of that persuasion would not consider it necessary to ask a girl's parents for the right to speak to their daughter about an issue that was a very private, family affair. She would stick her nose into it, and as Nora recalled Sylvia had a fairly large and ugly nose. A surge of anger welled in her chest like a thick bubble.

"Do you know what organization Mrs. Allison belongs to?" she asked.

Christine saw the anger and thought it was for her. She flinched a bit and said tentatively, "A pro-life group?"

Nora softened her voice. "An anti-abortion group, Christine. A group that is anti-feminist and anti all the things that women have fought for during the past ten years. And that's what this booklet is all about. It's not about biology or embryology or anything educational. It's about trying to persuade you not to have an abortion."

"But I didn't know what the baby looked like before. In my mind, it was a nothing. Just a thing. I mean, it didn't even have a shape."

"It's not a baby yet. It's a fetus," Nora corrected her. "It can't live by itself. It can't breathe alone."

"Mom, I just need some more time to think about it."

Nora took a gulp of her coffee. It was sour and no longer hot. "Listen, honey. I can understand you're feeling concerned about the ba— fetus. But think about yourself. Think what will happen if you don't have an abortion. You won't be able to go to school next fall."

Christine had slender, feathery, dark eyebrows. They pulled together into a frown. "I know."

"I don't think you do. I mean, think about it. While you're home, all by yourself, what are your friends going to be doing?" The question was merely rhetorical. Nora leaned forward to make her point. "They're going to be busy with school and each other, having a good time, going to dances, meeting other boys. . . ."

"I've been thinking about all that, too."

"Have you? Have you *really?*"

"Mom, I'm not stupid. You never give me credit for thinking."

"You don't understand the emotional impact this is going to have, Christine. Your life and your friends' lives are going to go in totally different directions. You're going to be all alone. And what about boys? What are they going to think about you? What kind of social life are you going to have when it's all over?"

"Mom . . ."

"And think about school. You might even have to repeat your junior year if you can't handle the schoolwork at home."

Christine's voice shook a bit. "Mom, I just don't think I can have an abortion today, okay?"

Nora took a deep breath. She had been striding so hard and purposefully through one of those children's drawings, so right and sure and vehement beneath the citron sun and azure sky, that she had quite forgotten where she was. A bell gave a trembling ring as the door to Sammy's Subs opened and shut, letting in two men. The smell of bitter coffee rose to her nostrils. She shifted in her seat, and the cracked vinyl rubbed against her buttocks.

"Just tell me one thing," she said. "You knew yesterday that you might not go through with the abortion, and you must have known that if you didn't, you wouldn't be able to wear that Ralph

Lauren skirt you wanted so badly. So why on earth did you pick a fight with me? Knowing what you did."

Christine gave her a small, guilty smile. "Uh, I guess the principle of the thing? And then, maybe, I'll change my mind."

Nora wearily rubbed the bridge of her nose with her thumb and forefinger. "Oh, Christine."

"Mom?"

"Mmmm?"

"Would you explain it to Daddy for me?"

Nora put her hand flat down on the table. "Oh, no," she said. "You're going to have to do all the explaining yourself."

3

◇   ◇   ◇   Nora parked her car at the back of the shopping mall and let herself in with her key. It was a Monday morning, the slowest business day of the week, and she would be taking care of The Kids' Place by herself until lunch, when Joanne came in to relieve her. They also had a part-time employee, Mrs. Hahnnecker, who worked some afternoons, Thursday and Friday evenings and Saturdays. At Christmas, when the store went wild, they hired temporary help.

Nora loved the store. She hadn't known that she was going to love it when it was just an idea that she and Joanne had shared while their children ate and played and bickered at their feet. Then she had been looking for a way to make money. Retailing had seemed easy to her then, a career that didn't require any specialized training. Even when they'd been putting a prospectus together for a bank loan, signing a lease and buying merchandise, it had all seemed like a game to her. Instead of playing house, she and Joanne were playing store.

Of course, it hadn't been a game at all. The first year they'd almost gone under. They'd been talked into an expensive line of fancy dress dolls that hadn't sold; how Nora had come to hate those dolls—their pink, pouty lips, the long-lashed blue eyes, the perfect porcelain faces—as they stared down at her from their glass perches. Nora and Joanne had also stocked too many books and not enough clothes: items like smocked dresses, tiny sweaters and quilted overalls, which sold like hotcakes and had a good markup. The fact that they'd opened three months before Christmas and had the feast of that season to hold them through the famine of the next was the only thing that saved them. After that, they'd learned caution, who their customers were and what they were good at. Nora, they'd discovered, had a knack for picking merchandise and an unexpected skill at displaying it to advantage. Joanne could resist the whiniest customer, the most persuasive salesman, and was able to cope with the toughest distributors and shippers.

She loved the store when it was packed with customers and the cash register was ringing like crazy, but she also loved it when it was empty and silent, which was why she took the quiet Monday morning shift that bored Joanne to tears. She got a lot of work done then, opening parcels, checking merchandise, re-arranging displays, putting together special orders. But that wasn't the reason she liked being in the quiet store. The mute toys, the obedient little dresses and overalls soothed her in a way that her own house and furniture never could. It wasn't just that the items, even though they were for sale, were possessions that she had chosen and cared about. Their value to her lay in their unceasing shiny and bright newness. The dresses and overalls never got dirty or worn; the toys were always whole; the pages of the books smooth and unblemished. She couldn't walk past a nook or cranny of the store without feeling that calming sense of being utterly in control.

She was addicted to it, Nora thought, as she switched on the lights, the fluorescent bulbs flaring one after the other so that bit by bit the interior of the store became visible. She hadn't been able to wait to go to work this morning; she'd rushed out early, without breakfast, before the children had left for school. Her spirit craved that fix of silence, of peace, of control. Since that futile drive to Syracuse a month before, the house on Cedarview Crescent had become a war zone, with a familial Maginot Line drawn right down the middle. On one side was Christine, with Danny in an unexpected alliance; on the other were Marty and Nora.

For days after they'd come back from Syracuse, Christine had wavered, a candle flame flickering between contradictory breezes. She had a frustrating way of agreeing with everything Nora and Marty said. Yes, she knew time was of the essence. Yes, she understood that nine months of pregnancy might jeopardize her school year. Yes, she realized that this was an important time that she should be devoting to school and friends and growing up. Yes, she even seemed to comprehend that she was throwing away the hard work of millions of women who had fought to give her the legal right to this abortion. But when it came down to brass tacks, to not only agreeing but *doing,* Christine balked.

"Well, what's stopping you?" Marty would ask, his tone reasonable. In Beeme family battles, Nora sometimes screamed like a fishwife, the children cried and had temper tantrums, but Marty always maintained his cool. "If you understand all that," he would go on, "then why aren't you willing to do something about it?"

"I don't think it's right."

"Let me put it to you this way," he said. "Is it right, do you suppose, to put yourself through this?"

"It's my choice," Christine answered. "I mean, it's me. It's my body."

"And who feeds that body and keeps it out of the rain?"

"I know it's you and Mom, spending your hard-earned money for my welfare. You don't have to tell me that."

"What about us then? Do you have a right to put us through it, too?"

"That's different."

"How's it different?"

Danny piped up. "We can take care of ourselves, Daddy, the baby can't. That's what she means."

"Shut up, Danny, and stay out of this." Marty would take a

big breath and then smile at Christine. "Let's look at the pros and cons again."

"We've done that already."

"I know, but . . ."

The discussions went round and round like spirals, forever turning on themselves and ending nowhere. Sometimes Christine held her ground without breaking down; other times, she held it, but was reduced to crying and blubbering. Either way, Marty would leave, while Nora mopped up after him.

"Why doesn't he listen?"

"He's thinking of you, Christine. He's worried about you."

"He doesn't understand anything. He doesn't want to."

"He understands that you're being stubborn and making the wrong choices."

"Who says they're wrong?"

"They're wrong for you, for our family."

"You can't assume that about me. You don't have the right!"

There were many talks like this. A few days would pass, and another would begin. It got so bad that Nora called a halt on discussing the abortion at mealtimes. Still, Christine's marks at school began to go down, and the atmosphere in the house was tense. One night, to escape it, Nora and Marty went out to dinner with Joanne and Grant at a seafood place in Burtonville. For a while the four of them talked about other things; the store and a summer merchandising promotion, a neighbor whose attic was being renovated ("the contractor is two months late already. . . . Three skylights, for Christ's sake"), and a law case Grant was working on involving the gravel pit two miles from Fairfax and a family that was suing the town after their child had fallen into it and broken both his legs. Nora always liked it when Grant talked. He was a tall, thin man to whom baldness had come early. Nora could never remember Grant with any more hair than the blond circlet on his scalp, but she thought he carried it well. He had one of those squarish faces that benefited from an overdose of forehead; his nose didn't appear as short as it was nor his jaw as shallow. He had penetrating blue eyes, and a calm, even way of speaking. If Nora hadn't known about the Whites' marital battles from Joanne, she would not have thought Grant ever raised his voice above a low, lawyerish decibel.

Although Nora had hoped that the subject of Christine's non-abortion wouldn't be brought up, they were discussing it by the end of dinner, when the table was littered with cracked lobster shells and spatters of butter. They dissected the problem, taking it apart as if it were a clock and analyzing all the coils and springs, gears and cogs, only to discover that they simply couldn't put it back together again.

"The thing is," Nora said, "that you can't chloroform her and carry her to the clinic, can you?"

"Under the law," Grant said, "she's in the driver's seat. You don't have any rights at all. Not in this situation. As the mother, she has the power to make all decisions regarding the child."

"If she broke her leg," Marty said, "and we didn't get it fixed, we could be brought up for negligence, right?"

"That's right. You're legally and financially responsible for her as a minor, but if she decides to keep the baby, you can't do anything."

"Is that crazy or what?" Marty said with disgust.

Grant took a sip of his coffee. "It has nothing to do with craziness," he said calmly. "It's the law."

"Has she talked about keeping the baby?" Joanne asked.

"Christ," Marty said.

Nora grimaced. "God forbid."

Joanne was leaning forward, her chin propped in the cup of her hand. Nora saw that look on her broad face, that curious, slightly amused look that always preceded a question designed for provocation. Joanne often had that appearance when the two couples were together and Marty was speaking. ("It's that incredibly flat, engineer's approach to life," she'd once said to Nora. "As long as I've known him, Marty's viewed the world like a flawed piece of machinery that he could fix if only people would let him." If anyone else had said this, Nora would have loyally bristled, but Joanne had a claim on Marty that went back much further than Nora's. She and Marty had known each other since the seventh grade.)

Now Joanne said, "I get the feeling, Marty, that underneath you're really furious about this."

He shrugged. "I'm not angry. What would be the point of that?"

"No one ever said there was any point to anger. I just think it would be a natural reaction."

Marty tended to ignore people he was indifferent to, but Joanne's provocations often got a response, because he was fond of her. "You know the trouble with you women, Joanne?" Marty asked, waving a spoon. "You're into this myth about men—that they aren't in touch with their feelings—and you're always ready to jump into a man's mind and tell him what's going on inside. As if he can't figure it out for himself."

"Oh, now you're going to turn this into a Battle of the Sexes thing. What I'm saying is that I can't believe you're taking this so calmly."

Grant came to Marty's aid. "He's not calm; he's upset. Can't you see that?"

"*You'd* be *furious* if one of our girls got pregnant and refused to have an abortion."

"I'd be like Marty, I'd try to make her see that her decision is based on purely emotional reasoning."

"What's wrong with emotional reasons?" Joanne asked. "The development of a moral sense has plenty to do with emotional reasons."

"A moral sense?" Marty said. "She's only fifteen."

"Fifteen has a good idea of what's right and wrong."

"This fifteen-year-old," Marty said, "isn't supposed to have food in her room, and we find empty bags of chocolate chip cookies under her bed all the time."

"That's immaturity. All kids do that kind of stuff."

"That's doing what's wrong, when she knows what's right."

"You can't compare chocolate chip cookies to aborting fetuses. In her eyes, that's murder."

Nora said, "The point is that Christine had no morals on this issue at all until she got that pro-life booklet. She didn't care about the abortion; she was quite willing to go through with it.

Now, all of a sudden, she's developed this ethical position. She's even gone to the Coalition for Life's office and picked up more literature. It's like she's being brainwashed."

Now Marty leaned forward. "And if she can be brainwashed in one direction, I think she can be brainwashed in another."

Joanne shook her head. "I don't know," she said. "I think it may be too late."

"No," Marty said. "I don't believe that. I think if we keep on talking to her"—his finger jabbed the air, emphasizing each point—"keep on explaining, keep on giving her the facts, she'll come around. She's a smart kid; she knows the score. Right, Nora?"

Nora smiled but changed the subject. She didn't have the faith that Marty had in his twin gods of fact and reason. There were other deities in the pantheon of modern life that commanded more of her attention and awe: the seductive Aphrodite-figure of love, the Pan of sentimentality with his sly, undermining smile, the wild, Gorgon-headed god of impulse. And then there was anger. Nora saw this god not as a fierce, armored Mars wielding his whip over a chariot of leaping horses, but as a fat, well-fed cherub with a quiverful of arrows that pierced unsuspecting breasts without impact or pain. Because Joanne, of course, was right. The mantle of calm and reason that Marty wrapped around himself was beginning to wear thin, so that bits and pieces of anger glimmered through—as if a flaming arrow had landed and a fire now burned within him, giving off heat and light.

The first person to visit the store that morning wasn't a customer, but a salesman, Bernie Cohen, who was a regional upstate representative for ten toy lines. He carried a briefcase full of catalogues and a suitcase of samples. He was a big, heavy man, close to fifty, with curly red hair that had turned to a speckled sand and a large Semitic nose hooked over a short upper lip. He wasn't handsome, but his face had a rich ethnicity that Nora enjoyed. He had grown up in a district of the Bronx not far from the Felsher bakery, and his voice, his looks, his intonations, his accent reminded her, in the pleasantest way possible, of events and people that she'd once thought of as vulgar, hateful and boring. When she was a child, attendance at the Felsher Passover and Chanukah celebrations had been mandatory. Nora had always been present in body, but her spirit had struggled to soar above the relatives who couldn't inhabit the same room without bickering and screaming, the great-uncle who had always pinched her cheeks until they were red and sore, her fat Aunt Malka who had once sat down, broken a chair and ended up sprawling on the carpet. She'd been mortified then by the antics, the jokes, the arguments, the appetites, the belching. Now that she was forty-three years old, however, a pink-tinted nostalgia had set in.

Bernie never just walked into the store. He blew in, as if a wind were gusting behind him, his curls wild and uncombed, his raincoat billowing out around him. "Sweetheart!" he exclaimed, dropping his bags on the floor in front of the counter. "Love of my life, how do you do it? You are looking as lovely as always. Turn around. Come on. . . ." He twirled his forefinger. "Amazing, *amazing,* not a gray hair, a wrinkle. A girl of twenty, no more. No, God forbid I should lie. Eighteen. Not a day over."

"Bernie," Nora said severely. "That line of games from Serendipitous is a washout."

He smacked the palm of his hand against his forehead. "Beauty and business, what a combination. It's a knockout."

"No one wants even an updated version of tiddlywinks."

"Did I tell you the one about the rabbi, the Pope, and the marbles?"

Nora couldn't help smiling. "It's too early for dirty jokes."

"It's never too early for dirty jokes. Okay, so you know the one about the marbles. I know I didn't tell you this one. Now listen. A guy who runs a sex shop has to leave his new assistant in the shop for the day. In comes a white girl. She looks over the merchandise and finally comes up to the assistant. 'I'll take a black one,' she says, pointing to the shelf of dildos behind him. An hour later, a black girl comes in. She comes up to the assistant. 'I'll take a white one,' she says, pointing to the dildos behind him. Finally, a Polack girl comes in. She looks around for a while, too, and then comes up to the assistant. 'I'll take the plaid one,' she says. At the end of the day, the boss comes back. 'How was business?' he says. 'Gee, boss,' the assistant says, 'we had a real run on dildos today. A black bought a white one; a white bought a black one; and a Polack bought my thermos.' "

"Very funny," Nora said.

"You're laughing. What do you call six epileptics in a bowl?"

"I don't think I want to know."

"A seizure salad."

"Groan."

"This is what I love about you, doll. You always make me work for my money." He brought the briefcase up onto the counter and opened it. "So tell me, how's life been treating you and the delightful Joanne?"

"Okay."

He looked up. Beneath bushy, sandy eyebrows, his eyes were a surprisingly soft brown. "You got troubles?" he asked.

"The usual. Family stuff."

"Yeah. Sure. I know all about that."

He did, too. Bernie and Nora had once gone for coffee together, and she'd learned the story of his life. He had a nervous wife prone to anxiety attacks and four children, all in their twenties now, but who'd given Bernie plenty of grief in their day.

"How's your wife?"

"Some days good. Some days not so good. The doctor gave her some pills."

"And your son? Christopher?"

"Crispen. What a name, huh? I said to my wife where'd you find that—on a cracker box? Crispen Cohen. No wonder the kid ended up on drugs."

"How is he now?"

Bernie held up his hand and showed her his crossed fingers. He had surprisingly shapely hands for such a big, burly man. "On the straight and narrow. Going back to school to be a refrigerator repairman. So tell me, sweetheart, what's happening in your house?"

On an impulse, Nora said, "It's my fifteen-year-old daughter. She's pregnant."

Bernie heaved a huge sigh. "Oy, oy, oy."

"We want her to have an abortion, but she doesn't think she wants to. It's a big mess."

"And the father?"

"No one we know. She met him at a party and that was that."

"My God, it's vomit from the mouth of God. These kids."

Nora found herself laughing, and then understood the impulse that had led her to confide in Bernie. He could always make her laugh.

He smiled. "I should have been a writer, huh? That's what my mother used to tell me. Although who knew from writers in those days? Who thought a scribbler could make a million dollars? So, now I'm a seller of lousy tiddlywinks games."

Nora forgave him. "Those wooden puzzles were a big hit. We've sold out."

"See? What did I tell you? Now, if you think those are good, you have to take a look at . . ."

Bernie left half an hour later, rushing out, his raincoat filled like a sail with wind that had veered in the opposite direction. Nora watched him go, smiled to herself and caught sight of her image in the mirror of the doll cabinet. Her cheeks were pink, and the tendrils of blond hair that had escaped from the tortoiseshell combs curled becomingly at her temples. She didn't look like the anxious mother of a pregnant fifteen-year-old; she looked young and vibrant, almost pretty. It wasn't only Bernie; being in the store did that to her, too. The lights, the shelves and mirrors, the bright and colorful merchandise became a backdrop for her, a setting, a stage on which she could work the illusion that she was someone other than the Nora Beeme who lived at 172 Cedarview Crescent. That Nora was reserved, a little shy, not a joiner, the kind of person who felt uncomfortable at parties, because she often couldn't think of what to say to strangers. The Nora of The Kids' Place was different. The merchandise provided her with conversation, the customers and salesmen with tiny, fleeting slices of sociability. In her store Nora was friendly, open, gregarious and chatty. She liked stepping into this persona; it felt good—like a dress that flattered her figure and face, eyes and hair, so that she appeared to be more than she was, more than the sum of those individual parts.

Nora had lost her taste for fantasizing during the Family Management Sessions. Although they were discussing, on this particular Sunday evening, the logistics of Danny's birthday party—the time and date, how many boys, what they'd do—the underlying tension was not conducive to any variety of eroticism. Christine was too quiet, too still. Her nails, bitten to the quick, were now ignored. She sat on the couch with her ankles crossed and her fingers twined together. Nora had begun to think she could see the pregnancy in Christine's face. She'd been nauseous lately, throwing up in the mornings and not sleeping well. Her face was narrower, paler. There were faint smudges of lavender below her eyes.

Marty had been hopeful that the physical discomfort of pregnancy would make Christine see the light, but much to their surprise it hadn't. This daughter, who complained vociferously over cuts and bruises, stomachaches and headaches, whose angling for affection when she was sick was incredibly blatant, who used every illness to stay out of school to the point of absurdity, had become a stoic. Nora hadn't known she was throwing up until Danny told her. She hadn't been aware that Christine wasn't sleeping until she herself had been up one night in the small hours and found her heating up milk for hot chocolate in the kitchen.

"How long has this been going on?" Nora had asked. She'd noticed the lowering level of chocolate powder in the Nestle's Quik box but had assumed the culprit was Danny, who had a disgusting habit of eating the stuff dry.

"I can't stay awake at school," Christine said, "but I can't seem to sleep at night either." She was wearing an old flannel nightgown with hearts all over it and torn lace at the collar. In the shadows cast by the fluorescent light, her face looked especially drawn.

"Would you put in some milk for me?" Nora said, perching on one of the stools at the counter, and then added, "When I can't sleep, it's usually because I'm worried about something."

Christine stirred the milk. "I guess I've got plenty to be worried about."

"I wish you didn't."

"I know, Mom. I wish I didn't, too, but everything's changed."

"It doesn't have to be that way. Everything could go back to the way it was."

"Do you really think that? You think that if I had an abortion, I'd be the same person I was before?"

It was at times like this that Nora wished herself back a month, two months, when the most crucial issue in Christine's life had been the addition of another expensive skirt to her wardrobe. "You might not be exactly the same *person,* but you'd be able to have the same *life* you had before."

"I find it really strange, Mom, that when I was little, you taught me to care about other people and not to only think about myself all the time, but when it comes to this baby, you want me to throw all that out the window."

"I don't think of it as a baby."

"Well, I do."

Nora sighed and studied her daughter's profile. "Christine, is what Daddy and I want for you too much?"

Christine glanced at her. "What do you mean?"

"Well, we want you to get good grades and go on to college. We want you to have a career and live an independent life. Do those expectations bother you?"

"Sometimes," Christine said slowly. "I guess I'm not sure I can live up to them."

"Is that why you're doing this, do you think? Because we're asking too much?"

Christine gave her an angry look. "Mom, I'm doing it because I can't *kill* something that's alive, that depends on *me* for its existence. And if I did have an abortion, I'd always know what I'd done. I'd never forget that I'd taken the easy way out."

Nora heard the mimicking singsong in her voice. "Is that what they tell you—over at the Coalition for Life?"

"Don't lay a heavy trip on me, Mom. Please."

"They have a one-sided, biased view of the world, Christine. They're trying to mold you into their own image. That's what I don't like about them."

"They're just trying to be helpful."

"Honey, let me put it to you this way. I don't think an abortion is the easy way out. I think it's a hard decision."

There was a silence between them, filled in by the kind of house noises that can only be heard in the dead of night: the hum of the refrigerator, the click of the oven clock, the gentle breathing of the furnace. Christine lifted the wooden spoon from the milk and sipped at it. Then she glanced at Nora.

"Daddy still thinks he can change my mind. He talks at me and talks at me. He never gives up. He thinks he's the only one in the world who knows what's right and wrong. Well you know something, Mom? I think there's a lot of rights and wrongs in this world, and nobody can know everything."

"That's my point!" Nora was quick to say. "The Coalition people think *they're* the only ones who know right from wrong."

"I'm not saying they're perfect. I know that."

"Christine, you still have time."

Christine lifted the pot and poured the milk into a mug. "It doesn't make any difference. I'm not going to have an abortion. You can tell Daddy that if you like."

Danny didn't want to go to the YMCA in Burtonville, which ran birthday parties for parents who couldn't face having ten eleven-year-old boys in the house. "That's really boring kid stuff, Dad. Nobody wants to do that anymore."

Marty was looking tired, too. His eyes had swollen pouches beneath them. He hadn't been sleeping well either, tossing and turning some nights or taking nightly prowls on others. Nora had a brief vision of the three of them, she and Christine and Marty, all wandering through the house, wraiths in nightclothes and bathrobes passing silently in the dark.

Marty rubbed a hand across his face. "Well, Danny, what are the options then? Bowling?"

"Yuck, we did that last year."

"Swimming?"

"Nah."

Marty looked imploringly at Nora. "A movie?" she said. "At the Odeon and then hot dogs and pizza at the restaurant next door?"

"Yeah," Danny said enthusiastically. He loved going out to restaurants. "Okay."

"Good," Marty said. "That's settled. Nora, you have anything more to say?"

"No, I think we've covered everything."

"Then I guess we can adjourn for—"

Christine sat up in her chair. "You haven't asked me yet."

Nora knew the oversight was deliberate. When Marty had finally realized that all of his mustered and organized and brilliant facts could not change Christine's mind, he'd begun to ignore her. He went to work in the morning, came home in the evening, sat at dinner, complimented Nora on a coffee cake she'd made, read the paper in the living room, discussed the beginning of the baseball season with Danny, and acted as if Christine had been erased from the family. If she tried to talk to him, he answered in monosyllables. If they passed in a hallway, he averted his head. Christine had taken to staying in her room most of the time, and Nora had found herself caught between two states, sympathizing with Marty one moment and being absolutely furious with him another.

Nora wasn't accustomed to being mad at Marty on a long-term basis. They'd had their fights and disagreements, but these had never been serious, and they had always talked things out to a point where they could compromise. To Nora, their marriage was a perpetual-motion machine that hummed and buzzed and clanked along, requiring minor adjustments now and then to keep the noise at the proper level. Marty, for example, had learned not to kick his dirty jockey shorts under the bed or to discuss his work at boring length at dinner parties. Nora had tidied up her Felsher table manners and rid herself of the habit of storing leftovers in tiny containers for so long that they grew a fuzz thick enough to spin into knitting yarn.

Occasionally, even though the machinery appeared to be in running order, a major overhaul was necessary. In the early seventies, Women's Lib had forced Nora into a close reexamination of the political aspects of her marriage and had inspired several debates over the division of household labor. The debates had been generally friendly, and Marty had been amenable to some persuasion. He'd agreed to change Danny's diapers now and then, to make one meal per weekend, to do the laundry when he saw the basket was full, to occasionally clean the bathroom. This political balance (or imbalance—Nora had known she was only making a dint in a vast, shining mass of inequities) had been impeccably maintained all during the time that they had lived in the small townhouse in Burtonville. But backsliding had begun to occur as soon as they moved to Cedarview Crescent. The allotment of household work had turned into a division of inside/ outside labor. Nora was now impresario of domestic details while Marty managed the externals: the cars, the garbage, the lawn work, the cleaning of gutters, the spraying of trees. Nora had the guilty sensation that she'd let down the movement, that she'd allowed suburbia to undermine the rhetoric, but the truth was she'd never really liked having Marty in the kitchen, he wasn't much of a cook, and besides she'd always hated mowing the lawn.

But this business with Christine was different. Nora felt the machinery of her marriage faltering. Small things about Marty had begun to irritate her out of all proportion: the length of time he took in the shower, the fact that he never turned the bathroom fan on after he'd had a shit, the discovery of a quarter-sized bald spot at the back of his head. She had small, irrational flare-ups of anger, most of which she immediately suppressed. But she wasn't able to hide the fact that she was finding it increasingly difficult to have orgasms. Fantasies didn't seem to work any more. Nor were all of Marty's generous efforts capable of bringing her to that wet, silky and ultimately satisfying point.

"I'm sorry," she had said one night, shifting in bed and feeling the sheets stick to her sweaty back. "I just can't."

"New position time. Turn over."

"I don't think that's going to work either. Just forget about me. It's okay."

But Marty had always taken Nora's orgasms or lack thereof to heart. "What's the matter, hon? This is about the fifth time you've had trouble coming."

Nora sighed. "I'm upset about you and Christine. No, not upset. Angry."

Marty, who had been lying sideways, his head propped up on his elbow, now lay on his back. "Angry at me?"

"You act like she doesn't exist."

"What am I supposed to do? Fold her into my arms and tell her it's all okay? She hasn't scraped her knee, Nora. She's doing something I profoundly disagree with."

"But can't you talk to her at least? Look at her as if she's there and not see-through?"

"Look," he said. "Work's been lousy lately. Peterson's software analysis was a waste of time, meaning the buck stops here. McAllister is on my back. Bariskofsky is still acting like a goddamned shark. Every day I'm snowed under with instructions from the top that don't make any sense to the guys out in the trenches. So when I come home, I don't want any more shit. You understand what I mean? I can't face any more problems."

"I think," Nora said, "that you're creating problems by ignoring her."

"All right, all right. I'm angry underneath, too, okay? This is the way I express it."

"Maybe it would be better to blow up and clear the air."

"Maybe it would, but it's not going to change anything."

"Are you going to treat her like this for the whole seven months? What kind of family life are we going to have if you do that?"

"I'm not a puppet," he said angrily. "I can't be jerked

around to suit everyone's emotional needs. I've got my own emotions to deal with."

Marty wasn't a man who talked often about his feelings and Nora had felt immediately contrite. She put her arm over his belly and slid her hand down to his groin. He'd gone limp, his penis curled up into itself. "Will you try though?" she asked.

Marty took a big breath. "I'll try," he said, "but you'll have to give me time."

But time hadn't solved the problem, only worsened it, and it seemed to Nora that the silence between Christine and Marty had grown so loud that it filled the house, spreading like fog, its tendrils creeping in and choking all parts of their life. But she hadn't expected Christine to be the one to stop that insidious creeping; Nora hadn't thought she'd have the courage.

Now Marty sat back in his chair. "Okay, Christine, what do you want to say?"

"I know you're real angry at me because of what I've decided, and I just want to say that I can understand that. Lots of parents can't handle it when a girl decides to go ahead and have a baby."

"You know what I can't stand," Marty said, "is when you sound like one of those damned brochures you brought home."

Christine looked down at her tightly clasped fingers. "Okay," she said, "then I'll tell you in my own way. The people at the Coalition sometimes have rooms that they rent for pregnant girls, ones that need to get away from home. I've thought about it a lot, and I'm wondering if it wouldn't be better for me to leave for a while."

To Nora, the silence had taken on a new and terrifying dimension. After Christine had spoken it was no longer a fog-like, creeping thing, but a raging animal roaring around the living room, howling in the corners, a violence that beat painfully around her ears.

Danny had blinked hard at Christine's words. Now he leaned over, peered into Christine's downturned face and said in a tiny, high-pitched voice, "You mean you wouldn't be here for my birthday?"

"No," Nora said quickly, "she'd not going anywhere. Christine, of course we want you to stay at home. You have to let us get used to the idea, that's all. Please don't think for a minute that we want you to go."

"Daddy does."

"No, he doesn't." Nora turned to Marty, wondering why he hadn't spoken, and saw that he had put his hand over his eyes as if to shield them from the light. "Marty?"

And then he took his hand away, and they could all see that he had started to cry.

Another Monday morning. When Nora had left the house this morning, she'd seen that her perennials were growing green and lush behind the clumps of mauve crocuses and waving red tulips. Usually she was an avid gardener, studying seed catalogues, planning what flats she would buy, making profound and important decisions about the location of this perennial or that. The fact that her garden was never entirely successful had not bothered her. The plants were like children, she'd always reasoned, growing in uneven, unpredictable patterns and requiring a firm hand through pruning, although she was always just a bit too lenient and the plants took advantage of her, spreading too far and trying to choke off their neighbors. Godlike, she would cut here and clip there, chatting as she went ("Oh no you don't. . . . This won't hurt a bit. . . . If you think I'm going to let you trail that vine halfway to Timbuktoo . . .") and thinking that, best of all, unlike children, the plants never talked back.

Now as she sat on a stool beside the cash register, adding up the tapes from the past week, Nora tried to envision her flower beds and decide if the coreopsis should be divided or that overly droopy bleeding heart removed once and for all, but this wasn't a typical Monday morning. A huge delivery had arrived from United Parcel, and there was a thin but steady stream of customers. At the moment two women were studying the crib toys: mobiles, bumper pads, stuffed animals. The older of the two, a white-haired woman, was holding onto a music box that hooked to crib rails and was showing it to the younger one, who was plump and looking happy.

"Isn't this just darling? My grandson has one of these. He loves it. Marion turns it on, and he just lays in the crib and smiles."

"I can't believe it, you know."

"Oh, it'll happen soon enough."

"I never thought Karen would have children. She was career, career, career, right from the beginning."

"It's that—what do they call it—the biological imperative. The clock just ticking away until they realize it's now or never."

"Bill can't believe it either. You know what he says to me? 'I'm going to be sleeping with a grandma. How do you like that?' Well, I'll be sleeping with a grandpa, I say. How do you like *that*? He just laughs. Oh, heavens, will you look at this mobile, the one with all the planets?"

"Educational," the older one said. "Start them right off in the crib."

Nora had been listening to this exchange and smiling, but now she gave an inadvertent shudder. *I'll be sleeping with a grandma.* Even if Christine was going to be giving up the baby the child would exist somewhere, and Nora would always be somebody's grandmother. In the past aging had not worried her a great deal. She hadn't liked the fact that her breasts now drooped into sagging lozenges or that her hips carried small squirrel-like pouches of fat, but because she had never considered herself a pretty woman Nora hadn't agonized over the loss of her looks. In fact sometimes she thought she looked better at forty-three than she had at twenty. Pictures of her then always showed her smiling, but the curve of her lips was tentative, as if she weren't exactly sure what the photograph would portray. But the jump from that girl to grandmother was too big for Nora to contemplate. She thought of her own grandmothers. They could have been twins, small women with large bosoms, liver spots and gray curls held firmly by hairnets that looked like spider webs.

The two women were still picking out crib toys, and Nora was idly wondering whether anyone wore those impossibly gossamer hairnets any more when Sylvia Allison walked into the store. She nodded to Nora, who found herself wearing a surprised and strained upward curve on her mouth, and then walked over to the section that held the children's clothing. Nora hadn't seen Sylvia since the Coalition for Life had taken down its booth several months before, and she remembered her as stout, big-nosed, heavy-faced. Sylvia was all these things, but to Nora's displeasure she also had that graceful, queenly carriage that characterizes some heavy women and lovely hair that swept in high wings of silvery-gray.

Nora didn't want to acknowledge anything positive about Sylvia, because in the week that had followed the last Family Management Session all the anger she'd felt for Marty had shifted. Like a large heavy wheel, it had turned slowly and awkwardly before coming to rest in another position, and Nora had discovered in herself a fierce hatred for the Coalition for Life in general and Sylvia Allison in particular. Without her interference, nothing would have been as it was. Christine wouldn't still be pregnant. Danny wouldn't be worried about things that no eleven-year-old should have to worry about.

("Would Christine still be part of the family if she left?"

"Of course she would. She'd still be your sister. But she's not going to leave. We've settled that."

"But if she *did,* who would take care of her?"

"Nobody, she'd take care of herself."

"What about her allowance? Would she get that?"

"Danny, it's not going to happen. There's no point in talking about it any more."

"If I left, I'd have to keep up my paper route, wouldn't I?"

"You're not going anywhere. Believe me.")

Marty would also not have been brought to the point of crying, and Nora wouldn't now be playing the role of the family Pollyanna, cheerfully and optimistically presiding over the uneasy truce that reigned in the Beeme house. She didn't like this Nora, who chattered on through awkward moments as if they didn't exist, who relentlessly commented on the bright side, who felt the need to buck up any morale that was sinking. ("Lay off," Marty said one night when Nora had effusively complimented him on how well he was handling Christine. "Just lay off.") But she couldn't help herself. A queen-of-the-mountain doesn't abdicate and a mender of cracks never, ever stops.

Sylvia picked off the rack an expensive smocked dress in a shade of the palest lavender and brought it over to the counter. There then ensued two simultaneous conversations. One, in real time, observed the niceties, the attitude that the customer is always right; the other was silent, one-sided and observed nothing at all.

"You're Danny's mother. Right?"

"Yes." Nora, seeing that they weren't going to mention Christine, thought: *you bitch.*

"I'm not sure about Mrs. Phelan," Sylvia went on, referring to Danny and Bobby Allison's teacher. "I don't think she has that class under control at all."

"I know what you mean." *You lousy bitch.*

"I haven't been in here before," Sylvia said, pulling out her checkbook. "You have a lovely store. It's just charming."

"Thank you." Nora rang up the purchase and noticed with a certain satisfaction that her hands were rock-steady.

"How long have you been here?"

"Five years." *Nosy bitch.*

"That long! I remember when this shopping mall was a hole in the ground." Sylvia was filling out the check; she had broad, capable hands, with short nails coated in a clear polish. "You know, my sister-in-law tells me that they don't really put baby girls in dresses like these any more. They're too impractical, she says, and when the baby learns to crawl, her knees go right up the dress. But I can't help myself. They're so pretty, I just have to buy them."

"They're wash-and-wear now," Nora said as she took the check. "No more ironing." *Ignorant bitch.*

"Well, that's something anyway. Do you gift-wrap, too?"

They did, but Nora would be damned first. "No, I'm sorry, we don't." *You lousy, nosy, ignorant, interfering bitch.*

The grandmother-to-be and her friend arrived at the counter

just as Sylvia left. They had chosen the astronomical mobile, bumper pads, several chewable toys, a blue bath sponge ("We know it's a boy already, but I think this amniocentesis business has taken some of the fun out of being pregnant, don't you?"), and a diaper bag that hung on the wall and had a face like a panda bear. Nora smiled, chatted, wrapped up the items, made change, and felt her heartbeat slowly gear down to a reasonable level. After they left she made a deliberate tour of the empty store, straightening the merchandise, rearranging a shelf of wooden animal puzzles, running her hand along the rack of dresses to even them out. She was seeking that addictive fix, that shot of soothing calm, that The Kids' Place always gave her. Except that this morning it didn't. No matter how many times she made the circuit Nora couldn't contain an unhappy restlessness, and it came to her, as she returned to her perch by the counter, that Sylvia hadn't just invaded her privacy, her marriage and her family. She had also left a stain, an ugly taint, in the one place that Nora had counted on to remain pure, untouched, undefiled.

It was the final straw.

For the first time since Christine had announced that she thought she was pregnant, Nora felt tears come to her eyes, stinging, salty, helpless tears, and folding her arms, she put her head down on the counter and wept.

4

◇   ◇   ◇   Joanne lived half a mile from Nora on a
street called Oakvale Mews. In their subdivision, Mews were
more prestigious than Crescents, having larger houses on quarter-
acre lots with three-car garages. The landscape around them had
not been razed as thoroughly during construction as it had been
on Nora's street, where the cedars of Cedarview Crescent had
been bulldozed into oblivion to make way for basements and
asphalt. On Oakvale Mews, oak trees still stood tall over mock-
Tudors and mock-Colonials—even, joked Joanne, mock-
Moderns. These houses were inhabited by lawyers, doctors and
investment bankers and often had swimming pools in the back-
yards. Joanne, who had reluctantly donned the coat of suburban
life in the first place, refused to button it up to her throat. No
matter how hard her children begged, she would not have a pool
installed. Which was why when Nora arrived at the Whites' on a
warm Sunday afternoon in late May, she found Joanne lounging
on a cushioned chaise on her back deck without a child in sight.

"You see? There's a method in my madness," she said with
satisfaction as Nora lowered herself onto the second chaise. "The

Beckwiths opened their pool early, and the entire neighborhood is in their backyard."

"And Grant—where's he?"

"At the—" Joanne paused. "The office."

Nora didn't catch the pause. She was thinking that if there had been room in her backyard, she would have gotten a pool. Unlike Joanne, she got a robust enjoyment from living in the heart of suburbia. She liked her house, which was duplicated in different pastel shades up and down her street. She liked having a garage full of bicycles and a station wagon that guzzled gas like a parched drunkard. She didn't even mind the fact that she could walk two miles in any direction and still be in a housing development. But then unlike Joanne, Nora had grown up in a cramped apartment over a bakery and had had to share a bedroom with her brother.

"He says," Joanne added.

"Says what?"

"That he's at the office." Joanne stood up. "Want some iced tea? I made up a pitcher."

"Sure. Well, isn't he?"

"I don't know. That's why I asked you to come over."

The screen door slid back over its tracks as Joanne went into the house. Nora heard the refrigerator door open and shut, and she could see the outline of Joanne's body through the screen. Joanne was wearing a red-and-green-striped bandeau that barely encased her melon-shaped breasts and left a solid rim of flesh exposed between her ribs and the waistband of baggy khaki shorts. Nora was already tan from hours working in the garden, but Joanne got rashes from the sun and always wore coolie-style hats and coated herself in sun-blocking creams. Her summer skin, Nora thought, was fashionably Victorian: pale, freckled and veined.

The screen door opened again, and Joanne reappeared with two glasses of iced tea. She handed one to Nora and then settled herself back on the chaise. "Of course I'm saying to myself that I must be paranoid. The man is a workaholic—right?"

"Why not phone him and find out if he's there?" Nora asked in some mystification.

"Because I found these." Joanne sighed as she pulled two paper napkins from between her breasts where they'd been tucked. "I guess I don't want to have my suspicions confirmed a hundred percent."

The napkins were the type found in metal dispensers in cheap restaurants, long and narrow and faintly ribbed. Nora unrolled them and laid them flat on her knees. Both bore a message in a round, childish script written in green ball-point pen. One said "I luv ya." The other, "You okay, babe?"

"Do you believe it?" Joanne said.

"These belong to Grant?"

"I found one in the pocket of his gray suit and the other in his brown coat. I was taking his winter clothes to the cleaners. The thing that gets me, Nora, is that I think he must have wanted me to find out. Why else would he have left them there? I'm the one who takes things to the cleaners."

Nora studied the napkins. "But this doesn't sound like Grant. 'You okay, babe?' *Babe?* Is that Grant?"

Joanne took a sip of iced tea. "Vulgar, isn't she?"

"You might be jumping to conclusions."

"I have an instinct about this," Joanne said grimly. "A sixth sense. I mean, in twenty-four years of marriage, I've never had a hint that Grant might be unfaithful. Not a breath. But now this, and all those Sunday afternoons at the office. And now that I think about it—what about the new interest in photography and the Camera Club on Thursday nights?"

"But Grant has been taking very interesting pictures," Nora felt obliged to point out. "The ones from your trip to the Bahamas were sort of artistic."

"All right. Maybe the Camera Club is legitimate. But Nora, things haven't been very good between us. Not for a while. Not since we had that blow-up in February over those stupid Australian stocks."

Grant had lost ten thousand dollars in penny metal stocks, an investment that he hadn't told Joanne about until the losses were too great to hide. Nora had been shocked when Joanne told her, not only because the amount was so large, but because Grant had always struck her as such a careful, unspeculative kind of man. But when she said this to Marty, he had just shrugged, saying that Grant had always been a bit of a gambler when it came to the stock market.

Joanne had been predictably enraged, accusing Grant of playing with family money and of pouring the children's future down a sinkhole. Grant had countered with instances of Joanne's own financial mismanagement: dresses bought and hardly worn, vegetables that rotted in the refrigerator, a Steinway purchased and expensive piano lessons paid for even though not one of their children had showed the slightest musical ability and all of them had hated practicing. He'd even pulled out check stubs and receipts and added up the cost of Joanne's maternal dreams. ("$13,562.67," Joanne had said wonderingly to Nora, "and not one kid can even play 'Chopsticks.' ")

"I thought that had blown over," Nora said.

"Oh, it did—sort of. But it left a bad taste. And the thing is, this isn't the first time. He's lost money before. Okay, he's made some too. But the amounts are getting bigger. Oh, I know he earns more now, too, especially since he became a partner, but how can I trust him? Honest to God, Nora, I've been reduced to sneaking into his den and going through his papers. And our sex life has been the shits, too."

Nora had always thought that if Joanne's marital sex life were graphed, it would look like a cross section of the Himalayas, with soaring heights and plunging crevasses. Her own, in comparison, would have been a gentle landscape of rolling hills and valleys.

"Of course, the first thing I thought of was revenge," Joanne went on. "I even considered Bernie Cohen for a small trip to the Aurora Motel."

"Bernie!"

"Oh, sure, he's available."

"He made a pass?"

"Not a pass. I just know. He gives off the vibes."

"Not to me, he doesn't."

"You're not available, that's the difference. If you were, you'd give off something, too. I don't know what it is—an odor or a sound—like the ones that dogs can hear but humans can't."

Nora supposed this was true. She had never physically committed adultery. This was not for lack of opportunity. Although she did not give off that whatever-it-was that let men know when a woman was available, there had been the odd man in the twenty years of her married life who hadn't noticed her antiseptic aura. Several of these she wouldn't have touched with a ten-foot pole; others she'd found sexy. She'd even incorporated a couple into her fantasy world and committed mental adultery. One man, an engineer who had worked at Devlin Electronics ten years ago, had actually driven her to murder. He'd never made a pass at her, but he had given Nora such looks from his striking blue eyes that she'd created a fantasy in which Marty was killed in a car accident and she became a grieving and lonely widow with deep sexual desires, which only the engineer could satisfy.

She had played this one out in all its variations—he comes to Marty's funeral where she is wearing becoming black, *no,* he arrives at her house late one night when the children are asleep, *no,* they've gone to visit her mother so the house is empty; the doorbell rings, of course she's dressed only in a negligee, *no,* wrapped in a towel, she's just come out of a sweet-scented bath; he enters, his eyes on the tops of her breasts, her legs, the peekaboo of dark-golden pubic hair beneath the towel's edge; they say nothing, he closes the door and then slowly releases her slackening grip on the towel until it drops, revealing . . .

Nora would have been the first to admit that if the metaphorical towel had ever been yanked from around her brain, her fantasies would have been revealed as hopelessly banal, a muddle of romantic longings and sleazy pornographic images, the latter shamelessly plagiarized from a few dirty magazines and *The Story of O,* which had circulated around her college dorm. Of course none of these fantasies bore the slightest relation to real life. She had finally spent a dinner party sitting next to this particular engineer, and he'd proved to be so dull that her fantasy had expired immediately. Which was no loss, she'd felt, because she had a thousand others to replace it.

Perhaps, Nora now thought, it was the fantasies that had kept her on the straight and narrow for twenty years. She was not, so to speak, open for business. Passes made sporadically during the years had fallen on the closed door of her loyalty and attachment to Marty, whom she might be quite willing to murder for a flight of fancy, but whom she loved so deeply that the thought of his real death frightened her terribly. Nora supposed her marital chastity was old-fashioned and slightly ridiculous, but she had never allowed it to color her perspective. If other people wanted to commit adultery, that was fine. It was simply off-bounds for Marty and herself.

"So why didn't you take Bernie to the Aurora Motel?" Nora asked.

Joanne gave an irritable shrug. "At first, I thought my reluctance had to do with the fact that I've always been unfaithful to Grant in the heat of an argument—as if that energy translated itself into a sort of reckless sexual energy. But you see, we're not fighting at the moment, just coexisting in space." She heaved a big sigh. "But then, I thought that maybe I was just getting old. I couldn't seem to drum up enthusiasm for poor old Bernie. Besides, with this AIDS business, you just don't jump into the sack with any— Oh, my God—" Joanne's glass was frozen in midair, its amber liquid tilted at a precarious angle toward her mouth. "Grant hasn't had to use a condom in twenty-five years."

Nora shook her head. "Joanne, this is crazy. You haven't proven anything yet."

"What would you think if you found those napkins in Marty's clothes?"

"I'd think— I don't know what I'd think actually. I guess I'd be suspicious, but I wouldn't jump to conclusions so fast."

"You know, the funny thing is that I always thought I wouldn't care if I found that Grant had been screwing around. I mean, it might even be tit for tat. I'd deserve it, wouldn't I?"

"Are you sure he's never known about your affairs?"

"Never," Joanne said with a trace of pride. "He's never even guessed. I don't bring home evidence. I don't fish off the company pier."

"You think it's someone in his office?"

"No, but I think it's someone he's meeting in one of the restaurants near his building. And I think she's young and not too smart and"—Joanne's eyes narrowed—"definitely tacky."

Nora tried to imagine Grant with a young, dumb, tacky someone and failed, but then she hadn't envisioned him as a gambler either. In fact, when she thought more about it, there seemed to be a lot she didn't know about Grant even though she had known him for more than twenty years of evenings together, summer barbecues, camping trips in the Adirondacks, and hundreds of co-joined children's activities. Nora had sat next to Grant at more school plays, ballet recitals, baseball games, and track and field events than she could count.

"Are you going to say anything to him?" she asked.

Joanne had picked up one of the napkins and was holding it from her with the extreme tips of her thumb and forefinger as if it were emitting an extremely bad odor. "What would you do?"

The same imagination that had failed Nora when she attempted to picture Grant cavorting with a woman did not fail her again. The vision of Marty making love to another woman was vivid: his hand on her breast, his fingers in her vagina, oh, God, his tongue grazing the pubic hair at that soft and sensitive juncture of her labia. Nora shivered and thought of how she would feel if she carried that vision, that possibility of reality, in her brain. There would be pain and fear and jealousy, all coalescing into one agonizing lump that would sit within her as if she had swallowed a heavy, sharp-edged stone. The pressure it exerted would be unbearable, the need to expel it overwhelming. She was accustomed to turning to Marty when she was in distress. He wasn't only her lover, her husband and the father of her children; he had also been her best friend—almost from the moment she had met him twenty years before.

"I'd ask," she finally said. "I'd have to."

* * *

1968. The night of Joanne and Grant's party. Nora had not been at all enthusiastic about going. She wasn't good at parties, and she knew her invitation was part of a matchmaking effort of Joanne's to pair her up with Marty Beeme. Nora had already resisted several previous similar attempts—blind dates and intimate dinner parties—not because Marty didn't sound appealing, but because she hated being measured, gauged and classified. "You're Marty's type," Joanne kept saying. "He goes for short, shy blondes."

Nora disliked the idea that a person had a type and that she matched it. Some days she seemed to herself to be energetic, sparkling, cheerful—a bon vivant; while on others she was gloomy, depressed, dowdy and a loser. These two personae appeared to have nothing to do with one another but lived side by side in her head, jostling one another as if they were cohabiting a small and cluttered apartment. (At forty-three, Nora would still be capable of these extremes of personality, but she would consider them as spokes in a wheel of which the hub was an unchangeable entity. At twenty-two, she felt helplessly caught in the swing of a pendulum, at the height one day, in free-fall the next.)

Nora's bon vivant personality rarely surfaced when she needed it the most, which was at bashes like the Whites' where the air was thick with music, smoke and chatter, and everyone else seemed to be having the time of their lives. Part of her problem, she knew, was that she didn't drink very much, she hated that feeling of losing control, and she didn't smoke—cigarettes or marijuana. The other part was that when it came to small talk, she seemed to have a fatal tendency to self-destruct, creating awkward silences or saying the wrong things. Consequently, Nora had ended up in baby Matthew's bedroom, rocking him on her shoulder, because he refused to go to sleep and had made a general nuisance of himself at the party.

Joanne felt guilty about this and, at periodic intervals, brought Nora more ginger ale, a plate of hors d'oeuvres and bits and pieces of conversation. "Not asleep yet?" she said on one such visit. "Christ, but that kid is such a pill. I'm going to owe you one for this." She was wearing a brightly patterned orange-and-red headband and a scarlet caftan that fell to her bare toes. In her right hand was a joint. "Here, want some dope?"

"No thanks," Nora said. "Great party though."

"I'm going to kill Marty when I see him. He said he was coming."

"That's okay." Matthew began to cry again, a thin buzz-saw rasping on Nora's shoulder. "Do you think he's hungry?"

"I fed him an hour ago. Both breasts. You'd have thought we were starving him."

There was a sudden, deep thumping sound in the wall. "What's that?" Nora asked.

Joanne pounded the wall back. "Give up, you old bat!" she hollered and then said, "The neighbor. She hates us. Oh, Jesus, I have to put those garlic and cheese things in the oven." She rushed to the doorway. "If you want to be relieved, just let me know, okay?"

"Okay," Nora said.

But Nora liked it in Matthew's room, which was on the second floor of the townhouse. Up here the cacophony of music and voices faded into a distant roar, and the air didn't smell of stale smoke or marijuana but of Matthew himself, a mixture of Johnson & Johnson baby talc with a slight undercurrent of ammonia, which wasn't unpleasant at all. Besides it was a nice room, painted in pale blue with nursery figures on the walls that reminded Nora of her own childhood: Little Bo Peep, Jack Sprat, Wee Willie Winkie, Little Miss Muffet. A plastic teddy bear night-light shed a dim illumination over the crib, which had a sheet with rows of yellow elephants marching across it and a mobile of farm animals dancing lightly over its bars. "I can't understand it," Nora said to three-month-old Matthew, whose bald head was resting on a diaper that lay across her shoulder. "It's such a nice bed. I wouldn't mind sleeping there." He whimpered and squirmed so she started rocking again.

She had kicked off her high heels, but she was still wearing her basic black cocktail dress, which she had gussied up with several cheap strands of pearls that filled the low neckline and hopefully distracted the eye from an absence of cleavage. The skirt, which was straight with a kick-pleat in the back, had always been just a bit too tight, forcing Nora to wear a panty girdle. As she rocked Matthew, supporting his awkward, terry-cloth lumpiness with one hand, she pulled down the side zipper of her dress with the other, tugged at the waistband of her girdle, and indulged in an orgy of scratching. Joanne had given up girdles, bras and high heels ("How the hell can you be liberated, when you're walking around in your own goddamned prison?"), but Nora just couldn't transform herself into a free spirit. She looked horrible in headbands, and caftans made her appear fat. No matter how hard she tried, she couldn't seem to let it all hang out, get with it, or be cool. She had, she thought unhappily as she rocked and scratched and rubbed her aching arches against the rung of the rocker, something of a girdle mentality: tight and cramped.

Matthew wiggled again, digging his toes into the top of her breasts, when the music from downstairs abruptly stopped with a screech of black vinyl and a woman's voice suddenly screamed, "My God! Police!" Then there was the sound of many feet rushing in various directions, and the doorbell rang over and over with such insistence that Nora knew someone's thumb was repeatedly jabbing the button as hard as possible. She quickly put Matthew down in the crib, ignoring his squeak of protest, zipped up her dress, and went to stand on the landing. Confusion reigned below her. The guests milled around, grabbing at coats and purses, their faces pale and frightened, their voices high. The three cops fanned out purposefully. They were New York State Troopers, tall and intimidating, wearing holstered guns and carrying billy clubs.

Nora sat on the stairs and, through the rails, watched the action. People were herded into small groups, interrogated and then let go. Those freed left as fast as they could, murmuring polite and sympathetic words to Joanne who was standing by the front door and looking alternately furious and dismayed. Grant was arguing with one of the cops, making lawyerish, stabbing gestures in the air, while a second cop led out one of the guests, another lawyer—Joseph, George, something like that—*his* hands, Nora saw with disbelief, in *handcuffs*.

"You don't understand," Grant was saying. "His father is Roger Pipkin, the county judge."

"I don't give a shit if his father is President of the United States," the cop said. "This here is cannabis, and I've got a job to do."

Joanne caught sight of Nora and ran up the stairs. "That goddamn old bat from next door. She called the cops on us, and they found some dope on Jeremy. Now they want Grant and me to come down to the station, too." She lowered her voice. "Thank God I got rid of mine before they came. I finished smoking it outside. Anyway, they've gone through everyone's pockets and all the women's purses. Christ, what a scene. Listen, would you stay with Matthew until we get back?"

"Sure."

"Thanks a million. I owe you another one."

"That's okay."

But when the front door slammed on the last of them, the silence only lasted for a second. Matthew began crying again. Nora went into his room and tried the old back-rubbing/soothing noises trick, but he would have none of it. His cries turned to screams, and his little legs thrashed. Nora finally walked him over to the window. "See the moon," she said. "See the sky. See the stars." Matthew's eyes were looking over her shoulder, so it was difficult to know whether he was appreciating the view, but he was silent for a minute so Nora persevered. "See the window. And the frame. See the curtains. See the doggies on the curtains. They're happy; they're not crying."

She shouldn't have mentioned it, because Matthew started wailing again. Sighing, Nora was about to start another tour of the bedroom when the doorbell rang. This time, instead of a New York State Trooper, it was a tall, handsome young man with tortoiseshell glasses and dark, curly hair that brushed his collar. He was wearing brown slacks with a sharp crease, a cream-colored, V-necked sweater and a white shirt.

"Hi," he said and, stepping in, surveyed the wreckage of the living room. Every available surface, including the arms of the sofa and chairs, was covered with dirty glasses, beer cans, ashtrays full of stubs, crumpled napkins and plates with half-eaten chips and hors d'oeuvres. "What happened to the party?"

"It got busted."

"No kidding."

"Joanne and Grant had to go down to the police station. I'm Nora Felsher, by the way."

"Marty Beeme. My car broke down. I'm late, but"—he studied the room once more—"lucky." He bestowed on her a smile that revealed very straight white teeth.

Nora shifted Matthew, who was still crying, to her other shoulder and shook Marty's hand. "I'm babysitting Matthew," she said. "He won't go to sleep."

Marty walked around her so that he could look at Matthew's face. "He doesn't seem to be very happy. Is he hungry?"

Nora lifted Matthew away from her. His eyes were squeezed shut, his cheeks red and furious. "He shouldn't be."

"Thirsty, maybe?"

"I could give him some water," Nora said dubiously. "Here, you hold him and I'll look for a bottle."

Marty took him gingerly and followed her into the kitchen. "Does he do anything dangerous?"

"He spits up," Nora said as she threw open cupboard doors. "Here they are. Now, I wonder where she keeps the nipples. In the drawers, do you think?"

"You wouldn't throw up on me, would you?" Marty inquired of Matthew, and then exclaimed, "Holy shit!"

Nora turned around and saw a dribble of white spit-up the texture of loose cottage cheese roll down the sleeve of Marty's sweater. She ripped a piece of paper towel from a roll on the wall and wiped Marty's sleeve. "You shouldn't jiggle him like that. It upsets his stomach."

Marty was giving Matthew a mournful look. "I thought we were friends," he said. "I thought we were pals."

Later, she would pick that moment out of all the others as the one when she had felt that first flutter of interest in Marty Beeme. Smiling to herself, Nora turned back to the kitchen drawers, found the nipples and fixed a bottle of water. Matthew adamantly refused not only the water, but the bottle of formula they hastily warmed up and the pacifier that Nora washed and dipped in sugar.

"I thought every kid liked sugar," Marty said, his voice loud over Matthew's howls. By this time, his sweater was off and his shirtsleeves rolled up. He had nice forearms, Nora noticed, pale skin with dark hair, long muscles and strong wrists.

She pushed back a strand of hair and tucked it behind her ear. "I'm getting desperate or deaf—or both."

"Let me trying walking him again."

"Don't jiggle!"

"Right. Here we go then, Matthew, old man. Over to the sofa. Back to the chair. No? Okay, back to the sofa. Over to the table." He passed Nora, who was slumped in the chair, and winked. "So, tell me, what do you do besides babysit Matthew?"

"I teach first grade."

"Oh, right, Joanne told me that. Actually, I've heard all about you."

Weariness made Nora candid. "I bet," she said with a sigh. "Joanne has spent the last three months trying to match us up."

Marty grinned. "Joanne's been matchmaking since kindergarten. It's in her blood."

"I wonder why it is that married people can't be content until their single friends aren't single anymore. Or why they think they can find you the perfect match." She reflected for a minute. "I mean, how many perfect matches can there be in this world?"

"You know what I think? Hey, Matthew, no need to get hysterical; if you don't like the doorway, just speak up next time. I think if we had a master machine, some kind of huge computer that could list all of us, it would find that each person could have thousands upon thousands of compatible mates."

Nora tried this thought on, but found it uncomfortable. She'd been brought up on a diet of rock 'n' roll love songs, books like *Gone With the Wind* and *Marjorie Morningstar,* beach blanket Grade-B movies, and the concept of Mr. Right. "What about true love? Don't you believe in that?"

"I don't think love has anything to do with it."

"That sounds sort of cynical to me."

"No, it's just a matter of mathematical probabilities." Marty wheeled smartly around, taking Matthew by surprise so that, for a brief moment, he stopped crying and simply blinked. "Just like Matthew here. You see, he's bound to stop, because the statistical probability of him still crying, say, two days from now, over precisely the same thing, is near zero."

As they had been talking, Matthew's cries had been evolving from howls into screeches. "Oh, God," Nora said. "How about the statistical probability in the next two minutes?"

Marty took Matthew off his shoulder and, cradling him in his arms, looked down at the small, distorted face. "Unlikely," he acknowledged. "Highly unlikely. Okay, back to shoulder position. Up we go and—"

But Matthew made a convulsive movement, stopped crying and a sound intervened. A distinct rumbling. Liquid thunder rolling in the vicinity of his diaper. Matthew looked from Marty to Nora and then gave them both a cheerful, toothless smile, while the air filled with a sour, almost musty odor.

"Christ Almighty," Marty said. "Are you any good at this?"

A yellow-brown stain had appeared at the back of Matthew's blue sleeper. "I always give him back to Joanne at this point," Nora confessed.

Marty took a deep breath. "A grown man shouldn't be afraid of a little shit, right?"

"Well," Nora said, as the stain spread down one leg, "statistical probabilities suggest that if we don't get him up to the bathtub or something, you're going to be covered in it."

Marty turned Matthew around, looked at the stain, and blanched. "You know what you've done?" he asked Matthew. "You've just set fatherhood back at least ten years. Minimum."

Later, when Nora and Marty would recall stripping Matthew down in the bathtub, they laughed and exchanged fond, nostalgic smiles. When they were actually doing it, the mood was quite different. Marty had to kneel before the tub, the crease in his pants crushed, his shirt wet, while Nora, also kneeling, tried to remove Matthew's diaper and rubber pants without coating herself in baby shit. Whenever she glanced at Marty, Nora could see that his face was strained and disbelieving. Her own face felt stretched into a grimace, and she knew she was a mess. Her dress was crumpled, her stocking had ripped at the left knee, and her hair, formerly a pert, upturned flip, had gone limp and stringy.

"God, to think I must have done this once," Marty said at one point as he stuck Matthew's slimy buttocks under the tap.

"And your mother still loved you."

"Amazing. Absolutely amazing."

Matthew was finally washed, wrapped in a towel and, looking none the worse for wear, placed on the changing table in his bedroom. Nora and Marty simultaneously took a deep breath.

"Mission accomplished," Marty said.

"Not yet," Nora said. "He has to be diapered."

"A piece of cake. Double in front for boys."

"Who told you that?"

"Joanne." He unwrapped the towel. "Ready?" Matthew blew a bubble and kicked his legs. "Thatsa a boy— Oops, what's this?"

Matthew's penis had risen up into a tiny white exclamation point. Nora felt a rush of heat fill her face, staining her cheeks red. She wasn't so much embarrassed by Matthew's immature erection as she was by a physical awareness of Marty, that fact that she thought he was sexy, and the thought of Marty's erections, rising even now onto the surface of her mind. To avoid looking at him, she leaned over and pulled a diaper out of a drawer.

"Jesus Christ!"

Nora stood up just in time to witness a small, glittering fountain of urine spurting out of Matthew and cascading onto his rotund belly. Hastily, she jammed the diaper over his penis, and looked up to find Marty doubled over and laughing so hard that not a sound was coming out of his mouth. And that's when she began to laugh, too, while the diaper turned warm and damp beneath her palm, and Matthew grinned happily, his small, plum-colored fists waving in the air.

*　*　*

As May turned into June, Nora began to notice that Danny was getting into more trouble at home than usual.

He was always in one form of trouble or another, because his personal habits were terrible. He hated soap and water, and his table manners were of the grab-and-gulp variety. But lately his behavior had sunk to a new low in hygiene. His private junk was no longer an inert mass confined to his bedroom, but had acquired a life of its own, extending itself, octopus-like, through the doorways of the house. Nora would find his soiled underwear in her closet, puzzle books and comics on the dining room chairs, game pieces ground into the carpet in the den. The irritation Danny caused her was like unpleasant music playing in the background of her life: it was always there, but there were times when she could ignore it or turn it off. Recently, however, Nora had the feeling that the volume of this unseen stereo had been turned too high. She found Danny drinking milk straight out of the carton, an unsanitary family no-no. He neglected to brush his teeth until they turned yellowish, and his breath was so bad that even the cat wouldn't talk to him. All of this was added to his bike lying in the driveway, his sports equipment dumped in the front hallway, and a constant and wearying legalistic battle over the mowing of their lawn.

"But, Mom, it doesn't need it yet. You see, the grass has to be at least an inch and a half high before it should be mowed again. See, here's this ruler— Mom, you're not looking."

"I'm not interested."

"And a piece of grass. See, it's only an inch and— What is that?"

"Three-eighths. Now, go mow the lawn."

"It's going to be ruined, you'll see."

"I'll take the responsibility."

"Daddy's going to be real mad."

"If you don't get out there and mow, *I'm* going to be real mad."

"But, M-o-m."

"Get going."

Danny did not confine his unpleasant behavior to home. One evening when Nora picked him up after choir practice, the minister, Reverend Bracken, took her aside. He was a man of large proportions, and so overweight that his belly strained the buttons of his jacket and his ecclesiastical collar appeared to cut cruelly into the heavy folds of skin at his neck. He also had a geniality that Nora often associated with big, blustery men—the sort that goes over well with young children and ladies beyond a certain age. He had a deep, booming pulpit voice, and when he spoke he rubbed the palms of his large, reddish hands back and forth, so that the friction of skin on skin formed a sibilant backdrop to his conversation. Nora, who had always felt alien and awkward in churches to begin with, found talking to Reverend Bracken difficult. She knew that he knew what she was—a woman of lapsed Jewish faith with a half-Jewish son who wanted to sing about Jesus.

Reverend Bracken smiled at her, put his hands in the prayer position and then—rub, rub, rub—began a long, rambling and roundabout conversation that Nora was first at pains to comprehend at all.

". . . Danny, a delight in the choir . . . a lovely voice and real enthusiasm . . . but restless . . . Understandable, of course, before the summer holidays. . . . Boys will always be boys. . . . So many years of dealing with youngsters of that age. . . . Spirits can get out of hand. . . . But a cautionary word . . ."

"What exactly has Danny done?" Nora asked this lightly, because she knew what Danny and his friend Billy could be like when they were together. They talked when they weren't supposed to, elbowed and poked one another, whispered and giggled and were generally disruptive.

Reverend Bracken cleared his throat. "It's not just Danny," he said. "I'm . . . uh, talking to all the parents involved."

A group of boys—a gaggle of them, all shifting and restless and not concentrating on their music; or perhaps not being suitably respectful in a House of God, running up and down the aisles, scrambling over pews, wearing their choir gowns backward.

Nora apologized in advance. "I know that Danny can get out of hand," she said. "Sometimes he's so immature."

"Yes. Well." Reverend Bracken's throat seemed to be in a permanent state of constriction. "You see, Mrs. Beeme, I found four of them behind the church last week. Before choir practice."

Four wild Indians, whooping around the immaculate church grounds, their heels digging holes in the expanse of emerald green lawn, hands tearing the branches of bushes, footsteps roughly planted next to delicate flowering annuals.

"Oh dear," Nora said.

Reverend Bracken's hands rubbed and hissed. "They appeared," he said, his hands rubbing and hissing, "to be having . . . uh, a contest . . . uh, urinating into the rhododendron bush."

Marty refused to take a peeing competition seriously. In fact, he laughed when Nora told him. "It might be the best thing that's happened to that rhododendron bush in years."

"This isn't funny."

"Come on, Nora. Boys do that kind of thing. I can remember sitting in someone's garage with a group of friends and having a jerking-off contest. Seeing how far you could spurt."

"Oh God," Nora said. "Did you win?"

"Nah. Andy Steinbekker always won. He could really shoot it."

Since Marty refused to believe that peeing on bushes was an offense, Nora reluctantly took on the responsibility of discussing it with Danny. He knew he was in trouble the minute Nora called him into the kitchen after school and said she wanted to talk to him, but he was particularly adept at assuming a saintly expression when under interrogation. Innocence widened his eyes; their pupils grew large and dark. His bottom lip jutted forth just a slight amount so that his mouth formed a small, sweet pout. Even his freckles seemed benign, like gold-dust sprinkled generously across the width of his nose.

Nora ignored that angelic look. "Reverend Bracken told me he found you and several other boys peeing in his garden."

"Me?"

"Danny, he saw you. Don't try to lie your way out of it."

"Aw, Mom, we were just fooling around."

"You call that fooling around? I call it disgusting."

"Billy was there, and Darryl and Bruce. It wasn't just me."

"That's no excuse, Danny. You know that. And I don't ever went to hear that you've done something like that again. Do you hear me?"

"Yeah."

"Danny?"

"What?"

"Why'd you do it anyway?"

Danny gave her a disbelieving look. " 'Cause it's fun, Mom. That's why."

Nora had always found it difficult to accept the feminist belief that boys and girls were essentially the same except for superficial anatomical differences. Having a child of each sex had confirmed her suspicion that there was a fundamental schism between maleness and femininity, a suspicion now reinforced by the church episode. No matter how far her imagination stretched, Nora could not see her teenage daughter and her friends stripping off panty hose and removing panties in order to form a circle and test urine flow, or for that matter, masturbate to see who could come first. The idea of it was not only ridiculous, but also nauseating. She could live with two males, Nora thought, make love regularly with one of them, and never really understand what it was about the male appendage that lent itself to public and theatrical display. Men scratched their genitals, fondled them, rearranged them, demonstrated with them, and if they were peculiar, flashed them. Being female, Nora remained mystified.

Matters with Danny turned more serious when Nora received a note from Mrs. Phelan, Danny's teacher, requesting that she and Marty come in for an interview. Mrs. Phelan reminded Nora of herself some twenty years earlier, when she had been starting out in teaching and held all sorts of illusions. Mrs. Phelan was young and concerned, and believed, as Nora once had, that she could single-handedly make intelligent, good citizens out of the malleable clay of children. The system had yet to wear her down, and she smiled encouragement at Marty and Nora as they entered the classroom, trying to make them feel at home as they sat down in the small, uncomfortable seats. She was petite, pretty, and had very large breasts, a fact which hadn't escaped either the sixth-grade boys or their fathers. Nora had noticed during previous parent-teacher meetings that Marty's eyes had kept straying to those enormous globes. It didn't help that Mrs. Phelan tended to wear silky blouses or that when she got enthusiastic her nipples grew hard and pressed against the fabric like small bottle caps.

According to Mrs. Phelan, Danny's behavior had been progressively deteriorating. He had neglected to do classroom assignments, displayed weak attention skills, was a disruptive element during class discussions, and had not handed in an important science project. Nora and Marty exchanged surprised glances at this; neither of them had even known that a science project was due. But this classroom behavior was far less serious than a recent event on the playground. A gang of boys, Mrs. Phelan told them, had been terrorizing a group of fourth-grade girls on a regular basis. The teasing had escalated to the point that one of the girls had been held over a fountain and forced to drink until she vomited.

"Are you saying that Danny is part of that gang?" Marty finally said after a shocked silence.

"He was there, Mr. Beeme. I'm sorry to say, but he was right in the middle of it."

Nora was having a hard time trying to imagine Danny holding some small girl's head over a fountain while she screamed and choked. He was an impulsive, careless child, it was true, and he delighted in torturing Christine whenever possible, but that was normal sibling rivalry, part of a mutual meanness that Nora was forced to tolerate. This deliberate cruelty to someone small and vulnerable was different. Helplessly, she looked around the classroom, as if some answer could be found in the neat, cursive handwriting that adorned the blackboard or the student essays hanging in orderly rows on the wall.

Crisis didn't leave Marty helpless. It brought out his management style. He put the tips of his fingers together and pressed them against the bottom of his chin. "Is appropriate action being taken against the boys?"

"They were all brought into the principal's office, and each has written an apology to the girl. Mr. Brilleau considered some form of suspension, but then decided the parents should be called in for a consultation."

"We'll deal with this at home as well. Of course. That goes without saying."

Mrs. Phelan smiled, showing dainty little teeth. "Yes, but we do feel that the boys are well aware of the *wrongness* of what they've done. Most of them feel pretty bad about it. A couple— that doesn't include Danny—are a little less willing to understand what a brutal thing it was, but I'm sure with time and explanation we can bring them around, too."

Nora could have cared less about any of the other boys. "You know, this just doesn't sound like Danny," she said. "I can't believe it."

Mrs. Phelan now leaned earnestly forward, the weight of those incredible breasts reclining on the desk blotter. "Mrs. Beeme, I was surprised myself. The classroom difficulties are relatively new; he's really had quite a good year otherwise. I just don't feel that Danny is quite the same boy as he was at the beginning of the school year." She paused. "To be honest with you, I've wondered if there are problems at home recently."

Nora felt Marty stiffen beside her. Quickly, she said, "We'll have a talk with him and try to see what's bothering him."

"Oh, I think that would be an excellent idea," Mrs. Phelan said. "You see, children are so affected by things happening outside the school situation. We can't always put our finger on the problems."

Marty was standing up, so Nora pushed herself out of the chair. "Yes," she said. "I know that. I was a teacher once myself."

Mrs. Phelan also stood up. "Really? Here in Fairfax?"

"Burtonville Elementary. First grade."

"Well, then you know precisely what I'm talking about. Communication. Talking things out. Discussing problems in a relaxed atmosphere. And it's so important for parents and teachers to communicate with one another as well."

Marty was edging toward the doorway. "Yes," Nora said. "Yes, it is."

"I also encourage the children to discuss their feelings and concerns in the classroom. I find it's a wonderful way of clearing the air. But of course, it's even more crucial in the home situation." Mrs. Phelan took a deep breath and gave Nora an intense, meaningful look while her nipples went into pop-up. "Children and parents need to be open and frank with one another. Don't you think?"

Marty was almost out the door. "Yes," Nora said. "You're so right. Thank you, Mrs. Phelan."

"Oh, not at all, Mr. and Mrs. Beeme. It was a pleasure to talk to you."

They didn't talk as Marty put his key into the ignition and drove out of the school driveway. While they'd been at the interview, dirty-white clouds had gathered, and it had begun to rain, the drops making dark circles on the pavement and spattering on the windshield. They headed home, down the hill and past the post office, the Exxon station, and Fairfax Drugs. As Marty made a left onto Mapleview Avenue the rain grew heavier and the sky darker. The wind was rising, and the branches of the huge maples began to whip back and forth, sending more rain against the car windows. Marty leaned forward and turned on the wipers and the headlights.

Nora was not thinking precisely about Danny, but trying to remember the definition of the pathetic fallacy, which she had learned about in a college course on literature, although which literature she could no longer precisely recall. She hadn't been very good in literature courses actually. The pathetic fallacy: wasn't that when a character's mood was expressed by nature? Sun for novelistically cheerful moments? Thunder and lightning for anger and depression? It was amazing, she thought as the rain drummed gloomily down on the car roof, how life could imitate art. She was immersed in her own private pathetic fallacy; the weather reflecting her mood, gray and heavy and overcast.

Sighing, she said, "Do you think that every family has such a delicate . . . well, equilibrium as ours?" Marty didn't say anything so she went on. "I mean, how do families manage when really bad things happen—like death and divorce? How come they don't go to pieces?"

"We're not going to pieces."

"Since when does Danny act like a juvenile delinquent?"

"You're exaggerating."

"Oh, come on. You were shocked. I saw your face when she was telling us about that little girl vomiting."

"Okay, I was surprised. But you know what eleven- and twelve-year-old boys are like. They form a gang and get that gang mentality. Half of them probably hated what they were doing— Danny included."

"I think there's more to it than that."

"Oh, Nora, for crying out loud."

"What?"

"You always have to find some deep, psychological reason for everything. Why can't you accept that boys will be boys sometimes?"

"Didn't you listen to Mrs. Phelan? His schoolwork is falling apart."

"Mine did at that age, too. I turned into the class clown. I thought I was a riot."

"You know what I'm talking about," she said angrily.

They were coming to a red light, but Marty stepped harder on the brake than was necessary. Nora was wearing a seatbelt, but as the car came to a shuddering halt, she instinctively made her arm rigid and pressed her hand against the dashboard.

Marty turned to her. "Nora, what the hell do you want from me?"

Marty had gone to work early that morning and had had high-level meetings all day. He was tired, Nora could see that. His face had extra lines on it, as if a hand had been penciling in old-age marks, and his eyes were pouched. But by now Nora was too upset and too agitated to let go. Mrs. Phelan had confirmed her worst fears, and Marty's evasiveness only compounded them. And what she hated most was the thin, slick veneer of politeness that Marty and Christine assumed when they were together. She wanted to tear it aside; she wanted the rawness below exposed, the private hurts meeting and touching and healing. Like Mrs. Phelan, Nora had a magical belief in communication.

"To admit that things aren't right," she said. "We're not the same, and that's why Danny's getting into trouble."

"Of course, we're not the same," Marty said impatiently. "We have a pregnant daughter."

"She isn't going to be pregnant forever."

The light turned green, and the car behind them honked. Marty drove ahead. "You know something, Nora, I must be a short-term kind of person, but I'm not thinking right now about two years down the line. I have to deal with today."

"Well, to be honest, I don't think you're dealing very well at all."

"God, but I wish I was a saint like you. It must be really nice."

"That's not fair," Nora protested. "I'm not a saint. I don't pretend to be one. I'm just trying my best to keep things on an even keel."

"Maybe life isn't supposed to be on an even keel. Have you ever thought of that?"

"Couldn't you be a little warmer toward her? Give her a hug now and then? A smile? Something?"

"You know what I think?" Marty said, and Nora saw the muscles clench in his jaw. "I think she's going to decide to keep the baby."

"What?" Nora said. "Oh, no, I don't think so. At her last appointment, Dr. Roya told her about a couple that can't have children and desperately want a baby. She said she'd arrange a private adoption if Christine wanted it."

"And what did Christine say?"

"She seemed interested."

"But she didn't say yes."

"Marty, she knows we're against it. I've told her that."

The car made a right on Thornbush and then a right again on Cedarview. "We told her we wanted her to have an abortion, too," Marty said. "She really listened, didn't she?"

"This is different."

"Uh-uh. This is the same thing. This is us not having any more control over our own kid." He punctuated his sentences by slapping his palm against the steering wheel. "This is our lives being screwed up by a fifteen-year-old whose brains are being scrambled by a group of right-wing fanatics."

"The Coalition doesn't encourage girls to keep their babies. They suggest adoption as an alternative."

"You know what you're doing, Nora? You're burying your head in the sand. Every time she goes there, she gets brainwashed about motherhood. Every single time. It's all hearts and flowers and sweetness. And they have a day care there, don't they? They're making it as easy as they can."

Nora watched their house come into view. A red-brick split-level with pale blue trim. A straight driveway to a two-car garage. A yew bush, neatly trimmed, on the front lawn. "You're anticipating something that may never happen," she said. "You're angry with Christine over a decision she hasn't made."

"Hasn't made—yet."

"You're not being fair."

"This is what my gut tells me, okay? This is what I have to live with."

As Marty drove closer to the house, Nora's focus seemed to narrow until all the other houses around theirs seemed to merge into the grayness, leaving 172 Cedarview isolated and separate, framed by nothing but mist and rain. Details of the house became clear and sharp; unpleasant details like the discoloration in the brick above the living room window, the bent edge of the rain gutter, the peeling paint on the garage door. Nora had always thought her house dignified in an ordinary way, but for a moment she saw nothing but ugly angles and garish colors, the suburban tract dwelling at its most vulgar. Quickly she blinked, bringing back the neighbors' houses, the mutual fence, the hedge that divided the lawns. The symmetry returned, the balance of lawn and house, garden and driveway, lamp post and paving stones.

"I don't think she will," Nora said. "I don't think she intends to keep the baby."

"Jesus Christ, Nora. You're living in a dream world." His voice filled with disgust. "A real dream world."

5

◇   ◇   ◇   As the school year came to an end, Nora noticed two things: that Jay's visits to their house had increased in frequency and duration, and that his presence paralleled another dip in Christine's already volatile moodiness. Nora couldn't tell if these two things were related, because Christine wasn't sullen and unhappy when Jay was actually there. Instead she was miserable at all other times, wearing a frown first thing in the morning as if a dark cloud were pressing down on her brows, and wrapped in a black sulk at night when she went to bed. She also talked back, giving Nora dirty looks when asked to do a task, and fought incessantly with Danny. Her room had gone from merely messy to absolute chaos, and she was flunking French and possibly Math.

Nora, who was in an unhappy search for her own emotional stability in the midst of this storm and all the others Christine had caused, thought she had found a safe haven in a thin veneer of calm. She sailed round and round this small harbor of equilibrium, denying entrance to any disturbing thought or event. She refused to get upset, raise her voice or be goaded into anger. But when Christine looked venomous and stamped her foot one Sunday morning simply because she'd been asked to help clean up the breakfast dishes, Nora discovered that she'd had enough.

"Would you like to tell me what's going on?"

"What?"

"With you."

Christine gave her a look of annoyance. "About what?"

"Stop looking at me like that," Nora said sharply. "I'm your mother, not one of your friends."

"Mom, just leave me alone."

Nora took her hands out of the sudsy water and dried them on a towel. "I'm not going to do that. Your behavior has been terrible. You stamp around here and yell at people and treat us like garbage. So I'd like to know what's going on."

Christine sighed. "I'm not very happy, okay?"

"That's obvious."

"So, don't I have a right to be unhappy?"

"You can be as unhappy as you please, but you can't take it out on everyone around you. Look, is it school?"

"No."

"Is it Daddy?" she asked.

If Nora thought that the mention of Marty was going to cause Christine to collapse into tears, she was wrong. Christine's face took on that peculiarly adolescent look that could be both blank and defiant at the same time.

"You know what gets me. You and Daddy talk about being liberals all the time and voting Democratic and all that stuff. And then you say you don't like the Coalition, because they're right-wing and you're pro-choice. Well, you know what I've noticed— you may say all those things, but when it comes to me, you only want the choice to go *your* way. That's not really being pro-choice is it?"

Nora ignored this. "You're not leaving this kitchen," she said, "until you tell me what's *really* bothering you."

"Mom . . ."

"I mean it."

"All right. If you really want to know, it's April and Marilyn. And Jessica, too." Now, tears filled those hazel eyes. "They're not my friends any more. Haven't you noticed?"

Actually, Nora had noticed the silent phone, the absence of that gaggle of girls, the weekends that Christine spent at home, but she'd been so wrapped up in work and problems that she hadn't put two and two together. "Because of the baby?"

"Yeah. They're scared. I guess maybe they're afraid babies are catching."

Nora watched as Christine grabbed a carton of milk off the counter and yanked open the refrigerator door, and what she saw made her throat ache. A little girl with skinny, freckled legs in a cotton nightie that came down to her thighs. An adolescent with jaunty pigtails and braces on her teeth. A pregnant woman with full breasts and a belly no longer concave, but swollen just enough to put that distinctive curve in her back.

"Oh, honey, I'm sorry."

Christine closed the refrigerator door. "I'm just glad school's going to be over soon. At least I don't have to see them anymore. I mean, April is really getting obnoxious. If she sees me coming, she just turns away. Marilyn acts as if I'm contaminated, and Jessica just follows along."

"But you told me that Jessica didn't believe in abortion and thought you were doing the right thing."

"She did, but she always does what Marilyn wants anyway. You know something? I wasn't surprised. I knew it was going to happen. The other girls at the Coalition warned me it might. One girl there—Elly, remember, I told you about her?—well, she said that when she got pregnant, it was like nobody noticed her anymore. When she walked down the halls at school, she could've been a ghost. Even her teachers kind of ignored her. You see, a lot of people just can't handle it."

"I know you don't want me to say it," Nora said gently, "but it still isn't too late to have an abortion."

Christine made a grimace. "You know what the baby is like now, Mom? It isn't just a bunch of cells anymore. It has a heartbeat. It has hands and fingers. It's a person. It can feel things—like pain."

"Christine, I don't think that last bit is true."

"It is. I've read about it."

Laura Ingalls Wilder had been banished from the shelf in Christine's bedroom, and in her place was a stack of information from the Coalition for Life. During one of her few ventures into Christine's room. Nora had sat down with this literature and gone through it. There were articles on the relationship between abortion and child abuse, abortion and euthanasia, abortion and fetal trauma. Articles written by medical doctors and Ph.D.'s and others with strings of authoritative initials after their names. Nora had to admit that some of these articles possessed a calm, scientific and persuasive air. Others were marked by a shrill hysteria.

Nora had been particularly horrified by one written by a Dr. Alice Stillman, called *A Former Abortionist Tells All.* In it, she wrote about a feminist convention she had attended in Cleveland before seeing the light and converting to the pro-life movement. Nora couldn't be sure when this convention had actually taken place or what its aims precisely were, because Dr. Stillman neglected to mention these details in her article. Instead, she attempted a lyrical description of atmospherics. The meeting was "wild and agitated," she wrote, "a bedlam of frenzied fanatics, all waving placards and screaming their messages of murder." Frightened by this, Dr. Stillman had stood in a corner and observed "bands of women with long, unkempt hair filling the halls with their high, loud voices. When the bands met, their members would embrace and kiss one another. At first I thought they were merely friends, but the embraces, the kisses, weren't those of mere friendship. Shocked, I realized that these women were Lesbians."

("You don't believe this, do you?" Nora had asked Christine.

"I didn't think much about it."

"It's full of out-and-out lies. It's disgusting propaganda!"

"Mom, don't yell at me. I didn't write it."

"I'm not yelling at you. I'm trying to get the point across that you've been given extremely biased information to read."

"I know you don't like the people at the Coalition."

"It has nothing to do with whether I like them personally or not. This offends my sense of what is right."

"Okay," Christine had said with a shrug, taking the pamphlet out of Nora's hand. "I'll throw it away.")

In defence, Nora had found and read a few articles of her own. Now, she took a deep breath and said, "There is no scientific or medical evidence that a fetus the size of yours feels any pain at all. It has an extremely underdeveloped cortex."

Christine clasped her hands tightly together. "I saw a film at the Coalition called *The Silent Scream*. It shows a baby being aborted, and you can see it trying hard to get away from that thing they use. That probe. You could tell it was hurting."

"I've heard about that film, Christine, and I heard there were a lot of things that weren't right about it."

"Mom, you should see it." Christine was fervent. "You might think differently then. You might change your mind."

Nora sighed and decided to go back to square one. "What I want to know now is whether your behavior is going to improve or not."

"I'll try, I guess."

"And aren't there any other friends from school besides April and Marilyn and Jessica?"

"There's Jay, Mom. He's being really supportive. He's a good person."

The Beemes had known Jay since he was the age Danny was now. At eleven, he'd been unusual for being exceptionally puny and for having an obsessive dream of being a rock star. Nora could remember talking to his mother at a PTA meeting and listening to her lament over Jay's three guitars, the drums he'd wanted to purchase and play in the basement, and his disinterest in school. At sixteen, nothing much had changed except that Jay was now a head taller than Nora, still skinny, and trying, without much success, to grow a mustache. He still had fine, almost feminine features and that rosy, beneath-the-skin flush that was part of childhood. His face, seen at certain angles and in certain lights, struck Nora not as handsome but as having that pure, ascetic beauty that one saw in medieval portraits of saints. His pride and glory was a thick head of blond hair—de rigueur, Nora understood, for rock celebrity—that he wore to his shoulders and had regularly streaked and permed.

He never arrived at the house without a guitar, and Nora would often come home after work to find Christine swinging in the hammock while Jay played. He had a nice singing voice as well, and Nora found that she could bear the kind of music he and Christine liked when it wasn't coming at her from a ghetto blaster or booming out of the radio.

"What's that?" she asked one afternoon, opening the screen door onto the patio. It was her day off, and she planned to spend it gardening. She wore rubber gloves and was carrying a spade and a plastic garbage bag.

"Oh, hi, Mrs. Beeme. It's a song by Huey Lewis and the News. 'Power of Love.'"

"It's not bad," she said.

"My mother," Christine said lazily as she pushed the hammock back and forth with one foot, "is musically illiterate."

Nora knelt down by the flower bed next to the back of the house and began to pull out weeds. "That's not true. It's just that you don't know anything about the music I liked when I was your age. Nobody listens to it any more."

"Oldies but goldies," Christine said with a yawn. "'I ain't nothin' but a hound dog.'"

The violets were trying to take over. Nora plucked a misguided shoot from beneath the rose bush. "There were a lot of nice songs then," she said. "Pretty ones."

"It's just that you don't really listen to today's stuff, Mom. If you got familiar with it, you'd like it better."

"I like a little melody," Nora said. "A bit of a tune. Something you can hum afterwards."

She didn't expect any support for this opinion, but Jay was nodding. "Some of that early rock 'n' roll was good stuff." He bent his head over the guitar so that the fair shining curls fell forward, and his fingers picked out an old melody.

Nora rocked back on her heels and let the sound sweep over her. The Everly Brothers. *Crying in the Rain.* It was astonishing what music like that could do. It brought back memories of a half-lit high school gymnasium strung with pastel streamers, a punch bowl filled with sticky pink liquid, and herself slow-dancing with Kenny Marshall in her first formal, a pale blue affair with embroidered pink and white flowers. She'd been wearing her mother's pearls and—a corsage on her left shoulder strap? Yes, a corsage with a pin that had been pricking her skin all through that dance, a sensation she'd ignored because she'd thought at the time that she was madly in love with Kenny and would gladly suffer the pinpricks rather than break away from his arms. The music could even bring back long-forgotten scents. She'd applied Shalimar to the five perfume spots: beneath each ear, on the base of the throat, at the inner wrists; Kenny had drenched his shaven cheeks with Old Spice cologne.

"Jay!" she said with delight. "Where'd you learn that?"

"My dad's been collecting sixties records. He's got Elvis and Paul Anka, Dion and the Belmonts . . . uh, Chubby Checker."

"How are your folks? I haven't seen them since New Year's."

"They're okay."

"And your sister? How old is she now?"

"Thirteen." He shrugged and gave his guitar strings a disharmonious strum. "She's okay."

Nora often had the feeling when talking with one of Christine's friends that the conversational ball was forever slipping through her fingers. She never quite got a hold of it, never quite knew its weight or heft.

"Last time I talked to your mother, she wanted you to sell your drums."

"I gave her a pair of those ear things that construction guys wear for her birthday. She wears them around the house when I'm home."

Nora pulled out a lanky weed that had grown taller in one week than her pink phlox had grown in a month. Is that fair? she silently demanded of her garden. Is it? "That was clever of you," she said.

Jay gave her a shy smile, and his face was no longer ascetic but suddenly young and sweet. "Yeah, except now she never hears anything I say."

"Mom, is there any more lemonade?" Christine said.

"In the fridge."

Christine twisted in the hammock and gave Jay a pleading glance. "J-a-y?"

"She's lazy," Nora warned.

"Yeah, well," Jay said, putting down his guitar and going to the door. "Now, she'll owe me one."

"A big glass," Christine said imperiously, "with lots of ice."

"Aw, shit!" Nora looked up, but Jay was already apologizing. "Excuse me, Mrs. Beeme. I just broke a nail on the door."

This, Nora knew, was a major catastrophe. Jay refused to use guitar picks and kept his nails long and polished. He had even come over one day with bits of Ping-Pong balls glued beneath them for strength. He and Christine often discussed the care and cultivation of their nails, and Nora had noticed that Christine had stopped biting hers and was letting them grow back. One afternoon, she had even found Jay slowly and carefully applying pink polish to Christine's nails. On another afternoon, she'd discovered Christine blowing Jay's hair dry in the bathroom, while he complained about his split ends. When she'd told Marty about this, he shook his head.

"That kid doesn't have his full quota of testosterone."

"Oh, Marty, I don't think he's gay."

"When I was in high school, we had a teacher that put polish on his nails. You know what we sent him once? A one-way ticket to Fire Island. Remember? That's where the homos went."

Nora was doubtful. "Christine told me he doesn't have a girl friend, but that doesn't necessarily mean anything, does it? The kids today don't seem to date the way we used to."

"You know what I think? I think he's an okay kid, but weird. Just a little weird."

But Nora didn't mind Jay's peculiarities or the angle of his sexual bent. She encouraged his presence; she invited him to dinner. She even took to baking cookies and cupcakes, which he could eat in voracious quantities. And she did all of this because she found Christine laughing when he was there. Swinging in the hammock and laughing at something he'd said or done. A girl's summery laugh that lifted on the warm air, as buoyant as a breeze.

On the last Sunday in June, during her regularly scheduled phone call, Nora finally got up enough nerve to tell her mother about Christine's pregnancy. Esther had moved to Miami in 1982 after Leo's fatal heart attack. When the bakery had been sold off, she'd proved to be, if not a rich, seventy-five-year-old widow, a comfortably well-off one. She immediately bought a mink jacket on sale at Alexander's and bought a condominium near Ben, who was unmarried and in swimming pool sales. Nora found a guilty comfort in the fifteen hundred miles that lay between Fairfax and Miami, a no-man's-land that only required a communications traverse once a week and actual face-to-face confrontation once a year.

On the Sunday night that she phoned, her mother had just come back from a bridge session in which she and her partner, Helen, had won two rubbers. This had put Esther in a good mood, despite the state of her health and Ben's latest behavior.

"I went to the rear admiral."

"Who?" Nora asked in mystification.

"The hemorrhoid doctor."

"Oh."

"So you know what he tells me? Take hot baths. What kind of advice is that?"

Nora knew better than to say anything. Esther delighted in medical dilemmas involving herself, family, neighbors, and perfect strangers. And she thoroughly enjoyed anecdotes that involved fearful operations, doctor incompetence, and hospital outrage. She would express horror, but in truth nothing pleased her more than proof that some doctor, preferably gentile, had once again misdiagnosed, mistreated and mismanaged some woman's insides. ("So he took out everything. Not just the womb. Oh, no, that wasn't enough for him. No, he had to have the works. Ovaries. Tubes. She's lucky to have her privates left.")

"And on top of that your brother is going to give me heart failure."

"Ben? I thought he was doing well."

"He's taken up with a nurse who's been divorced three times."

"If she's a nice—"

"Three times! Three times and you're out. That's what I told him. What does he want with such a loser? And she's not even pretty. If she were pretty, I could understand. At least there would be a good reason for spending so much money. By the way, did you know your brother thinks money grows on trees? He takes her out for dinner and guess how much he spends? Come on, guess."

"A hundred and twenty-five."

"Wrong. Three hundred. *Three hundred dollars.* A family can eat on that for a month!" What Nora couldn't see she could imagine—Esther's round face in its halo of permed white curls, her chin quivering with outrage. "He spends it in one night! Well, what can I do? He wants to make a big impression. Why, I don't know. She's got nothing that I can see, except he says she makes him feel good. So—she can make him feel good a lot cheaper, can't she?"

Nora didn't know how Ben stood it, but then her brother had always been able to ignore both Esther and Leo. As a wiry little kid with good hand-eye coordination, he'd spent as much time as he could out of the apartment and the bakery, playing baseball at the corner lot. As an adult, he'd hopped from job to job and city to city, keeping one step ahead of any possible complaints, recriminations or marital prospects. He'd finally settled in Miami and spent ten years with Aquarius Pools. Nora kept waiting for him to light out once again, particularly with Esther now virtually parked on his doorstep, but Ben had maintained that enviable quality of indifference. "Nah, she doesn't bother me," he'd said, during a rare phone conversation with Nora. "I just let her talk. It makes her feel good."

Esther was still chattering on, but now she'd switched back to her bridge game. "So I bid three diamonds, and Helen said three spades. I say four spades. She says four no. I tell you, Nora. I knew we had a slam like nobody's business."

"Mom?"

"Anyway, we made six diamonds and—"

"Mom, Christine is pregnant."

There was a brief silence, during which Nora rearranged the sheet over her legs. She always called her mother from the telephone in the bedroom, propping herself up on the bedrest and two pillows. In the winter, she turned her side of the electric blanket up to six.

"My God." All the spring had gone from Esther's voice.

"She's planning to put it up for adoption," Nora said with forceful cheer. "So we're thinking, all's well that—"

"And the boy?"

"Just someone at a party. Nobody important."

"You let her go to such a party?"

"It was at a friend's house. It was an accident."

"My God. A fifteen-year-old girl."

"Yes, well—"

"You know, when you were fifteen, you told me I was too strict. You wanted to go out and do God knows what. I said, a fifteen-year-old girl should be at home by nine o'clock. Of course, you didn't like it. You got angry with me; you said hurtful things."

Nora cleared her throat. "Anyway, Christine's doing fine. Of course she can't go to camp this summer. But she's taking prenatal classes, and I've hired two tutors to help her with French and Math. Unfortunately, she didn't do too well in those this year, and we thought a good head start on next year wouldn't be a bad idea."

Esther hadn't heard a word. "The shame of it," she said heavily, "would have killed your father."

"Mom, Marty isn't dying. I think Daddy would have survived."

"Oh, I know what you're going to say. Things are different

today. Well, in my day she would have been spoiled goods. Of course, who am I to pass judgment? But when I look at your brother and that woman, I'm not stupid. If she thinks he's going to marry her, she'd better think twice. Why buy the cow when you can get the milk free? That's what I say and . . ."

When she finally hung up the phone, Nora put her head back on the pillow and, closing her eyes, idly wondered what the symptoms of death by shame would be. Measle-like spots? Psoriasis spelling a flaky S on the forehead? Perhaps something more genteel, like a lingering, wasting depression. Or maybe a heart attack—robust health one moment, collapse by disgrace the next. She felt a hand fall gently on top of her head and opened her eyes.

"You okay?" Marty said.

"I hate to say it, but you're really lucky your parents are dead." Nora put her hands on top of Marty's so that his was pressed tightly against her scalp. "She said when I was fifteen, she didn't let me go to parties."

"The Esther Felsher School of Revisionist History?"

"I made out like a bandit with David Aaronson at Linda Meyer's Passover party when I was fifteen and a half. On top of the coats piled on her parents' bed."

"You never told me about that."

"He kept trying to unhook my bra. I finally let him."

"If your parents had known what a hot number you were, they would have locked you away."

Nora gave him a tired smile. "In a Jewish convent?"

"You bet. With nine-foot walls."

The official version of Nora and Marty's courtship—the one Nora told the children—was that they had met at the Whites', started dating and found out that they loved one another. The real version was that, after the Whites got back from the police station, Marty and Nora went straight to her apartment where they banged like bunnies on her Murphy bed. This was a scenario which they played out almost every night for two weeks straight until Marty had to leave on a business trip.

To the outside world, Nora seemed quite normal. She went to school, taught her first-graders, had three parent-teacher interviews, grocery-shopped, paid her phone bill and wrote to her parents. Inside, she was assailed at the most inconvenient moments by the most vivid moments of recall. "The capital G," she said to her class while standing at the blackboard, "is a C with a difference." But when she demonstrated this, her fingers felt not the rigid chalk, but the soft, hairy weight of Marty's scrotum. When Michael Minsky's father put his hand on her desk during an interview, and Nora saw that his fingernails were shaped like Marty's, a wave of faintness swept over her and black spots appeared before her eyes. And any item vaguely resembling a body part could set her off. One afternoon she found herself transfixed by a cellophane bag of macaroni in the A & P, seeing not the innocent noodles, but the dark curls of Marty's pubic hair and the blond ones of her own damply entwined at their groins.

After four months of orgiastic liaison, Nora and Marty got engaged and did the obligatory parental tour. Marty was the only child of a father who was a professor of Mathematics at Hunter College and a mother who taught piano. He had been born when both were in their forties, and they were already elderly when Nora met them. Stephen Beeme was tall, angular and slightly stooped. His was the original Beeme face, with its narrow flat cheeks and square chin, topped with white curly hair. He was kind to Nora in a vague way when he happened to notice she was there, but he spent most of the weekend in his book-lined den.

Mary Beeme was friendlier, but had that air of distracted politeness that often accompanies people who are extremely busy and have a lot on their minds. She was impressive physically, a tall and commanding presence with straight, iron-gray hair that she wore pulled into a smooth chignon, a prominent, high-arched nose, and a formidable bosom. She still taught piano privately, guest-lectured at several local colleges and served as Chairman of the Board of the Forest Hills Symphony. Nora tried to like both the Beemes, but everything about them intimidated her, from their intellectualism to the impeccable high shine of their dark oak floors. When they looked down at her from their towering Beeme height, she was sure they saw something small and insignificant and unworthy.

"They don't like me," she whispered to Marty one night. The Beemes had a big old house with bay windows and bedrooms with slanted walls on the third floor. Nora was put in one of those, while Marty was supposed to be sleeping in his old room on the second floor. At midnight, he had crept up to her room and crawled into bed with her.

"Sure they do. My mother told me you were very appropriate."

"Appropriate? What does that mean?"

"That she likes you."

"Not where I come from, it doesn't. It's called damning with faint praise."

"I thought my mother got a kick out of showing you my baby pictures," Marty said. "I thought you were both having fun."

This had been Mary Beeme's only maternal moment. She had sat Nora down on the plump, floral sofa and brought out the family album. The pictures in it were turning sepia and had scalloped edges. Nora had seen Marty as a crying infant, his face contorted with rage, as a toddler outfitted in a cowboy outfit and brandishing twin six-shooters, as a boy of six playing with a Civil War army set he'd received at Christmas. "Such powers of concentration," Mary had said proudly. "He'd play with that set for hours and hours." Nora had been far more struck by the neatness with which Marty had laid out the lines of men and horses and tents. The kneeling infantrymen had been placed at perfect right angles to the standing riflemen, the cannons positioned in a precise circle.

"It was fun," she conceded. "You were pretty cute, although that crew cut was something. What did the barber use—a chain saw?"

"I had curls like a girl. I would have been the sweetest thing."

She nibbled on his earlobe. "Mmmm—I think you're tasty."

Marty gave her a squeeze. "Look, the thing you have to understand about my parents is that if I'm happy, they're happy."

Nora sighed. "They're so reserved. They never talk."

"Yes they do. My father talked all through dinner."

"About politics."

"Nora, you're making this a lot more complicated than it really is. My parents have always done their own thing, and I've done mine. They don't interfere with me, and I don't interfere with them. It's simple."

"But I don't know what they're thinking."

"You don't have to as long as you know what *I'm* thinking."

Marty's erections had a way of working themselves out of the open fly front of his pajama pants. In the moonlight, she could see this particular one beckoning her, a slender white wand.

"I can guess," she said.

"So?"

"So?"

"What do I have do to—beg?"

"Plead. Grovel. And kiss my feet."

The springs creaked and whined as he made his way down to the bottom of the bed under the covers.

"Marty, stop it. You'll wake up your parents."

His voice was muffled by the covers. "Then you'll know what they're thinking."

"And no tickling. Marty, don't."

"Say uncle."

"Stop it! Uncle!"

"Say aunt."

"Aunt!"

He emerged. "Do you give up?"

Nora threw her arms around him. "I surrender."

Like Marty, Nora and her brother Ben were the products of a late marriage. Both her parents had been the oldest children of immigrants who had come to the United States just before the twenties and whose family fortunes, albeit small, had tumbled to next-to-nothing during the Depression. Esther had been the first in her family to finish high school, but had not gone to college, working instead as a seamstress in a clothing factory. She had been engaged for a short time before the war, but her fiancé had died of meningitis.

Nora had always considered this tragedy as romantic, envisioning a dramatic deathbed scene, but as Esther refused to talk about it her imagination had nothing to feed upon except a few skimpy details: that the fiancé had been a university graduate, had been called Max, short for Maximillian, had possessed handsome blue eyes. Those blue eyes had caused Nora to wonder if her mother had married this fiancé, whether she would have had blue eyes, too. Of course she'd known that if Esther hadn't met Leo through friends of friends when the war was over and married him, she wouldn't *be* Nora exactly. In fact, she wouldn't even exist as she knew herself. At this point in her childhood thinking, Nora had always lost interest in genetic speculation.

Leo came from a family of small entrepreneurs: tailors, shoemakers, milliners, but he'd dreamed of being a financier in the style of the Rothschilds. When he was seventeen, his father had died, and Leo had been forced to work in a cousin's bakery. He never spoke of his past without a bitter edge to his voice, and Nora had always understood that her small, bald father had been born to greater things than braiding crullers and kneading pumpernickel bread. As a child, she had marveled at the fact that if the letter "n" could have been added to "baker," then the Felshers wouldn't be living in a cramped apartment in the Bronx but in a fancy suburban ranch house, and she could have had a room of her own.

Nora had warned Marty that there would be no horsing around when they visited the Felshers for the obligatory weekend, and the sleeping arrangements were just as she expected. Marty slept on the couch in the living room while she was in the bedroom she had once shared with Ben and which now housed a small washing machine, her mother's Singer and the ironing board. The hallway connecting the two rooms ran right in front of Esther and Leo's bedroom door and had a linoleum floor with a sub-layer that creaked when anyone tiptoed down it to the bathroom. So Nora spent two chaste nights in her narrow, girlish bed, feeling lonely and bereft without Marty beside her and desperately counting the hours until they could drive back to Fairfax.

As she had expected, Leo spent the weekend trying to make Marty as uncomfortable as possible. Esther didn't approve of their engagement either, but her method of attack was more private. She came into Nora's bedroom while she was unpacking and sat down heavily on the bed. She had put on weight since going through menopause and had become stout through the torso. Only the lower half of her legs remained slender; beneath her housedress with its large floral pattern, her calves retained the shapeliness of her youth.

"So," Esther said, "he seems like a nice boy."

"He's very nice."

"You know what I always say?"

Nora sighed and unfolded a pair of slacks. "What?"

"Like should marry like."

"We love each other."

"Love," Esther said with disgust. "It's here today, gone tomorrow. What lasts is background."

"I'm marrying him."

"You couldn't have found a nice Jewish boy?"

"It doesn't matter that he isn't Jewish."

"If the Germans should knock on your door, what do you think would happen?"

"Oh, please."

"Don't oh please me. You know what would happen."

"Mom, this is the United States!"

"Let me tell you what would happen. They'd take you. Not him. To save his own neck, he'd sacrifice yours."

Nora refused to even acknowledge this absurd statement. In silence, she continued to unpack, lifting her underwear out of the suitcase and putting it on the chair beside the bed. Esther lifted up a lacy white bra.

"Very fancy."

"It's a Bali."

Esther contemplated the frothy wisp in her hands, and her lips pursed together into that moue they always acquired when she was about to dispense sexual advice. Nora had learned to hate that expression. It combined a sly knowingness with a self-conscious audacity.

"You have to be careful with a man who's not Jewish. There are things you have to be very careful about."

"Like what?" Nora said warily.

"He may not be clean."

"What? Of course he's clean. He showers every day."

"That's not what I mean. You know what I'm saying?"

"No, I don't."

"He may not be"—Esther lowered her voice and gave a small shudder—"circumcised."

"Oh, for God's sake, Mom."

"Have you thought about that?"

"He's circumcised."

Esther gave Nora a suspicious look. "How do you know?"

Nora smiled innocently. "He told me."

Esther sublimated the rest of her anxieties that weekend by cooking round the clock. She attacked the food and forced it to surrender, giving it no opportunity to yield gracefully. She peeled, chopped, diced, kneaded, pounded, scraped and sliced, her elbows cutting vicious circles in the air. Beneath her small hands, carrots and potatoes were stripped bare, onions tamed into thin rings and chickens gutted of their bones. There was always a pot bubbling on the stove and something baking in the oven. The windows in the kitchen were constantly steamed over, and Leo sat in his undershirt at the formica table, eating and talking at the same time and trying to wear Marty down.

"So you're working for New York Bell," Leo said. Once he had been blond like Nora, but now he had a freckled, bald head with a thin fringe of gray hair. "How much do you make?"

"Ten thousand."

"That's all?"

"It's a starting salary. I'm due for a raise."

"How much will you be getting then?"

"Ten five."

"That's all?"

Marty didn't bother to respond. ("Just sit it out," he'd said to Nora. "There isn't anything they can do.") He leaned back in the kitchen chair, crossed one leg over the other, and looked elegant and aristocratic in his white shirt and tweed sports jacket. Nora, who had never dared fight with her father openly and had never had anybody fight for her, was incredibly proud of Marty's bravery and nonchalance.

Leo went on, "The death of John Kennedy was the greatest tragedy this country will ever know."

"Yes," Marty said.

"Who knows what he could have done?"

"Who knows?" Marty echoed.

"You voted for Johnson?"

"Yes."

The fact that Marty had voted Democrat didn't satisfy Leo. He jabbed a stubby finger at the center of Marty's chest. "You know what I think about Nixon?"

Marty shook his head again.

"He's a crook. He's always been a crook. He'd have ruined this country if he'd gotten his hands on it. He'd have destroyed it."

And so on and so forth all weekend: Esther attacking food, Leo attacking Marty, and Nora desperately wishing herself away. Of course there was nothing Leo and Esther could say or do that would change her mind anyway, so the entire weekend was an exercise in futility.

Nora would be many years into her marriage before she would understand why she had so stubbornly defied convention and her parents. The Nora of the two seemingly disparate personalities, the bon vivant and the shy loser, had fallen into love with Marty in much the same way she had tumbled into bed with him: willy-nilly, no regrets, no questions asked. And having arrived at that state, she had found it lined with mirrors, reflecting her in ways she'd never seen before. There was Nora the blond bombshell, the sexiest woman on earth. Nora, who was cute and funny and made Marty laugh. Nora, of the significant opinions and highly respected concerns. Nora, suddenly maternal and happily domestic, scrubbing Marty's back in the bathtub, trimming his toenails, making elaborate little dinners for him from her Fanny Farmer cookbook.

Nora had thought she loved Marty madly. At the time, she had felt that she would have died for Marty given the chance. She had imagined herself cast as the heroine of romantic tragedies, speaking gracious, lingering lines: " 'Tis a far, far better thing I do . . ." But four months of lust, she would someday realize, hardly justified a lifetime of loyalty. What she had fallen for so hard wasn't Marty at all, but the self-image he had given her: a Nora who was whole, framed and mirrored in his eyes.

Nora hated to take Danny shopping. He was especially annoying in a shoe store, where he was supposed to sit still until they got served. This particular shoe store, Wegman's, was always busy, and they had to wait no matter how early Nora got there. Danny sat obediently back in his chair for only a few seconds. Then he slid forward and tried to see if the tip of his sneaker could kick against the back of another chair. When he found that it couldn't, he swung himself back and forth, holding himself up by his hands. The enjoyment of that finally palled, and he drummed his heels on the floor in a rhythm backed up by a staccato frenzy of knuckle-cracking.

"Cut that out," Nora said.

"Mom, I don't need new sneakers."

Nora contemplated the torn canvas of the ones he was wearing, the rubber worn off at the tips, the grimy color and the lack of shoelaces. "You can't go to camp in those ratty things. They're disgusting."

"I like them when they're like this. They're neat."

"Forget it."

"New ones aren't cool."

"Too bad."

"Ma'am, are you being helped?"

Nora shook her head at the young man, explained what they wanted and then winced when he pulled off Danny's sneakers.

"Those socks," she said. They had once been white, but were now black on the bottom and had a hole through which Danny could wiggle his big toe. "Where did you find them?"

"In my drawer, Mom."

"They're grotesque."

"Would you also like to buy some socks today, ma'am?" The young man gave her a polite smile.

She smiled politely back. "I guess we'll have to, won't we?" When he had gone over to the rack of socks, she turned and glared at Danny. "And when was the last time you washed your feet?"

"Yesterday, Mom."

His toenail was ragged and had a ridge of dirt beneath it. "I'd believe you when thousands wouldn't."

"It's true!"

"Sure."

Nothing she and Marty had said to Danny since meeting with his teacher had made an impression. He'd been genuinely repentant about the incident in the playground and had taken a two-week grounding punishment with more grace than usual, but he still went blithely on spreading his mess through the house, avoiding soap and water and acting badly in the classroom. His refusal to shape up had prompted Nora to attempt a delicate probe of his psyche.

("Danny, I have the feeling that something is bothering you."

"Like what?"

"You're still getting into trouble. What about that last detention?"

"I didn't do anything! Mrs. Phelan just likes to pick on me. She's really mean to me."

"Mrs. Phelan is a good teacher."

"How do you know? She doesn't teach you."

"She said you were bothering the class."

"I wasn't."

"Come on."

"Why don't you ever believe me? Why do you always take her side?"

"Danny, I just wonder if you're upset about Christine and the baby."

"Christine's *really* mean. *She* picks on me all the time." He paused. "Mom, could I go now? Disney is on."

"Danny . . ."

"You said I could watch. You promised.")

Danny was getting on Nora's nerves, and she admitted to herself that she couldn't wait for him to go to camp. She contemplated with pleasure the vacation camp would give her—three weeks of Dannyless bliss. No more sibling rivalry, no more bicycles lying in the driveway, no more doors slamming and dirt tramped in on her clean kitchen floor. Best of all, no more complaints from teachers and ministers.

"Nora! I haven't seen you in ages."

She turned to find Bev Perry beside her chair and stood up to say hello. Bev, a tall blonde with a wide smile and forthright manner, had been the mastermind behind a three-year, multi-mother car pool that Nora had participated in when Christine was nine years old and thought she wanted to be Gelsey Kirkland. After Christine had dropped out of Mrs. Edelson's Ballet School for Tots 'n' Teens, Nora never quite lost track of Bev, but would run into her at places like the library and the post office and at community events like rummage sales. Their meetings were always a flurry of hellos, breathless exchanges of information and exclamations over the children.

"Danny! My goodness, I wouldn't have recognized him. And this is Charity. Yes, she's eight now. The time goes by so fast, doesn't it? Oh, and Zachary's eighteen—do you believe it? Yes, to SUNY in Binghamton. He didn't want to go too far from home. Easier to bring his dirty laundry home, of course."

Nora shook her head. "Zachary in college. And how's Sara doing?"

"We're so pleased. She's still dancing, you know, and her

teacher just recommended that she try out for the American Ballet School."

Nora felt the muscles in her face going rigid. "That's wonderful."

"Of course, the chances are very slight. Still, after all those years of paying for lessons and shoes and leotards, you can imagine how we feel. So, tell me—what's Christine up to?"

"Oh, she's just fine."

"Going to camp again? She was going to be a junior counselor this year, wasn't she?"

"No, she decided not to." It actually hurt to smile; the upward curve of Nora's lips cut painfully into her cheeks. "She got bored with camp. You know how it is, she's been going since she was five. She says she needs a change."

"Oh God, fifteen's the worst, isn't it? If Sara wasn't in ballet, I don't know what I'd do."

They were interrupted by the arrival of the young man with a pair of socks and several boxes of sneakers. They exchanged good-byes and see-you-agains, and Nora tried to concentrate on choosing the right pair of sneakers for Danny's continually growing feet.

"You'd be taller," she said to him at one point, when the young man had gone into the back to get a size larger, "if so much of you wasn't feet."

"Mom, Christine isn't going to camp because of the baby, right?"

"Yes."

"So how come you said that she was bored with it?"

How come? Because Nora hadn't been able to find the strength within herself to bear the shock and the pity. That awful, condescending pity. The there-but-for-the-grace-of-God pity. The Bev Perry, thrilled mother of Sara, budding ballerina, pity. Nora had once dreamed of Christine's being a ballerina. She had looked so pretty in her black leotards and pink tights, her delicately leathered toe pointed, her arms in a big, graceful O above her head. And Nora had dreamed of Christine as a Broadway actress, when she'd dramatically recited a poem in the school assembly at age eleven. And of Christine the great writer, when she'd written that lovely story about the wounded sparrow for her ninth-grade English class. Even the English teacher had been impressed. She'd given Christine an A+, and Nora had preserved the story in a scrapbook, carefully putting each page between its own plastic sheets.

How come? Because Marty had been right: Nora did live in a dream world, and she was now discovering that dreams don't die easily. It didn't matter if they were silly and extravagant or much more ordinary, like Christine going to college, choosing a career, meeting a nice young man, getting married, having children. The dreams gasped for breath like fish out of water; they arched and stretched and flailed, smacking painfully against the hard surface of reality. Anger that Nora had suppressed within the calm harbor of her emotions now broke loose, and she found herself hating Christine. And hating herself for hating.

"Huh, Mom? How come?"

"Because," Nora snapped, "what we do in our family is nobody's business. And if I ever catch you wearing socks like that again when we're going to a shoe store, you'll find yourself in deep shit. Do you understand? *Do you?*"

6

◇ ◇ ◇ In July, Nora and Marty went to Washington for a weekend. Devlin Electronics was participating in a seminar held by the military, since the company had received the contract to build part of a communications device for a new satellite. The seminar was a perk for management types like Marty, who were now working long hours and had been forced to sacrifice their summer vacations, because the contract was so massive and had such heavy deadlines. It wasn't really a holiday for Marty, but Nora intended to enjoy the free air fare, the complimentary hotel room, the moratorium on family problems, and the chance the trip gave her to see her best friend from high school, Stacey Epstein, sharer of erotic adolescent imaginings.

She didn't even care that the temperature in Washington was a hundred and three degrees in the shade, with a humidity reading near ninety. The heat was so great that the layer of air above the sidewalks shimmered in the heat, and the buildings on the Smithsonian Mall appeared to be bleached of all color. When Nora stepped out of one air-conditioned museum building to walk to another, a fine perspiration would break out on her body so that the fabric of her blouse, a formerly crisp cotton, stuck to her back and the waistband of her skirt was wet. By the time she met Stacey at one of the bistros near the Capitol Building, Nora felt limp, damp and flushed.

Stacey, on the other hand, looked as if she had stepped out of an air-conditioned magazine article advising women how to dress for success. She wore an unwrinkled beige linen suit with shoulders the exact width prescribed by the current fashion season, a silk blouse with swirls of red and beige, pearls at her neckline and her ears, and streaked blond hair that had been permed, moussed and back-combed to achieve that look of carefree wildness. Nora, who had never been able to do clever things with scarves or belts and who had been ten years late in understanding that blue eyeshadow was out of fashion, always envied the way Stacey, whose face was plain and narrow, could make herself so attractive.

"You look wonderful," Nora said after they had hugged one another. "You really do. How long has it been?"

"Three years," Stacey said. "Waiter, two Perriers, please. With lemon. They have wonderful salads here, by the way. I should know; I've become an expert on salads. That's all I eat now. That or tuna fish. I'm getting too fat."

"You don't look it."

"Only my mirror, my doctor and my masseuse know the truth."

"Remember those sundaes we used to eat?"

"Don't remind me. Oh, Nora, those were the days, weren't they? All you had to worry about then was zits." Stacey opened her purse and pulled out a cigarette case. "Do you still smoke? No? I wish I could give it up. I'm sure my lungs look like the inside of a coal mine." She lit a cigarette. Her fingernails were a beautifully manicured red. "So tell me, how are the kids and Marty?"

"You first," Nora said. "You're the one with the exciting life."

Stacey, who had never married, was the veteran of many affairs and a constant traveler. She always sent Nora postcards from far-flung corners of the world. Mixed in with the junk mail, advertising brochures from Allstate and bills from the electric company, Mastercard and New York Bell, Nora would find messages from New Delhi, Sydney, Rio de Janeiro, Katmandu, Paris: "Am blowing the budget but loving every minute!" or "My first mountain climb. I'm utterly exhausted!" or "Everything we ever heard about French (Spanish, German, Danish, Japanese) lovers is absolutely, fantastically true!"

"Me? You have to be joking. I'm a cog in the bureaucracy." Actually, Stacey was a lawyer who worked for the FCC. "I push paper this way, then I push it that. It's extremely boring."

"But it's a good job, isn't it?" Nora had always envied Stacey her jobs. She had worked in New York City and Boston as well as Washington, and her paychecks were bigger than Marty's.

"It pays the bills. Actually, Nora, I never save a penny." She picked up her cigarette case, which had a mirror on it, and gazed at her reflection. "I'm going to be a bag lady one day. You know, unwashed, uncombed and god-help-me, unmade-up."

"What happened to what's his name?"

"Which what's his name?"

"The one from Los Angeles."

"Oh, him. Eddie."

The last time they had met, Stacey had been heavily involved with a married man with scads of money. Nora had listened— enviously, she couldn't help it—to stories of weekends at Lake Tahoe, Frederick's of Hollywood underwear sent by UPS, orgiastic encounters in airplanes thirty thousand feet over Kansas City.

"That was over years ago. He decided to stay with his wife. I knew he would. They all do, you know. No, I vowed that Eddie would be my last married man. You want to know something, Nora? He wasn't even that good in bed. Of course, the illicit thrill carried it a long way, but you can't imagine what an energy drain it is to be involved with someone who's married. You know, there was a time I thought his wife had put a detective on to me?"

Nora made a sympathetic murmur as the Perriers arrived.

"It was absolutely wild. I kept seeing men in trenchcoats lurking behind me everywhere." Stacey stubbed out her cigarette, took a sip of her Perrier and closed her eyes as if to ward off a momentary stab of pain. Nora noticed that she wore three separate shades of eye shadow—a pale pink next to her eyebrows, rose-red across her lids, and a mauve line at the lashes. "No, never again. The trouble is that there are so few other, *decent* men. Nora, you have no idea what the pickings are like out there. It's an absolute desert. The men are gay, or separated and still carrying around all that emotional baggage from their marriages, or unattached but unwilling to make a commitment. You want to know the truth? I've been celibate for thirteen months. I sublimate. I have a cat now and three guppies. I grow herbs on my balcony. I belong to a video club." She paused and then lowered her voice. "Oh, Nora, remember when we figured out that we had both learned to masturbate? Well, it's like bicycle riding. Thank goodness, you never forget how."

The shame of it. The fear that Ben, sleeping across the room, would hear her. The wetness and that sea smell. Nora hadn't wanted to do it, but she hadn't been able to stop herself either. It hadn't been enough anymore just to dream about Rock Hudson or Troy Donahue or Fabian, clutching a pillow in her arms and experimentally pressing her mouth against the crumpled cotton. She could remember the way the need seemed to creep upon her unawares, not a distinctly physical sensation at first, but something that settled in the vicinity of her pubic bone and would not go away. From there it would spread, a clamoring and a wanting that she had never been able to ignore.

At the time, she had guiltily thought she was the only girl in Benjamin Franklin High School who was doing it. And then, one night during a sleepover, when the lights were out, Stacey had brought the subject up. They'd been discussing the hard-to-imagine sex life of their parents.

("Nora, do you think your mother has orgasms?"

"God, no. I don't even think she and my father make love any more. I'd hear them, wouldn't I?"

"I don't know. I mean, I know my parents do, because I checked my mother's diaphragm."

"You didn't!"

"Shhh, yes, I did. And it was wet."

"Oh—disgusting."

"Not from *that*. She washes it off afterwards. Anyway, I think she has orgasms. I think she likes sex. Do you think we will?"

"It depends on who you're doing it with."

"Yeah . . . but it should feel good. I mean, sometimes, I— Oh, forget it."

"What?"

"No, forget it."

"Come on, Stacey."

"Well, sometimes I . . . touch myself down there."

"You do?"

"Don't you?"

"Well . . . actually . . . I have."

"Have you ever had an orgasm?"

"Stacey, you promise you won't ever tell anyone?"

"Of course, I promise."

"Really promise?"

"Really, *really* promise."

"I think I have.")

Nora's relief at finding a co-conspirator had been overwhelming. After that mutual confession, she'd still hated succumbing to that sharp sexual need, but had given in to it more easily. Nora had masturbated all during high school and college, even when she was sleeping with Andrew Stone. It wasn't until she met Marty that the frequency of her masturbating had decreased, until now she couldn't remember when she had last felt the desire.

The waiter arrived and looked expectant. "Sorry," Stacey said, "we're not ready yet. Can you give us a few minutes?" She picked up the menu but didn't look at it. Instead, she leaned forward and said, "You want to know how bad things really are? My biological clock ticked out last year, and I think I'm going into menopause. My internist told me I'm arthritic." She now held the menu at arm's length and squinted. "And I can't see without glasses anymore either. Honest to God, Nora, isn't life the pits?"

Nora liked hotel rooms and all the nifty take-home items that she found in the bathrooms. In this one, there were packages of soap, bottles of shampoo and mouthwash, a sewing kit, a shoeshine cloth, and a plastic shower cap. The scaled-down size of some of these objects made her think of the pleasure she had felt when she was very small and had spent long hours playing house. When Christine had been born Esther had given her several boxes of her own toys: five child-sized place settings with the Blue Willow pattern, miniature knives and forks, and kitchen utensils like spatulas and hand-beaters. There had also been tiny packages of pretend-food: a small and perpetually brown plastic turkey, domino-size boxes of Rice Crispies and thimble cans of Campbell's Tomato Soup. As a toddler, Christine had loved to set out the dishes and flatware and serve Nora make-believe meals of dry Cheerios and Ritz crackers. "You've had enough of that," she would say, her fat hand grabbing a plate out from under Nora's nose. "Time for your vejables."

Nora also liked the hotel room's graceful designer anonymity, the maid service that had invisibly vacuumed the floor and scrubbed the toilet, and especially the two thick, white terry cloth robes hanging side by side on the bathroom door. She had finished with her shower and was feeling cool and pampered as she examined the contents of the small refrigerator, whose front had been so cunningly concealed in the wall of closets. More little things lay inside: chocolates in glittering silver-and-gold wrappings, a glass bowl of sliced lemons and olives, a jar of maraschino cherries, narrow-necked bottles of whiskey and aperitifs, and cans of juices and selzter. Nora nibbled an olive and mixed herself a Bloody Mary. When Marty arrived she was lying on the bed, naked beneath her robe, sipping at her drink and studying the pornographic movie selections.

"What a day," he said, pulling off his jacket and yanking at his tie.

"Pandora's Box," Nora said. "I suppose that's a pun, right? Oh, darn, they're only showing that on Tuesday nights. *Hot Kisses* is on tonight. What do you think? Will it have a plot? Should we try it?"

Marty threw his jacket over a chair. "Does it need a plot?"

Nora got up from the bed and put her arms around him. Even though he'd been in air conditioning all day, he had a sharp sweaty smell at the armpits. "You stink," she said, giving him a wifely kiss. "Hard day at the ranch?"

"Bariskofsky is such an asshole. He drones on and on. Christ Almighty, talk about rising to your level of incompetence. And we just found out they want the software a lot faster than we thought. It's going to be hell on wheels." He paused as his hands patted her on the buttocks. "Hey, a naked lady." He tugged at the front of her robe and eyed her breasts. Then he started marching her back to the bed. "Let's make our own porno film."

"Hold it," Nora said. "A bath and then me."

"In that order?"

"Yup."

"You're a hard woman, but I guess I can handle it."

While Marty was soaking in the tub and nursing a Scotch on the rocks, Nora called Joanne to see how the store was doing and to check up on Christine, who was staying with the Whites.

"Hi. Having a good time?" Joanne said.

"It's great."

"Christine is doing fine. She and Nina spent the afternoon baking peanut butter cookies. Jay showed up, and he and Matthew consumed them all. Which was a blessing, because God knows I don't need them. She's gone, by the way. They all went over to the tennis courts."

"And the store?"

"Surviving without you. We got a big shipment of books from Mallet. Oh, and guess what? We sold that damned rocking horse."

The rocking horse had been made of five different kinds of wood, had a real horsehair mane, and cost a bundle. Nora had insisted on buying it over Joanne's dead body. "See. I told you. Neiman-Marcus, here we come."

"Don't pat yourself on the back yet. Mrs. Caraccato returned all those party goods. Remember that order? Well, she said her daughter doesn't like Smurfs any more."

"You couldn't sell her something else—Strawberry Short-cake, Peanuts, Barbie?"

"She wouldn't bite. You know what I think? She found the stuff cheaper at The Papery."

The Papery was a new store in downtown Burtonville. "Oh, shit."

"Anyway, Bernie stopped by. He sends you love and kisses. And that's all the news."

"Okay, see you day after tomorrow."

"Oh, and Nora?"

"Yes?"

"Remember, you can do everything I would do—plus."

"Plus? I might get arrested."

"That's the idea."

When Nora went back to the bathroom, Marty was stretched out in the bath with his eyes closed and, because he was too tall for the tub, his knees bent. She looked with affection at his naked body: the hairy legs and the hairless, rough kneecaps, the small, soft paunch with its bull's-eye navel, the penis curled limply on his floating scrotum. As she stood there, he farted, and the fart came up in pops, rocking his balls from side to side and releasing tiny bubbles from his pubic hair that broke on the surface like champagne.

"Well, thanks," Nora said, "and hello to you, too."

Marty grinned and kept his eyes closed. "Wash my back."

Nora sat down on the toilet seat and picked up a washcloth. "What happened to last year's slave?"

"She died of overwork."

"I'll bet. Lean forward."

Marty obediently hunched over, presenting Nora with his curved back. She began to lather it, scrubbing the knobs of his spine, the arched shoulder blades, the patches of hair. "When you

were a teenager, did you ever wonder if your mother had orgasms?"

"*What?* Never. Christ, in those days, I didn't even know
how women were built, much less whether they had orgasms or
not."

"Did you wonder if your parents had sex?"

"Nora, what on earth did you do today?"

"Had lunch with Stacey. We used to talk about stuff like
that."

"How is Stacey anyway? Still the wild single?"

"She says there are no more good men. She says she's been
celibate for thirteen months."

"Maybe some of us married types should take pity on these
poor lonely women. I mean, spread the wealth around a little
bit."

Nora gave him a pinch. "She's off married men. They're
more trouble than they're worth. Besides, Eddie wasn't any good
in bed."

"Is that what you women talk about? What we're like in
bed? Boy, would I like to be a fly on the wall."

"You know what they say about eavesdroppers."

"Nah, I'm not worried. You don't have anything to com-
plain about."

"That's what you think. Now, in comparison to my twenty-
five fabulous lovers . . ."

"Twenty-five?" Marty gave a snort. "You can hardly manage
me. I mean, things have been pretty few and far between lately."

The Beeme marriage, that perpetual motion machine, had
lately been sputtering along on four of its six cylinders. Nora and
Marty's sex life consisted of quickies in the morning and perfunc-
tory performances at night—hasty, last-minute couplings with no
other function than to relieve the odd itch. Nora hadn't been able
to indulge in a long, leisurely orgasm or satisfying fantasy in
weeks, and she knew the fault was hers. She had read many
articles on the frailty of the male erection, that visible banner of
masculine happiness and security, which waved proudly in good
times and flagged impotently at bad ones. No one, it seemed to

her, discussed the fragility of the female orgasm, a state that could be difficult to achieve at the best of times and, when she was uptight about anything—the store, the kids, Marty—proved elusive altogether.

"I know," she said, leaning forward and kissing the back of his soapy neck. "I'm going to make it up to you."

"What are you going to do?"

"Mmmm. Mutter. Mumble."

"Oh, really?"

"Really."

Which was how Nora found herself sitting naked on a cushioned chair by the bed with her legs spread wide over the arms, while Marty, also naked, lay on his side on the bed, facing her. Her tube of K-Y Jelly lay on the night table with its cap off, and a good portion of its contents were spread on her, in her, and on Marty's fingers. She was holding her labia apart with both hands while Marty ran a forefinger over her engorged clitoris, down to her vagina, inside as deeply as he could go, back out, and then up again. A circular, probing motion—round and round and round. Nora's head was tilted against the chair's back, and her eyes were closed.

She is in a semi-seated position on a huge circular platform, her body pinioned at the ankles and wrists, her back and head supported by a cushioned form, her legs bent and held apart by stirrups. There are other women on the platform, each shackled in the same position, and it is slowly revolving around, stopping at small windows so that each woman is displayed at one before she moves on to the next. She understands that the windows have been placed at such a level that a viewer will be unable to see her upper body or face, but only her wide-open vagina, which has been generously coated with a lubricant. Sometimes the light reflects off the windows in such a way that she can see not the eyes of the men peering in, but the reflection of her own vagina in the small square of glass. It is red, glistening and swollen.

The platform has been moving slowly and steadily around, but now it comes to a full stop. She hears a clicking sound, then a creaking as the window before her is unlocked and opened. She has heard that this can happen, that for enough money a viewer can touch what lies vulnerable before him. She has also heard that nothing she can do will stop this. She can moan or cry or scream, but no one will listen. She stiffens as fingers touch and probe her, pulling on flesh here, pushing flesh there. A finger is inserted, then two, three and four, stretching her wider than she has ever been stretched before. The hand twists so that the thumb presses down on her clitoris. She moans, and suddenly the fingers are gone, and the air is cool on her exposed, moist skin. Waiting, she shivers and her knees tremble. Then a finger touches her lightly at the very bottom edge of the vaginal opening and slides downward toward her anus. She takes in a shuddering breath.

"You like that—huh?"

Nora opened her eyes and blinked. "Are you getting lonely over there?"

Marty rolled over onto his back, his penis pointing toward the ceiling in purple priapic splendor. "I could be," he said. "Want to join me?"

She is lying naked on a bed, her legs spread wide, her head forced back. She is being held down by several women, all of whom are dressed in simple, loose-fitting, long white smocks. They could be nurses or merely servants; their hands are cool, noncommittal. A man enters. He is tall and muscular, dressed totally in black and masked so she can't see any part of his face. He is wearing a tunic and tight-fitting pants and gloves. Every part of him is covered except for his genitals, which protrude through a slit in the fabric of his pants. His erection is enormous, terrifying. She only catches a glimpse of it before a gauzy scarf is tied across her eyes.

Although she can't see him through the blindfold, she knows what he is doing. He coldly inspects the flesh between her wide-open legs, examines and disdainfully touches her breasts. Her nipples are hard and aching, but he ignores these and moves closer to her head. She feels hands on the sides of her face, fingers pressing against her cheeks. Her head is angled to one side, and hard, hot flesh pokes at her mouth, forcing it open, and she takes him in, the huge, swollen sword sliding past her tongue toward the back of her helpless throat.

Marty put his hand on Nora's head, stopping its up-and-down motion. "If you don't quit," he said, "I'm going to come."

Nora let his penis slide out of her mouth. "We can't have that, can we?" She gave a quick good-bye lick to the sensitive flesh below the glans, making his stomach muscles flutter, and then slid up his body so that their faces were together. He wrapped his arms around her and gave an affectionate squeeze.

"How come," she said, "sex in hotels is always better than at home?"

"I don't know."

Nora said, "A different bed, maybe?"

"Does it matter?" He put his hand down between their bodies and fingered her clitoris.

"Maybe it's the air." Marty didn't say anything, but pulled her on top of him, and Nora eased herself onto his penis. "Well, I was just wondering."

"Would you prefer to talk or to get down to brass tacks?"

"Brass tacks," she said.

"That's what I thought."

He pushes the labia apart and enters her, her legs held firmly in place by the women so that there is no way she can squirm or move backward and avoid the immensity of him. Once he is in her, he begins to move slowly in and out. In order to keep her lubricated and receptive, someone strokes her clitoris in the same steady rhythm, and she becomes part of a spiral, spinning up an endless curve in a velvety blackness. The faster she spins, the higher she goes, and the spiral begins to thin, from wire to thread, from thread to filament, from filament to something so delicate and so fragile that when the finger slides into her anus, it shatters, breaking like glass into a million glittering bits of crystal. She comes hard, jerking and shuddering, over and over again.

Below Nora, Marty arched and cried out and then was quiet. They lay together for a silent moment in the tumble of sheets and blankets, their bodies cooling, and then Nora bit his earlobe. "Thanks," she said.

"Thank *you.*"

Nora slipped off him, reached for a tissue and tucked it in her crotch. Then she pulled the blankets over both of them. "I could sleep," she said.

Marty pulled her close so that her back was against his warm belly, and tucked an arm around her, his hand spread across both her breasts. "So how was that compared to your twenty-five fabulous lovers?"

Nora wiggled closer to him. "Let's put it this way. I'm not planning on firing you yet."

"That good, huh?"

"Mmmm," she hummed drowsily.

"You got anything left for later?"

"Later? You couldn't get it up again."

"That's what you think."

"Well, if you're really, really lucky . . ."

Marty gave a gentle tweak to her left nipple, and Nora closed her eyes. In a few seconds, she was asleep.

Within a minute—Nora knew because she checked her watch—of the Beemes' arrival at the cocktail party, Marty abandoned her. The party was being given by Devlin, the military and two other companies, Simca, Inc. and Microtel, as the final get-together for the seminar, and it was held in one of the conference rooms of the hotel. Nora had bought a dress especially for the occasion. Like many of the fancier clothes she owned, it seemed to have been designed with discomfort in mind. The waist pinched, (her fault—she should lose five pounds), one of the jutting shoulder pads kept slipping backward, and an interfacing along the front of the bodice scratched her chest. Although the fabric, a paisley, nonnatural fiber, had been touted by the saleslady as wonderfully crease-free, the back of the skirt was already crinkled. Nora knew she would spend a good portion of the evening shifting uncomfortably from foot to foot—her new high heels were already putting the squeeze on her toes—and surreptitiously stroking her buttocks.

With Marty already deep into an enthusiastic discussion of Delta V Maneuvers and Momentum Dumps with two military types, Nora wandered alone through the crowd to the bar for a glass of white wine, and followed that with a visit to the food table, where a collection of highly caloric tidbits had been artistically placed on crackers. As she nibbled at a crab-mayo something and gazed around the room, it struck her that people smiled harder, gestured more emphatically and talked louder at cocktail parties. She could hear brays of laughter and snatches of conversations from as far as three feet away.

". . . always go to Aspen in the . . ."

". . . a fifty-percent-off sale that . . ."

". . . too much in stocks. Bonds were . . ."

On the other hand, it was also clear to Nora that not every conversation was trivial. Certain VIPs from Devlin had been cornered by senior-looking military types with stars on their epaulets and lots of spaghetti on their chests. Their faces had that portentous look of people who are convinced of the solemn worth of their mission. Even Marty had it. From where she was standing, Nora could see that his square chin had acquired that self-important, professorial crumple without the fingertips pushing it in place.

"Are you a spouse?" someone said, and Nora turned to find a woman standing beside her. She had pale skin, brown eyes and fine, chin-length hair which resembled in color and curl the fur on a spaniel's ears.

"A spouse," Nora confirmed. "You too?"

The woman nodded and smiled. She had a bright-red fleck of pimento caught between a canine and bicuspid. "My husband's with Simca—from Chicago."

Nora smiled and tried hard not to notice the pimento. "Devlin. Upstate New York."

The woman's smile increased in width. "We went once to Lake Placid. A skiing vacation. It was very nice. My children really enjoyed it."

Nora stretched her smile likewise and felt her lipstick crack.

"We don't live near there, but it *is* a very nice place. So you have children?"

"A boy and a girl."

"Oh, me too. What ages?"

"The girl's sixteen and the boy's twelve."

As if this were the most wonderful coincidence in the world, Nora assumed an amazed look. "Almost the same as my kids!" And immediately felt her left shoulder pad slide backward toward her shoulder blade.

"So you're here just for the seminar, too?"

Could she shrug it back into place? Nora masked the shrug by leaning forward and picking up another hors d'oeuvre. This wasn't an easy maneuver, as she had a wine glass in her other hand and a purse hanging from a strap off her right shoulder. As she leaned, the purse fell toward the table, the strap dislodging the other shoulder pad and pushing it forward so that it pressed it against her collar bone.

Nora straightened, her smile now as lopsided as her pads. "Yes, I can't be away for too long. I have a store back home."

"A store. You mean, a retail store?"

"Yes, a children's store. Toys, some clothes, that sort of thing."

The woman ran her tongue over her teeth so that when she smiled again, the pimento, thank God, was gone. "A store. Isn't that interesting."

"Yes, it is. I really enjoy it."

There was no telling what height of inanity this conversation might have achieved, because they were interrupted by the arrival of another woman. This one was tall, thin and elegant, a Stacey clone, except that she was prettier. Her shoulder pads, Nora could see, were the kind that never budged.

"Sandra, how are you?"

"Oh, Moira, this is—I'm sorry, I didn't catch your name."

"Nora. Nora Beeme."

"This is Nora Beeme from upstate New York. Moira Wilkes." They nodded hello to one another. "Moira's husband is also with Simca."

"How nice."

"Moira used to run a feminist reading group that I belonged to, but she's gone back to school for a Ph.D. in Human Sexuality."

"Really," Nora murmured.

"And it's so interesting. Her research is in—what was it?—historical patterns of female sexual response."

Moira reached across Nora and picked up an hors d'oeuvre. Her fingernails were a gleaming, dark umber. "Actually, Sandra, I hadn't had a chance to tell you, but I've decided to change my dissertation topic."

"Really? That talk you gave the group was so fascinating."

"I decided I wanted to study a more contemporary issue. So now I'm looking into female sexual fantasies."

Nora forgot all about the mess at her shoulders, the crimp at her waist and the pinch at her toes.

Moira leaned forward as if imparting a secret to them, and an expensive scent wafted across Nora's nose. "It's a neglected field of study, which is amazing when you consider how many women fantasize. Can you guess?" Nora and Sandra shook their heads. "An estimated 88 percent. Is that incredible?"

Nora was feeling sorry for the 12 percent of nonindulgers. She wondered what they did to keep their sex life exciting, but she didn't dare ask. "Incredible," she echoed.

"But," Sandra said, "is that so surprising? I mean, I've read so many articles about how it's a good thing for women to fantasize. Well, and men too, for that matter."

Moira bit delicately into her tidbit on a cracker. "The thing is," she said, "the truly *disturbing* thing, is not that so many women feel the need to fantasize, that's okay, but what they're fantasizing *about*. We are discovering, in fact, that their fantasies are based on male images of pornography."

"Is that bad?"

"Would you believe that I'm finding that many women fantasize about rape?"

Nora tried to imitate Sandra's look of shock.

"And what we have to ask ourselves is whether it's a good

thing for a woman to do this. In my opinion, it just reinforces women's self-images of being passive, submissive societal victims."

Nora, who had been fantastically raped more times than she could count, now ventured, "But a rape fantasy isn't . . . um, about a woman in an underground garage being thrown on cement by some creep. I mean, that's *reality,* but a fantasy is different. In a fantasy, you have control."

"It comes to the same thing," Moira said. "The violence, the power imagery—it's the same."

But now Nora thought of something else. "Maybe fantasies like that arise from something . . . well, more primal," she ventured. "I mean, in all animal societies, males are aggressive and dominant. Maybe, it has something to do with instinct."

Moira ignored this. "Part of the problem is that women haven't developed their own erotic images. The body of female erotica is based primarily on already existing pornographic elements—rape, female bondage, violence, penetration, huge genitalia, etcetera. Elements that are degrading to women."

"Well," Sandra said, "I have to confess that I do fantasize, but it's always something romantic. Flowers and candlelight, that sort of stuff."

Nora had always believed that her fantasies were harmless, innocent indulgences that offended no one. She'd never thought of them as being degrading. In fact, they possessed an inherent selfishness; in them, she was The Star, the center of whirling constellations, the focal point in an absorbing production staged just for her benefit. It's true that early in her marriage she'd felt slightly guilty that she didn't always fantasize about Marty, but he'd never known that, so her guilt had finally dissipated and she'd continued merrily on, creating new fantasies with abandon. Never once had she given any thought to their political content. For a brief, wild moment, Nora considered what a noble thing it would be to give them up: a one-woman, private, unsung sacrifice in the name of feminism. She'd be able to hold her head up in conversations; she'd be a stronger woman for it.

Moira was now going on at length, her head thrust forward,

authoritatively waving a caviared cracker in the air. ". . . so you see, things have to change. Women have to be educated to understand how masochistic they are. If fantasies are necessary, and I think they are, women must be taught to fantasize about men and their relationships with men in a totally different way. If they don't, we're never going to be equal. Never."

But what would she do without them? Nora took a sip of her wine and tried to imagine going to bed with Marty for the next thirty years without all of her favorite sexual scenarios, politically incorrect and degrading though they might be. She immediately felt bereft and panicky. Her wine went down in a gulp, burning her throat. There was no way she was going to be able to ruthlessly cut away the rank undergrowth that flourished in her brain. She needed her fantasies, Nora realized, she wanted them. The truth was—she was addicted. Shamefully and secretly addicted to unauthorized, illegal, contraband fantasies.

7

◇   ◇   ◇   August was the month of the propaganda baby.

The propaganda baby was named Melissa, and at the age when an infant is at its most charming. She was seven months old and had rolls of creamy skin at her neck, elbows, wrists and the backs of her knees. She could sit up, roll over, suck on her own toes and play peekaboo, pattycake and how-big-is-the-baby. She also had an endearing way of tilting her dark, curly head to one side, lowering the incredible sweep of her lashes until they grazed her cheeks and then opening her blue eyes as wide as possible, as if what she'd seen behind her plump eyelids was astonishing beyond measure. When she was holding Melissa, Nora had the sensation that the baby was a bonbon, a talcum-scented sweet-meat, a pink and white, almost edible, confection.

Melissa belonged to Elly, an unwed mother of seventeen, whom Christine had met at the Coalition and with whom she'd become close friends. To Nora, Elly gave off an air of competence that was almost frightening in one so young. She had quick, neat movements and long, narrow fingers that were always busy. Dur-

◇   131

ing a half-hour's stay, Nora had seen her apply two coats of bright red polish to her toenails, daub zinc cream on Melissa's buttocks as she expertly changed a diaper and swiftly twist her fine, dark straight hair into one of those complicated French braids. No matter how hot it was, Elly always arrived at the Beemes' in the same outfit: jeans and an oversized white man's shirt that she cinched at her waist with a wide belt and accented with a carelessly tied scarf at the neck. She somehow managed to make this outfit look more stylish than anything Nora had gone to great lengths and expense to purchase for herself.

When she had first been introduced to Elly and Melissa, Nora hadn't been quite able to believe that one was the mother of the other. The fat, bouncing baby bore no resemblance to the tall, thin girl with the dark, precise features. Nor did it seem possible that Elly had physically given birth. Beneath jeans tighter than any girdle that Nora had ever endured, Elly had an abdomen so concave and narrow that it was hard to imagine a pregnancy filling that bony unaccommodating space. But pregnant she had been, conception having taken place one night when her stepfather was drunk and out cold, her mother was partying with friends and her boyfriend, Darren, finally got her to "do it." She was still seeing him now and then, but had no intention of marrying him.

"I mean, sometimes Darren thinks he wants to, but then the idea of it freaks him out. Besides, he can't keep a steady job, and I don't want him hanging around with nothing to do."

Elly's natural father lived in California, and she hadn't heard from him in years. Her mother hadn't guessed that she was pregnant until she was five months gone.

"I didn't show for the longest time, so she never even noticed. Of course she was really mad at me when she found out, because she'd gotten me a prescription for pills even before I'd slept with Darren. You see, she figured I was already doing it. Anyway, I'd thrown the pills out. I didn't want her telling me what to do."

Her stepfather, who seemed to be chronically drunk and unemployed, had tried to fondle her while she was pregnant, but

Elly'd known just how to handle him. "I'd tell him to shove off. I'd say, 'Get your dirty hands off of me!' and he'd leave me alone." She finally did move out after Melissa was born and was now living in one of the apartments that the Coalition found for girls who had nowhere to go. "My Mom started telling me how to do everything with the baby. Plus I had to clean and help with dinner. Actually, I had to make it most of the time since she was too busy with work and her friends. But if I wanted to go out with *my* friends, she'd tell me that I was a mother now and just couldn't leave because I wanted to. I wouldn't put up with it any more."

These bits and pieces of history were spoken in a sharp voice amidst a flurry of baby care—the careful mixing of rice cereal with strained peaches, the replacement of a dirty bib with a snowy white one—and were placed like chips of mosaic into the larger picture that was Elly's life. She knew every social agency within a hundred-mile radius and how to obtain cheap food, medicine and clothing. She was an authority on childbirth and obstetrical lore and had firm opinions on the proper care and feeding of babies. She had her future set out in front of her like a map with marker pins at crucial intersections of time and space.

"I'm going to get a part-time sales job at either the Drug Mart or Mr. Grocer when Melissa is a year old. They don't charge you for uniforms and the time is flexible. When she's two and out of diapers, I'm going to study to be a nurse's aide at Syracuse Community College. They have a really good program there with day care. There's a waiting list, but I'm on that already. When I finish that, I can work shifts while Melissa is sleeping and pay someone to look after her. Meanwhile I'm going to study real nursing so that when she goes to kindergarten, I'll be able to make good money and she can have everything she needs."

Nora listened to Elly with an uneasy fascination. There was something incongruous between Elly's messy family background (Nora imagined a thin, waspish mother who smoked too much and a fat slob of a stepfather) and this absolute and impeccable control over her present existence. Nora didn't think there had ever been a time in her own life when she'd ever had everything as together as Elly, unwed teenaged mother. Despite the fact that she'd had a husband, a good family income and a diaper service, Nora remembered early motherhood as exhausting and stressful. Marty had taken photographs of her with two-month-old Christine in which her eyes had been circled in black and her normally round face had been angular and thin. She had loved her babies with ferocity, but it was the horrific details of infant care that remained in her mind: breast-feeding at all hours, the shitty midnight diapers, Christine's nonstop crying, rocking Danny and having him vomit into the open neckline of her nightgown.

But if Nora wasn't quite convinced by Elly's facade, Christine was taken in completely. She admired Elly and talked about her, and repeated the many pearls of wisdom that Elly let drop during her visits.

"Mom, would you buy that bran cereal?" she said at dinner one night.

"Which cereal?"

"Bran Nuggets."

"Bran Nuggets? The last box I bought died of neglect."

"Elly says it's good for constipation during pregnancy."

"Oh, for Christ's sake," Marty said. "Do we have to discuss this at the dinner table?"

"What's constipation?" Danny said.

Nor could Christine be convinced that Elly's life wasn't exactly a bed of carefully planted roses, all blooming at the same time.

"Where is Elly's apartment, exactly?" Nora asked one afternoon after Elly had left. It was too hot to sit out on the patio anymore, and she'd taken the magazine she was reading into the air-conditioned living room.

Christine flopped down on the couch and lay on her back, her abdomen a small hard hill beneath a loose, pale blue top. She could no longer wear her own clothes, or even Nora's, and had acquired a small wardrobe of maternity hand-me-downs from the Coalition. "West Burtonville, I think."

"Over by the tire plant."

"I don't know, Mom, I've never been there."

"It's not a very good neighborhood."

"Elly says she really likes it. Elly says it's neat."

"I'm very happy for her."

Christine bristled. She was no longer as moody or angry as she had been, but she searched for attacks even in the most innocent questions and was quick and snappy on the defense. "Why don't you ever believe anything Elly says?"

"Who said I didn't?"

"I can tell. You get that look on your face."

Nora thought of the smiles she'd bestowed on Elly, the nods of admiration, the quick agreement with all those pompous adolescent opinions. She sighed. "I have to confess I find it a little hard to believe that everything is going so well for her."

"Why?"

"Because she's all alone, and it's hard to bring up a baby all by yourself."

"She has the people at the Coalition. Mrs. Allison visits her at least once a week."

"And she's on welfare."

"Elly is incredibly economical. She clips coupons and only buys things on special. She gets food from the church. She writes down every penny that she spends so she knows where it's going."

So that's where Christine's new budget had come from. Nora had wondered. Four allowances ago, Christine had purchased a small black ledger book with two columns, one for assets and one for debits. Nora had found it in the children's bathroom when she'd been cleaning. Entries had included "Ledger book— $6.95," "Baskin and Robbins—$1.10," "Movie—$4.50."

"She doesn't have much of a chance," Nora went on, "of accomplishing all those things she wants to. Not with a baby on her hands. Not with government cutbacks in social services."

Christine turned on her side, her hair swinging. The perm had grown out, and she was wearing it longer now, to her shoulders. She'd also had rubber bands added to her braces so that when she spoke it was through a web of rubber and bubbles. "Why can't you even give her any credit for wanting to get ahead?"

"I do. I just think she's going to find it a lot harder than she expects."

"You're so negative. I hate it."

"Not negative. Realistic."

Christine was silent for a moment, as if regrouping her forces, and then she said, "Don't you think Melissa is cute?"

Nora was about to say "of course," when it hit her. That's what Elly's visits really meant. *You're living in a dream world.* She hadn't believed Marty, clinging instead to her own, more pleasing, version of reality. Christine would give up the baby; she'd go back to school, Marty would stop being angry, Danny wouldn't get into trouble. Were those all dreams? Dreams so soft that she hadn't noticed how opaque they were? Dreams that had blinded her to what Melissa represented? A propaganda baby, a sweet and luscious candy treat designed to whet the appetite.

"Christine, you aren't seriously thinking about keeping the baby, are you?"

Christine looked away. "I haven't decided."

Nora felt a dizziness come over her, as if her mountain had moved and her mother-perch was swaying dangerously back and forth. She clutched her magazine, holding on for dear life. "It's a very bad idea."

"Why?"

"You're not Elly. You know that. You're disorganized and—"

"My room's been clean lately. Haven't you noticed?"

Nora had noticed the neat dresser top, the expanse of unlittered floor, the bed actually made, but the pleasure she'd found in those smooth surfaces now turned sour. "It's one thing to keep your room neat and another to have to take care of a baby."

Christine shrugged. "I knew you wouldn't think I could do it."

"Suppose you don't have a nice and easy baby like Melissa? Suppose you have a cranky, colicky baby that cries all the time? That's what you were like. Or a sick baby? Or just a plain difficult baby?"

"I know it's not easy, but Elly—"

"You have to finish school; you want to go to college. Do you have any idea what the chances are of being a single mother and achieving those things? Do you?"

"I know."

"No, you don't. Not really, because you have no idea of the responsibilities involved. You have some silly, sentimental idea that bringing up a baby is all sweetness and light. Well, it isn't; it's also hard, hard work."

"But—"

Nora ignored her. "And I'm not prepared to do it for you. Do you understand? I can remember that dog you wanted and how you promised us you'd feed and walk it and brush it and wash it. Well, what happened? Come on, tell me."

"I don't want to talk about it."

"You don't want to talk about it, because Daddy ended up feeding it and walking it and brushing it and washing it. That's why you don't want to talk about it. Well, a baby's a lot bigger responsibility than a dog."

"I know that!"

"Do you? You won't clean up the kitchen without a fight. You won't learn how to cook a meal because it's boring. You still fight with your brother as if you were two years old. You still want to spend all your money on Calvin Klein jeans!"

Christine sat up straight and gave Nora an angry, defiant look. "I wouldn't do that. That stuff wouldn't be important anymore."

"You're dreaming if you think that."

"I can change, you know," she said vehemently. "I'm not going to be the *same* person forever. I can be *different.*"

There was silence for a moment and then Nora said wearily, "Just tell me why you want to keep this baby."

Christine sank back against the couch cushions. "Why? I don't know. . . . Well, I think . . . I guess I want something of my own."

"You have a lot of things of your own—a room, clothes, friends, parents, a brother."

"That's not the same."

"You know, your father and I have tried to give you every-thing you need."

"I know that, Mom."

"So what's missing?"

"It's hard to explain. You see, it's like all the outside stuff doesn't really add up to anything. It's like . . . well, having an emptiness inside."

Emptiness? Nora wanted to scream. *What emptiness?* Where did it come from? Why hadn't she heard about it before? Nora had never believed that bringing up children was easy, but she had thought she'd done her best. Now she wondered help-lessly which parental misstep had caused that emptiness. Inade-quate breastfeeding? Too strict toilet training? Lack of quality time?

Nora sighed. "What sort of emptiness?"

"I can't explain it, Mom, it's just there. It's like there's noth-ing in the center."

"If you're talking about an identity crisis, everyone has those."

"I don't know what it is. I can't put a name on it."

"Is this . . . emptiness a good reason to keep a baby?"

Christine gave her a crafty look. "Why did you have me?"

"Because—" Nora paused, looking at her daughter's face and seeing it not at fifteen but at three months, a small circle of flesh and tiny features surrounded by a hat brim and a blanket of pale yellow with green yarn trim. The memory of that face car-ried with it a sliver of time, an afternoon when she and Marty had gone shopping and he was carrying a sleeping Christine in his arms. He had been walking very carefully on an icy sidewalk, and Nora had been following in his footsteps when she'd suddenly had a horrific vision, a slow-reel scenario of a car swerving off the road, hitting Marty so that he fell and Christine flew out of his hands. Nothing of the sort had happened, of course, but Nora could remember the way her heart had leapt, the flinching of her muscles, the sensation that *she* was that small, sleeping baby, crashing and breaking on the pavement.

"Just tell me one thing," she said. "Do you think you're

ready to be a mother? Honestly, now. And I don't want to hear about Elly and all the ways you can possibly change. Come on, tell me: are *you* ready to be somebody's mother?"

Christine's hands dropped to her abdomen. Her fingernails were manicured now and polished a pale pink. At first she cupped the weight of the baby she was carrying in her palms. Then she ran her fingertips around and around in small, soothing circles as if the child beneath were agitated and kicking.

"I think I love it like a mother," she said slowly, frowning as she looked down. "I don't know. . . . I think I love it already."

Nora had loved Christine even before she'd been conceived. Or rather she had loved the idea of a Christine. She'd had hazy, pleasurable visions of a small baby, a crib, a rocker, all colored in sweet pastels. She imagined herself standing for a photograph with Marty behind her and a child in her arms—a family, a cohesive unit, three dots joined by strong, black lines into a perfect triangle. Marty didn't share those visions exactly, Nora knew that, but he said he loved her and he wanted her to be happy. Besides, all their friends were having babies. It seemed the thing to do.

But much to Nora's surprise, she didn't get pregnant right away. Esther had always warned her that a baby could come from Just One Time. Joanne had bragged that she'd conceived when Grant hung his pants over the end of the bed. Another acquaintance of Nora's got pregnant despite a diaphragm. It was a shock to discover that she and Marty could make love frequently, and nothing would happen. Not even when Marty stayed inside of her until he shrank into a soft bud and slipped out. Not even when she kept her hips raised on a pillow après-sex for a good half hour.

Nora consulted a gynecologist. Dr. Sullivan, a tall, distinguished man in his fifties, was cloyingly paternal. "Now, my dear," he would say from the vantage point of her naked posterior, "there's nothing wrong with you that your hubby can't cure." Later in her life Nora would remember with resentment the endearments and the reassuring taps, but at the time she clung to his fatherly presence as if he were the only means by which she could climb the invisible wall that separated the wasteland of her barrenness from the lush terrain of fertility.

Dr. Sullivan didn't feel that eight months of non-conception was anything to panic over, but Nora had become so convinced that the birth control pill had upset her system that he finally agreed to do some tests. ("Healthy hormones, my dear," he'd said, tapping the back of her hand. "Just as I told you—ovulation right on schedule.") But Nora's fears were catching and even Marty was vulnerable to fertility anxiety. He went secretly to a friend, who, being a teacher of high school biology, had access to microscopes.

("You didn't!" Nora said.

"Sure, I jerked off in the boys' bathroom onto a glass slide."

"What did Brian think?"

"He said he'd checked his sperm once, too."

Nora couldn't help envisioning thousands of men in solitary cubicles, hunkered over as they masturbated, worrying about the contents of that viscous white fluid. Which was odd, because she'd always envied men their no muss-no fuss reproductive system. It now occurred to her that perhaps it was women who were lucky with their cramps and odors, pads and tampons. At least, they knew *something* was going on.)

Marty's semen, under magnification, had proved to be swarming with spermatozoa, all busily engaged in swimming hither and thither, all happily ignorant of the futility of their existence. Nora and Marty agreed that they'd reached some limit of absurdity, that they were two normal adults, and that there was no good reason why they couldn't conceive. This mutual reassurance helped Nora for a while, but nothing came of it. Month after month slipped by, her period came and went like clockwork, and the hated red stain would once more appear. She cried when a sixth-grader in her school became pregnant from a rape, cried not because she felt badly for the girl but because the irony of it was so painful. And she was tormented by the proliferation of pregnancies all around her. It was as if almost every young woman in America had decided to have a child all at once. She saw them everywhere: in her doctor's office, on television, in the stores, on the sidewalks and at parties, their stomachs proudly ballooned out before them. She imagined they could see her emptiness; she imagined their pity, and a black column of envy rose within her, filling her throat until she thought she would choke.

Nora and Marty now began to make love according to the commands of the basal body temperature thermometer, a slim, imperious dictator who brooked no dissent—not even when one of them was sick, exhausted or unwilling. Every morning Nora took her temperature and recorded it on a chart, a small zigzag of minor ups and downs. Once a month, with great regularity, her temperature flew up like a swallow, a dramatic change in tenths of a degree. It was then, according to the directions that came with the thermometer, that marital relations *must* take place if conception were to occur.

"When we get home? *Tonight?*" Marty said one night. "You have to be kidding."

Nora shook her head as she turned on the car's ignition and peered through the windshield at the darkness and the thickly falling snow. Marty had been on a business trip, and his return flight had arrived in the middle of a storm, three hours late. It was now past midnight. She was tired, having worked all day and then having spent three hours in the airport lounge, alternately pacing the floor or sitting in the uncomfortable chairs and trying to read. Marty looked absolutely beat, his face dark with the shadow of his beard, his eyes red-rimmed. Nora supposed that she should be expressing wifely concern over his well-being, just thankful he'd made it home safely, but all she could think about was the fact that, according to the tyrannical thermometer, there were only a few hours left before her system closed down for the month.

"It's now or never," she said.

"I'm on California time, remember? I've been up for eighteen solid hours."

"We have to."

" 'Have to,' " he echoed, taking off his glasses and rubbing his eyes. "Possibly considered by *other* people as the two sexiest words in the English language?"

Nora was not amused. "It's not my fault."

"I didn't say it was."

"You implied it."

"Now, hold it for just a—"

"You could have come back yesterday."

"Oh, that's what's bothering you."

Nora stubbornly stared out the window. She'd turned on the headlights, and snowflakes danced through the beams. "Well, you could have. Fletcher didn't care."

"This is a job, Nora, not a hobby. This keeps a roof over our heads—remember?"

"You *knew* it was the right time."

"Oh, sure, I can see it now. Fletcher asks me to stay an extra day. 'No sir,' I say, 'I have to get home. Why, sir? No, no one's sick. No, the house hasn't burned down. No, sir, it's because my wife needs me. I'm on fuck duty.' "

"Marty—"

" 'Fuck duty, sir? Let me explain. We undress, we get into bed, we put a pillow beneath my wife's hips, we turn out the lights, I insert my gland into my wife's gland. In a few seconds, it's all over.' "

Nora's anger crumpled beneath the weight of his bitterness, and she turned off the ignition. "Oh Marty, it isn't as bad as that, is it?"

He sighed. "It's getting pretty grim."

Nora cried easily at this point in her life. Tears came into her eyes and her voice quavered. "I'm . . . sorry."

Marty reached over and took her mittened hands into his gloved ones. "You're right—it's not your fault."

"I'm the one that wants a baby."

"I do, too."

"Not as much as me."

"Suppose we never have a kid," he said gently. "Would it be the end of the world?"

"It would be awful."

"We'd still have each other, wouldn't we?"

Nora blurted out the words. "You might leave me some day for . . . someone else . . . who could give you kids."

"I wouldn't."

"My mother's cousin Herschel did. He was married for seventeen years, and then left his wife for a younger woman. He's got three kids now." The tears came back, and Nora began to sob.

The front seat of a car wasn't the easiest place for two people in bulky winter coats to hug. Marty drew Nora as close to him as possible. "Am I Herschel?" he demanded. "Am I?"

Nora shook her head and buried her face in his coat.

"Look, it's true—I don't want kids as badly as you do. It isn't going to be the end of my life if we don't have any."

Nora lifted her head and wiped the end of her nose on her mitten. "We can forget this month. It probably wouldn't work anyway."

"Nah, let's give it a whirl. What've we got to lose? I'll think sexy thoughts all the way home; I'll make mad, passionate love to you; than I'll collapse. How's your resuscitation technique?"

Nora began to cry again.

"Now what's the matter?"

"I love you," she wailed.

Of course, Christine was conceived that night, when the two of them were so tired that it was a quick fumble under the blankets and an immediate drop into sleep. They couldn't even stay awake long enough to perform the other rituals: the wait for Marty to subside, the propping of Nora's buttocks at a helpful angle. But while they slept, the magic occurred: that unseen conjuring, that noiseless connection, in the shadow of the swallow's wing.

Nora couldn't bear to tell Marty that he'd been right—that Christine wanted to keep the baby. It seemed easier to let the hot summer days slide by. The store wasn't especially busy; they were running an August sale on summer clothes. The only excitement came from putting in the final orders for Christmas merchandise.

Joanne and Nora each took a two weeks' vacation, the Grants going to Europe, the Beemes going nowhere. Marty was now working six days a week. Devlin Electronics had promised everyone on the satellite project that they'd get a month off when it was over, but there was no end in sight. There were constant complications, changes of plans, deadlines not met. Marty was too distracted to notice what was going on in the house or with the children, and Nora could see that so much of his energy was being spent at work that he didn't have any left for worrying over Christine. He didn't even seem to notice that she was pregnant anymore, treating her with the same casual attention that he bestowed on Danny.

Then Devlin decided to close down for the Labor Day weekend, and it rained for the three days, a chilly downpour that marked the end of summer. On Saturday Nora worked, the store doing a brisk business in school items. Danny spent Saturday night over at a friend's house, and Christine went to the mall with Jay. Marty repaired things: the screen door that wouldn't close properly, the broken blade on the lawn mower, the doorbell that no longer rang, the master bedroom toilet that gurgled and burped after flushing. On Sunday, no one got up until almost noon, Marty and Nora making love at nine o'clock and then falling asleep again. The children rented movies for the VCR in the afternoon, and Nora baked while Marty read the Burtonville-Fairfax *Leader* and the New York *Times.* There was a serenity to that Sunday that lulled Nora into a state that almost could be described as happiness. She hummed to herself as she cooked, an atonal, pleasing hum.

Then, after dinner that night, Danny brought it all to a crashing end.

He wandered into the den where Nora and Marty were watching television and said, "I was thinking about my room."

This was nothing new. Danny had come back from camp with an obsession about his room. He'd decided it was too babyish for him, and he no longer liked the curtains or the bedspread. He also wanted to change the arrangement of furniture, although he was not sure how. Nora thought Danny himself had changed over the summer. When she'd taken him shopping for school clothes, he'd displayed a new interest in style, insisting on incredibly tight jeans and "not gross" shirts, a category that Nora discovered she had no skill in locating. He'd also acquired a new vocabulary of swear words ("I don't like Jimmy any more. He's an asshole— Oh, excuse me, Mom, but he is.") and had grown an inch at least and developed huge, knobby elbows and knees. Nora regarded these changes with both alarm and love. *My son, the almost-man.*

Marty glanced at Danny and then back to the television. "What about your room?" he said absently.

Danny frowned. "I decided that I'm willing to share with the baby if it's a boy. And I'm not going to throw out all my old toys and comics, because he might like them."

Marty picked up the remote control and clicked off the television. "What baby?" he said, looking at Nora.

"You've been so busy," she said, "that I—"

"Christine's decided to keep it, hasn't she?"

"And it's going to need a place to sleep, right?" Danny said eagerly. "If it was in my room, I could help take care of it."

Marty blew—that was the only way Nora could express it— like a volcano. He sprang up, his mouth opened, and a roaring came out. "There're going to be no babies in this house!" he shouted. "She'd better know that!"

"Wait," Nora said quickly. "I've already talked to her."

"And what good did that do?"

"She's not a hundred percent sure. She's—"

But Marty was already heading for Christine's room, walking down the hallway with long, angry strides. Nora ran after him and grabbed him by the arm. "Please, Marty—"

He yanked his arm from her grasp. "Forget it," he said. "It's my turn now."

Nora couldn't do anything but follow with Danny trailing behind, his worried voice trying to catch up to her. "But where would the baby go then, Mom? If it couldn't live here. Where would it sleep?"

Christine was on the telephone when they arrived. She was

wearing a fuzzy blue bathrobe, and her hair was still damp from the shower. Her room was neater than Nora had ever seen it. Not an item of clothing was anywhere in sight. There were no crumpled bits of paper and candy wrappers on the floor. The surface of her desk held neat piles of books and papers and several pencils laid out in orderly, parallel lines.

She glanced up when Marty walked in, got a frightened look on her face and said hurriedly into the receiver, "Sorry, Jay, got to go. . . . Yeah, okay. . . . See you."

Then she looked quickly at Nora and then back to Marty. "What's the matter?"

"You know damned, fucking well."

Marty never swore before the children—never. Nora flinched, feeling as if those words had dragged the four of them from safety into dangerous, hostile territory.

Christine felt it, too, and she immediately burst out, "If it's the baby you're talking about— Well, I thought I'd give it up, but I can't. I just can't."

"There'll be no babies here. This is my house and that's the way it's going to be."

Nora sat down on the bed. "Just a minute, let's talk about this. Let's not just deliver ultimatums."

"But where will the baby go?" Danny said.

"Butt out, Danny," Marty said. "This is none of your business."

"But, Dad—"

Nora said, "Let's try to be reasonable."

Marty ignored both of them. "You hear what I'm saying?" he said to Christine. "You hear me?"

Christine was standing now so that she faced Marty, and Nora saw a new resemblance. Their eyebrows were pulled together in the same V; their chins jutted out at the same angle.

"I can't help but hear you," Christine said haughtily. "You're yelling."

"I've had it," Marty said. "I'm not going to let *my* life be ruined by you and those people!"

"Nobody's ruining your life."

"No? Who do you think's going to support this kid? Who?"

"I'm not asking you to."

"No? So then what's going to happen to you? You going to ask the *state* to buy you, what is it—Ralph Lauren—jeans? Or those Coalition people? You think money grows on goddamned trees?"

"We've had this conversation before."

"And a lot of good it did. You don't want to listen, that's the trouble. You have some misguided, crazy notion that you have a selfish right to do what you want and the hell with everyone else."

"I have a right to keep my baby. A legal right."

"I'm not arguing the law here. I'm arguing us: this family, your mother and me and your brother. We have rights, too."

"You know what?" Christine said. "You know what? I think you're selfish, that's what. You want everything *your* way. You don't want anything to interfere with *your* life!"

"You're damned right I'm selfish!" Marty roared. "I did my bit. I paid my dues. I've worked hard to give this family a home and food and clothing, and I think I've earned a right to have the future the way *I* want it. What have *you* earned, Christine? What have you done that gives you the right to go around making decisions that are going to affect your mother and brother and myself? You want to have a baby, you go ahead! Just don't do it on my back, you understand?"

Christine's face flushed a hot pink. "All right, I won't! I'll keep you right out of it. I'll leave, that's what. I'll move out!"

Nora's lips were trembling. "Hold it!" she said. "Everybody calm down and stop! Let's think about what we're saying, all right?"

Danny had been standing in the doorway looking scared. Now, he said, "Could I have your room, Chris, if you move out?"

"Mom, *do* something about him!"

Marty turned to him. "Danny, get out of here."

"But—"

"Get out!"

"You don't want to understand," Christine said as Danny disappeared. "You don't want to hear my side."

"You're right," Marty said sarcastically. "I don't want to listen to all the garbage those people have been force-feeding you. I'm sick and tired of it. You know what I've thought since the beginning of this fiasco, and you know what I'm thinking now."

"This is my baby. It's half *me.*"

"Half you and half some goddamned, stupid jerk."

Tears sprang into Christine's eyes. "I love my baby!"

"Well I don't!" he yelled. "Understand? And I don't want it in this house!"

He turned and walked out. Christine slumped back in her chair, crying, while Nora looked helplessly around the room, thinking that she'd give anything, *anything,* for it to be messy again.

"I'll try to talk to him," she said, shakily. "I'll see what I can do."

"I hate him. *I hate him.*"

By the time she was eighteen months old, Christine had developed the prettiest way of getting Marty's attention. Nora remembered how she would look at him with adoring eyes, grasp one of his fingers in her small, fat hand and tug hard. Marty had never been able to ignore her, had never been able to deny her.

"Listen, Christine, he's angry right now and tired—you know how hard he's been working—but when he calms down he'll think things over. I'm sure he will."

"He wants me to leave."

"No, no, he doesn't. Remember when you said you'd go before? Remember how upset he was?"

"I think things are different now, Mom."

"Let's not jump to conclusions."

"Mrs. Allison said this might happen. She said lots of fathers can't face things."

Nora couldn't help it. The mention of Sylvia Allison was like a small hook of irritation catching in her throat.

"You know, Christine, we're all selfish in our own way. Daddy doesn't want his life changed, Danny wants your room because it's bigger, and you're a little selfish, too—don't you think?—wanting to keep the baby because you love it. You know the best thing for it is adoption by some couple who can give it a good home."

Christine wiped her eyes with her fingers and then gave Nora a bitter look. "You're on his side," she said. "I should've known you'd be."

Nora rushed to placate and patch. She was reminded of an anthill that she had once disturbed by stepping on it, caving in the entrance with her heel. Ants had poured out from some other opening and frantically scurried around, repairing the damage. They'd climbed over themselves in their haste, legs entangling, antennae twitching madly. She was one of those ants, busily running hither and thither, applying balm here, a calming logic there, an appeal to finer emotions wherever she could.

Patch.

"Why doesn't Daddy want the baby?"

"He thinks Christine isn't ready to be a Mommy."

"Maybe he hates babies."

"No, Daddy loved you when you were a baby."

"Maybe he doesn't like *this* baby."

"It isn't born yet, Danny. It's too early to tell."

Patch.

"There's still time."

"Christ, when will you give up?"

"You're important to her. Don't turn your back. You're hurting her."

"Maybe that'll make her think twice."

"This wasn't a snap decision on her part, you know. She's given it a lot of thought."

"Get her away from those people, and she might be able to think straight then."

"You're angrier at them than you are at her. You are, Marty, admit it."

"I'm angry at everybody, but it doesn't change anything, does it?"

Patch.

"Daddy loves you."

"He has a funny way of showing it."

"This is as hard for him as it is for you."

"Oh, sure. He's not being kicked out of his own house."

"Nobody's kicking you out."

"He's kicking the baby out—that's the same thing."

"That's how he feels right now. Things can always change if people work at it."

"Boy, Mom, you're really an optimist, aren't you?"

"I'm trying to be, Christine. I'm trying."

But Nora discovered that she'd undertaken an impossible task. She'd patch in one place only to find a crack somewhere else. She'd shore up one section only to discover that another had collapsed. It was as if the whole structure of her family, the mountain of her mother-perch, had been supported by a framework too weak to bear the sudden shifting weight of unexpected burdens.

Marty was the core of the problem. In the past Nora had been able to persuade him, pressure him—not consciously, she realized, but instinctively—to mold him into the husband/father she'd thought he should be. And he had been malleable clay in her hands, yielding, shaping himself to fit her vision of the family. It was a shock to Nora to discover that he could be so obdurate, fired to an unexpected hardness, stubborn and rigid.

"But think how young she is."

"Nora, you remember *Fiddler on the Roof?* You remember how Tevye refused the daughter who married the gentile? He loved her, but she'd gone too far. He'd bent, but he couldn't bend any more. Well, that's how I feel. I bent when she got pregnant. I bent when she refused to have an abortion. But this is my limit. I can't bend any more."

"But, Marty, what then? Do we really let her go?"

"You know, I can't help what I am. Middle class. And you know what the basis of the middle class is? Deferred gratification. I work my ass off, and I bring home a pay check. But do I use that money for myself? No, I defer my own pleasure for my kids.

I don't take vacations, I pay for hockey equipment and ballet lessons and nice clothes. Do I buy the car I want? Of course not, I put the money in the bank to pay for college. Why do I do it, Nora? Why do you?"

Nora gave a helpless shrug. "Because we have to."

"Because we have dreams for our kids, right? We want them to grow up and be successful. Well, Nora, she's throwing that dream right down the fucking drain, and I don't want to defer forever. And, let's be honest, okay? If she has a kid, is she really going to be happy in some crummy apartment on welfare? No, she's going to want to live with us, and if we let her, you and I are going to end up bringing that baby up and deferring for the millionth time."

"I don't want to bring up a baby either," Nora said, "but I guess I have a sentimental streak. After all, it will be our grandchild, won't it?"

"Well, I'm not sentimental. And Christ, I don't need any grandchildren right now."

"That's part of it, isn't it, Marty? The growing old thing."

"I don't want to be a grandfather, all right? I hate the thought of it. I'm only forty-five years old. It's bad enough I'm losing my hair. It's bad enough I have a permanent pot. And, Christ Almighty, isn't it bad enough I don't get erections the way I used to? I don't want to have a kid around, reminding me that I'm getting old every single day of the week. There, does that satisfy you? Can you lay off now?"

But Nora couldn't, because she was too terrified to stop. Too afraid that if she weren't busily patching, patching, patching, the rift that ran right down the middle of the Beeme family might widen so far that nothing would hold the mountain together.

Nothing at all.

8

◇   ◇   ◇   Nora and Joanne rarely lunched together, because they had to fill in for one another at the store, but one Wednesday in September, Joanne insisted that Mrs. Hahnnecker come in an hour early and that Nora accompany her for lunch at a downtown Burtonville restaurant called The Diner. It was one of those places where the management tried to conceal the mediocrity of the food with flashy decor. In this case, they were attempting to cash in on fifties nostalgia by decorating the walls with blown-up photos of Elvis and girls in ponytails and flaring skirts. Small jukeboxes were attached to each booth, the kind that once took a quarter and were connected to a larger jukebox that actually played the record. Nora, flipping through the list of songs, thought she might like to listen to something, but Joanne told her that they were all fakes, like the neon signs in the windows that winked *Miller Hi-Life* in pink script, and the huge cardboard cut-out of the Rheingold Girl that stood in one corner.

"Made by a company in Utica," Joanne said. "I know because the owners asked Grant to write a letter to the manufacturer when the stuff wasn't delivered on time. Anyway, it's all crummy, imitation nostalgia."

Joanne was irritable, but then Nora thought she had just cause. The Whites were going through one of those bad times. It had begun during their European vacation with Patrick, who had developed diarrhea so severely that they'd had to cancel half of their reservations and stay in Amsterdam for four extra days. On their return Matthew was supposed to come to grips with college applications, but instead he began talking about getting a job at a gas station and buying a car. In the meantime, Nina was miserably besotted with a boy who was flunking out of high school, getting wasted on the weekends and seeing three girls at once. Of course, their big freezer also went on the blink without anyone noticing, and hundreds of pounds of steaks, cutlets, wings, roasts and frozen vegetables were ruined. Nora wasn't surprised that relations between Grant and Joanne had now reached an all-time low. Grant was still working six or seven days a week, and while Joanne hadn't found any more annotated napkins, she remained convinced that he was in the midst of a torrid affair. ("Torrid? How do you know it's torrid?" Nora had asked. "Cause I'm getting damn little action at home, that's why.")

Joanne was also convinced that she'd discovered the identity of the napkin jotter. In casual conversations with Grant's secretary, she'd found that he didn't always take his lunch at the more elegant Brokerage Restaurant which was near his office and had cloth napkins, but had been spotted going into The Diner on several occasions. The Diner had paper napkins in dispensers, precisely the sort that she'd found in his pockets. Joanne began to frequent The Diner in the late afternoon, and found a waitress who used a pen with green ink and had roughly the same handwriting as that which had appeared on Grant's napkins.

("What's she like?" Nora had asked.

"You wouldn't believe it. I mean, give me a break."

"She's that bad?"

"Nora, I want you to see her. I want you to tell me if I'm crazy or not.")

But the waitress, Rhonda, hadn't been there when they'd

arrived, so they ordered lunch—over-mayonnaised club sand-
wiches accompanied by greasy french fries—and talked about
Nora's problems.

". . . and I finally found a home tutor for Christine, well,
actually two. One will do Math and Science, the other History
and English. We're not going to worry about French right now."

"Does she miss school?"

"Not school. She could care less about her classes. It's the
social life. She gets bored and cranky. Thank God for Jay,
though. He still comes around."

"I'd have thought the pregnancy would have scared him
off."

Nora thought of how she'd seen Jay and Christine watching
television one evening. They had been lounging on the den sofa,
each leaning against an arm, their legs stretched toward one another, the soles of their bare feet touching. The blue-white light
of the television had flickered on Jay's face, etching its pure lines,
making him look like a ghostly blond angel.

"They've become very close. More than friends in a funny
kind of a way. I think he feels kind of fatherly toward her. She
tells him everything, all the gritty details of being pregnant, when
the baby's moving, how constipated she was last week. And he
listens. He really is such a gentle soul. Anyway, there's also Elly.
She and Christine talk on the phone every night, and Christine
babysat for her on the weekend."

"How did that go?"

"Oh, she loved it," Nora said with a sigh. "She thought it
was really neat."

"Neat." Joanne made a face. "I don't think I would ever
describe my children's infancies as 'neat.' Gruesome, maybe, exhausting, definitely, but never 'neat.' "

"Well, she had a great time. And I have to admit it was good
to have her out of the house."

"A small détente?"

Nora had not thought it would be possible for the atmosphere in the Beeme house to be any icier than it had been in

April when Christine decided not to have the abortion. But she had been wrong.

"A very small one," she said. "Marty managed to relax a bit."

"He still busting his ass at Devlin?"

"It keeps getting worse. The pressure on those guys is terrible. I'm trying to get him to jog or something, because he's under so much stress. Oh, and I haven't told you about Danny."

"You mean there's more?"

"You think the Whites have a monopoly on misery?"

"Just wait until your freezer dies on you. Then you'll know from misery."

They smiled at one another, and Nora went on, "Danny's taken up with this boy he met in camp. Peter Meltzer."

"Meltzer . . . Meltzer . . . Why does that name ring a bell?"

"Remember the puppet theater that got returned? About two years ago? The one that went out in perfect condition, but suddenly its stage floor was broken? That was Mrs. Meltzer."

"Right. How did that end up?"

"Who was going to argue with her? We had to take it back. Anyway, Peter doesn't go to Danny's school, but he lives just off Maple Avenue. There's something about him that I—" Nora paused, as she tried to put into words the feeling that Peter Meltzer gave her. He wasn't sinister-looking at all, but handsome, with dark wavy hair and a cleft chin. "Well, he's one of those kids who can't look you in the eye when you talk to him. You know what I mean? You don't feel like you're getting through."

"And you think he's a bad influence?"

Nora grimaced. "Worse. I think he drinks."

"Drinks? You mean, like Scotch or gin?"

"Canadian Club. I just happened to be getting a tablecloth from the closet where we keep the liquor, and I found the bottle had been opened. It was new. Neither Marty or I had used it yet."

"It could be Jay or Christine."

"Not Christine—she's fanatic about her diet. And Jay's fanatic about his singing voice in case fame beckons. He won't even drink soda."

"So—did you ask Danny about it?"

"Of course. He denied it." Vehemently shaking his head, his freckles dark with indignation, and looking so horribly offended ("Mom, it's the truth! The real truth!") that Nora had almost lost faith in the facts. By the time she and Danny had finished arguing she was no longer sure that the bottle hadn't been opened before. But Nora still had an uneasy feeling, a sense of secrets withheld and dangers present, and when Peter visited she found herself surreptitiously watching Danny, even though she knew that her surveillance was useless. She was only his mother; she couldn't penetrate the surface of skin, not when he refused her entrance, his face blank and smooth, his eyes that impermeable blue.

The weight of her worries—Danny, Marty's anger, Christine's pregnancy—was such that Nora now felt a constant pressure. Some days it felt like an immense brick lying on her back, bending her over; some days it was in her skull, its sharp edges pushing against her temples and making them ache. Today it was filling her head, and she wearily pressed her fingers against her eyes. "Explain something to me, Joanne. Why is it that when we have a roof over our heads, when we don't have to worry about where our next meal is coming from, when everybody is healthy and we have it better than most of the people on this earth, that our lives are so stressful?"

"You thought there were happy endings?"

Nora dropped her hands and opened her eyes. On the wall next to her was an enlarged photo of a girl being kissed on the cheek by Elvis, her eyes squeezed shut, her mouth an O of ecstasy. "I think I did. I think I believed that if I was a good girl, I'd reap some kind of reward: marriage, children, a beautiful sunset, *something*. I can tell you one thing: when I was sixteen, I never guessed it would be like this."

"When I was sixteen," Joanne said, reflectively, "I thought being a good girl meant being a virgin when you were married. Maybe that's why I haven't had a happy ending."

"I can't think of anyone I know who was a virgin on her wedding night."

"Mona McLaughlin. Remember her? She taught with us. Second grade."

Nora remembered—vaguely. A plump person with glasses and flyaway brown hair. "How did you know that?"

"She told me. She was convinced that she had the world's thickest hymen, because she'd done so much horseback riding as a kid—don't ask me how that makes any sense—and was so worried about her wedding night that she went to a doctor and had it cut."

"What happened to her?"

Joanne grinned. "She's a bag lady in Albany."

"She is not."

"Okay, the truth. She got divorced after two years and went home to Queens to live with her mother."

"And then what happened to her?"

"I don't know, but the point is, is that a happy ending?"

Nora sighed. "Maybe there is no such thing as a happy ending."

"Maybe it's all a state of mind."

"Maybe it's french fries without grease."

"Maybe it's having your kids grow up and move out."

"Maybe it's never getting married in the first place. Wouldn't that be ironic?"

There was a pause. "Maybe," Joanne said, "it's having The Other Woman walk in the door and deciding that, yes, you have to be out of your mind."

"She's here?" Nora twisted around in her seat. "That's her?"

"That," Joanne confirmed grimly, "is her."

By Nora's standards, The Other Woman wasn't even a woman. Rhonda didn't appear to be much older than Christine, although that judgment could be erroneous, Nora conceded, because she was so tiny. Tiny and perfect. Not so much pretty as doll-like, a girl with fragile wrist bones, fine blond curls and large blue eyes. Her white waitress's outfit displayed a small but ample bustline, narrow hips and firm, slender calves. Nora looked back at Joanne, with her heavy flesh and wide, Slavic features. In comparison, she appeared huge.

"I don't know," Nora said faintly, "but I wouldn't say she was Grant's type, would you?"

"Who knows what Grant's type in philandering is?" Joanne gave an unhappy shrug. "I'm only his wife."

"But she's so . . . young. What would she talk to him about?"

"Do they talk? I mean, am I *crazy* or not?"

"I'd be shocked if it were Marty."

"Would you? She's cute in a way. And God knows but she's never had to worry about a calorie in all of her short little life."

Rhonda, who was talking with another waitress, now laughed with a high, tinny shriek that was followed by a burst of giggles and then a smothered noise when she clasped a hand over her mouth. It wasn't the laugh of a grown woman, but a giddy, adolescent range of sounds, the kind Christine used to make when she and her friends were comparing notes on boys.

Nora winced. "She may be cute, but who could stand a diet of that?"

"A middle-aged man seeking his lost youth?"

"Surely Grant has better taste."

"I don't know," Joanne said glumly. "Maybe that's just wishful thinking."

"Have you thought about asking him?"

"Of course I have."

"Well . . . ?"

Joanne frowned, as if pain were pulling her eyebrows together. "If this is the truth, I'm not sure I want to know it."

One Sunday afternoon at the beginning of October, Nora was working in her garden and pulling out the tender annuals like lobelia and impatiens that hadn't survived the first frost. At the same time, she was idly thinking about a number of things: repairs (replacing the blown fluorescent light bulb in the store), dinner (making chicken curry—did she have any rice?), and clothing (she had to press her cream blouse for tomorrow), when it occurred to her that she and Marty hadn't heard about the fall potluck barbecue.

This affair was a gathering of several neighborhood families that usually took place in mid-September. Invitations were issued by phone and the atmosphere was always casual. As Nora wondered if she and Marty had been left off the guest list, she continued to pluck out wilted foliage, but her pleasure in gardening was slowly seeping away. It seemed to her that acquaintances and neighbors had been avoiding her lately. Of course they all knew about Christine now. Some quick glances and then averted eyes in the grocery store had made her aware of that. Maybe she was being paranoid, she told herself, maybe the barbecue had been postponed. But she couldn't get it out of her mind that she and Marty hadn't been invited because the neighbors were embarrassed and afraid that they could only make mangled and awkward offers of sympathy, all the while thinking gratefully that there, but for the grace of God, goes— She grabbed for a clump of lobelia and, by mistake, also pulled out some of her violets.

"Fuck," she said under her breath, staring at their limp roots.

Which immediately brought to mind another depressing fact: that she and Marty hadn't made love for a long time. She'd been avoiding counting the days, but when she looked back, their last sexual encounter quickly receded into the mists of time. She sat on her heels and brushed a strand of hair out of her eyes with her gloved hand. When *was* the last time they'd made love? Was it really Labor Day weekend? Why, that would be . . . a month ago. No, that couldn't be. She tried to remember what else had happened during September, but the days were a blur, a hodgepodge of events piled on top of each other—Danny's soccer team games, Christine's appointments with Dr. Roya, Marzipan's attack of worms—all layered with hours of hard work.

After a leisurely and not terribly profitable summer, The Kids Place had burst into action. Traffic in the mall had almost tripled since the beginning of September and, at Joanne's suggestion, she and Nora had aggressively gone after some extra business. They'd gotten the contract to supply a nursery school with specialty toys and had finally been invited to the Junior League's annual Christmas Bazaar, a retailing honor in Burtonville that would introduce the store to that hard-to-reach clientele, the wealthy, who often looked down their noses at the locals and preferred to go to the city to shop at Bloomingdale's and Neiman-Marcus. Stores that participated were expected to outdo one another in booth decoration and merchandise. As a result, Nora and Joanne were now both working six days a week and some evenings. They hired on two part-timers to ease the load, but both required training and that was Nora's task. She was exhausted most nights now and fell asleep before the eleven o'clock news. Which, considering that Marty went to work at seven-thirty in the morning, they both worked on Saturdays, and Sundays were devoted to shopping and fixing things around the house and yard, didn't leave a lot of time for anything as recreational as sex.

Nora could remember only one other time in their marriage, other than post-childbirth, when she and Marty had not made love for as long as a month. It had been in 1979, three months after Marty's mother had died of a stroke. Both of them had been worried that his father, Stephen, would be unable to take care of himself, having spent most of his adult life cocooned in an academic world of journals and teaching, his needs efficiently looked after by Mary Beeme. Although shaky after his wife's death, Stephen had, to their surprise, handled the housekeeping problems well. He'd hired a maid who came in three days a week, and he himself displayed an unexpected interest in cooking. That plus the fact that he was still teaching part-time and busily involved in his learned societies lulled them into believing that all was under control.

Then Stephen had two heart attacks: the first put him into the hospital, the second a week later killed him. To Nora, Marty appeared to deal with the second death in the same calm manner as he had the first. He buried himself in details: executing the will, making all the arrangements necessary to selling his parents' house, and getting rid of the furniture, heavy mahogany pieces with frayed upholstery that no one wanted anymore. The money his father had bequeathed to the university was put into a trust to create a Mathematics scholarship in Stephen's name. Marty even saw to it that his father's last article was edited and submitted for publication, the abstract of it written by a colleague. When this flurry of activity was over, Marty returned home and Nora assumed that life would now go back to normal.

Then they discovered he was impotent.

At first Nora and Marty took this lightly, considering it a temporary aberration that would disappear as soon as he got back into a regular routine, had enough sleep, relaxed, took it easy. When Marty was once again playing squash with his buddies from work and not falling asleep right after dinner, they tried again, choosing an ideal time—a warm summer's afternoon when both kids were away and they had the house to themselves for hours. To their dismay, it didn't work.

"Are you sure?" Nora finally asked, after having tried everything short of doing the Dance of the Seven Veils.

Marty covered his eyes in a weary gesture. "I'm sure. It's not your fault."

She lay back, and picking up Marty's hand, entwined her fingers with his. His palm was sweaty. "You okay?"

"Yeah, I'm okay." He paused and then added, "I mean, the spirit's willing, but the body won't work. I just don't feel anything. But, listen, that doesn't mean that you—"

"Marty, maybe you should see a doctor?"

He shook his head.

"But something's wrong, don't you think?"

"I'm not sick."

"But it has to be a symptom."

"Of what?"

"I don't know, but it doesn't have to be something physical. Maybe it's your parents dying like that—one after the other."

He shifted restlessly. "You know something, Nora? I was sad, but I wasn't overwhelmed with grief or anything like that. We weren't close."

"Maybe it doesn't matter whether you were close or not."

Nora was warming to her thesis now. She sat up. "Maybe, it's just losing your parents that's important."

Marty hated psychological talk. "The old hard-on/death connection, huh?" he said with a false jauntiness. "I can see it now. 'Burial Zaps Erection—Is This Prick Too Soft to Fight Back?' "

Nora looked down at his penis. It was small, telescoped in on itself so that the glans, ringed with flesh, resembled an un-opened flower bud. "I'm just trying to help," she said.

Impatiently, Marty pulled his hand out of hers, swung his legs sideways, and stood up. "Let's forget it," he said. "Okay?"

Nora hadn't mentioned it again, and one night three weeks later he had pulled her over and made love to her, a satisfactory performance that only suffered from a little rushing, as if Marty had been afraid that if he let things go on too long he might lose what he had.

Nora, remembering this, also recalled how unhappy she'd been for those three weeks and how relieved she'd been when it was over. It hadn't been the sex she missed so much as the affec-tion that came with it: the hugs, the little flirtations, the casual early-morning fondling of genitals that usually went nowhere but was always pleasing. She was missing that now, Nora realized, but she'd been too busy to notice. And admittedly, relations be-tween Marty and herself were a little strained at the moment. They weren't fighting anymore; they weren't even arguing. A silence on the subject of Christine had set in and gelled, holding in its center their respective positions: Nora angry and not approv-ing of Marty's implacability, Marty angry and not giving a damn whether she approved or not.

It was a standoff.

Christine and her unborn baby, Nora now thought, had introduced this new element into her marriage. Before this, she and Marty had solved differences of opinion by talking them out. Fights were usually over quickly, angers doused like small, con-trollable conflagrations. But Christine—and for a brief second Nora vehemently wished Christine out of her sight like a hateful irritant, a speck of dirt in the eye—but Christine had changed all that. The workings of the Beeme marriage had shifted, the machinery still clanking and rattling along, but with a different rhythm, a faltering now and then, a dissonant sound beneath the hum. Nora had never thought before how odd it was that she should choose an engine as a metaphor for her life with Marty. She didn't like machinery; she'd never understood how an engine worked; she was bored when anyone talked about pistons or carburetors. For all the years of her married life Nora had ignored the Beeme cars, letting Marty deal with the tune-ups and breakdowns.

Machinery and mountains: and wasn't she still frantically patching whenever possible? Even though new rifts and cracks were constantly appearing?

Marty no longer talked to Christine. Nor would he discuss the problem with Nora when she tried to bring it up. "Forget it, Nora, I have nothing more to say to her."

Christine no longer ate meals with the family and spent most of her time, especially when Marty was home; holed up in her bedroom, listening to tapes or talking on the phone to Jay or Elly. Her room remained clean, and her budget book held long columns of neatly penciled-in figures. She and Nora were polite to one another, like two cats who inhabit the same house but have set out invisible lines of territory that should not be crossed. Nora never asked Christine to do any housework or cooking beyond already defined limits. Christine did what she was asked sullenly, but without displaying so much overt displeasure as to incur Nora's anger. But these two cats in the same domicile couldn't help treading on sensitive boundaries, and occasionally there were spats, quick, hissing moments that ended abruptly and without resolution.

Haircuts. Christine was not only tired of having her hair long, but she also wanted gold highlights put in. Nora tartly informed her that hairdressers were expensive and that her hair was just fine. Christine said she was insensitive and mean. Nora said she didn't care.

Maternity clothes. Christine was beginning to hate the hand-me-downs from the Coalition. What was the point, Nora wanted to know, of spending money on clothing that would only be worn for a couple of months? "So I won't look so *gross*," Christine said. Nora said she didn't look gross. Christine said she was cruel.

The Baby.

"Interesting, isn't it?" Nora said, giving Christine an article that she'd clipped out of the newspaper about infertile women in their late thirties.

Christine glanced at the headline. "What's interesting about it?"

"How desperate they are."

Christine shrugged.

"Think what good parents these people would make."

"Why should I?"

"I want you to keep an open mind."

"I'm not giving my baby away!"

"Christine . . ."

"Leave me alone!"

And then there was Danny, who had immediately gotten into trouble the first week of school, causing a disturbance by pushing another boy to the floor, jumping on him, and hitting as hard as he could until a teacher pried him away.

"Since when do you hit someone like that?" Marty had demanded. He and Nora had already spent fifteen minutes trying to get to the bottom of this episode without much success.

"He got me mad," Danny finally revealed.

"Well, what did he say?"

"Nothing much."

"Come on. He must have said something."

A stubborn shaking of the head.

Marty gave Nora an exasperated look and then turned back. "Okay, you're going to sit here until you tell me. I don't care if it's going to take all night."

A nonchalant shrug.

So Danny had sat there on a stool in the kitchen after supper from seven until nine-thirty, doodling on a pad, playing with the telephone cord, sometimes putting his head down on his folded arms.

Finally Nora couldn't stand it any longer. "Does it matter what was said?" she asked Marty. "Hasn't he been punished by now?"

"Jesus, but that kid is stubborn. I give up."

Danny went to bed, and Nora tucked him in. She sat on the edge of his bed and smoothed his hair back from his forehead. "You must have really been mad," she said. "You gave that boy a black eye."

"I hate him! He's an a-hole. He sucks."

"Danny, your language, please."

"Well, he is. He's a perverted nerd jerk."

"Okay, I'll take your word for it. But listen, honey, you can't go around punching people you hate. It's not acceptable."

"Even when he says really mean things?"

"Sticks and stones . . . remember?"

"It was a *lot* worse than that."

"It doesn't matter. You don't hit. You just walk away, turn your back and ignore. . . ."

"That's easy for you to say."

"I know, sweetie, but you're going to have to. What would happen in our society if people were allowed to attack anyone who made them angry? Think how dangerous that would be. People would use knives and guns and—"

"Mom?"

"Yes?"

"Is Christine a cheap hooker? Is she?"

Nora had discovered early on in her marriage that nothing, other than orgasm, made Marty quite as happy as a back-rub. The minute she began to rub her palms against his skin he would close his eyes, settle further into the mattress and make small, contented murmurs. She often gave him back rubs at night, after they'd turned off the lights and were supposed to be going to sleep.

"Mmmm, that feels good." Nora dug her fingers into the

muscles at his neck. "Right there . . . No, to the left . . . To the right . . . Up . . . Ummm, that's it."

"Marty?"

"Mmmm?"

"Are you angry with me?"

"No."

"You're sure?"

"Uh-huh."

"Because I don't think we've made love since Labor Day." He was silent as she kneaded his shoulder. "Am I right?"

"Has it been that long? I suppose so. I've been too tired, I guess."

"I just wondered if maybe this business with Christine was sort of getting between us."

"No."

"You sure?"

"I thought we'd agreed to disagree."

"Are you . . . depressed about it?"

He sighed. "Nora, Nora, Nora."

"But a month," she said. "The last time we went that long was after your father died."

"You want a performance, I'll give you a performance."

"I don't want a per*for*mance. I just want to go back to the way we were."

Marty turned over. In the dark, his face was a pale oval. "You know how many times I've heard you say that? 'The way we were.' Didn't they make a movie with that title?"

"Robert Redford. Barbra Streisand." Under the covers, Nora wiggled her feet until their soles rested on the top of Marty's. "I can't help it, the past always seems so much safer than the present."

"Look, I'm not happy about Christine. I admit that. I don't like the thought of her having the baby and moving into some dump in Burtonville like her friend. I didn't work this hard all my life because I support downward mobility for my kids."

"Then why be so . . . so adamant? Why not give a little?"

"Because I can't. Look what we're doing if we just pat her

on the head and tell her it's fine to have the baby and bring it home. We're teaching her and Danny that they can do anything, and no matter how strongly we disapprove, there'll be no repercussions, no responsibilities, no consequences. That's where I draw the line, Nora. I have values, and she's trampling all over them."

"But she has values, too."

"Fine, but they're in direct opposition to mine. I don't believe in fifteen-year-olds having babies and keeping them. I don't think that the ability to conceive entitles her to motherhood. I don't think she's earned the right to keep that kid."

"She loves it."

Marty snorted. "If she really cared about the welfare of that baby, she'd give it up for adoption."

"Okay, Marty, I agree with what you're saying. And it's all very rational, but if push comes to shove, are you really going to be able to watch her go? I don't know if *I* can."

"Listen, Nora, this isn't just rationality speaking. This is me; this is what I stand for. She's rejected my values, my beliefs, *me.* Don't you see?"

The obstacle. The wall. The standoff. Nora kept banging her head against it—hard. "Oh, Marty, I don't want to talk about it anymore." She snuggled close to him and sighed. "A whole month."

"Horny?"

"I don't know. Are you?"

"I can't remember what it feels like."

"Me either."

"Okay," he said. "You want to then?"

"Please." Please, she prayed silently, let's erase Christine, the month of emptiness, the wall between us. She placed a palm over his penis, judging its state of readiness. *"Al dente,"* she said lightly. "I give it . . . um, a six out of ten."

"The poor thing needs attention."

"Is that so?"

And Nora tried; she really tried. She caressed and stroked. She arched her back, moved her hips and spread her legs. She did everything she was supposed to at the appropriate time and in the appropriate places, but none of it worked. At least, not for her. Marty seemed to do just fine. He grew hard, grunted and ejaculated, all the while tenderly concerned that she too was following suit. Nora didn't let him down, because the moment seemed far too fragile to break with yet another failure of love. So for the first time in her twenty-odd years of sleeping with Marty, she faked it. He didn't seem to notice.

"From the beginning of time," Dr. Stillman was saying, "there has been a societal and familial taboo against aggression toward the helpless young. When that taboo is violated, it affects our hearts, the morals we live by, the structure of our society. Imagine what happens to those who deal in abortion day in and day out. They know the struggle of the unborn baby who is trying to survive against the brutal force of vacuum aspiration, or those born from saline injections, desperately trying to draw a breath. Any abortionist can tell you of the whimpering of aborted infants that can be heard daily in the garbage cans of our hospitals."

As the audience sucked in its collective breath, Nora squirmed on her seat. She hadn't taken off her raincoat, and the auditorium was too warm. Her skin had that prickly-heat sensation all over, but most strongly under her arms and between her breasts, where it gathered into a sticky dampness. Her discomfort wasn't just confined to the physical either. She knew she didn't belong. She wasn't exactly a wolf in sheep's clothing, more like a Democrat at a Republican gathering or an atheist at church. She didn't like meetings; she didn't agree with the pro-life ideology; and if she had really wanted to cut the enemy off at the pass, her attendance now was too little too late. She should have been studying the Coalition's strategies months ago, when Christine had first announced that she was pregnant.

"Those who deal with abortion become hardened against human suffering, passive in the face of violence, helpless against the murder of children. And these attitudes, entering our society, spread like a poisonous gas, infiltrating every corner, every nook and cranny, every niche of our national psyche. Its effect has been a diminishing of the value of children in our society. After all, when the destruction of children is sanctioned by the government, by religious leaders, by the press, and by the man and woman on the street—and not only sanctioned, but let's face it, even applauded—then no child can have any value."

So why was she here? The reasons prickled like her skin, uncomfortable needle-like reasons that goaded and jabbed. Despite all her efforts, her soothing and calming, her shuttling back and forth between one person and another, nothing had altered in the Beeme household. Marty wouldn't change his mind, their sex life was nonexistent again, Christine was talking about moving out, Danny was rebellious and stubborn. Nora, feeling helpless, had suggested the family go to a counselor, but Marty had refused. ("You know what counselors study, Nora? Psychology. Social work. And you know what those are? Soft sciences. So soft they can never prove a damn thing.")

Helplessness had now been compounded by a sense of desperation so strong that Nora found herself doing odd things: driving aimlessly through the streets of Fairfax and talking to herself; losing items like car keys, her wallet, her spring jacket— she'd left it *some*where; forgetting meetings like the one she and Joanne had set up with the nursery school; and always, always, being late. Late picking up Danny for a dentist's appointment, late getting dinner on the table, and late for work, because while she was putting on her makeup and looking into the mirror her mind would slip into another space, and the next thing she knew she was watching her half-lipsticked mouth silently shaping words ("I can't quite . . . Things have reached a . . . Yes, I understand that such . . .") and ten minutes had disappeared out of her life.

Was her presence at a Coalition for Life meeting any crazier than all that?

"And, if you extend this logic one step further, into the twilight zone of our national neurosis, then it becomes defensible not only to destroy the unborn, but to kill living children as well. Absurd, you say? It couldn't happen in the United States of

America? Well, statistics show, my friends, that if we haven't actually reached the slaughter of living children, our society has taken one step along the way. The abuse and battering of living children is at an all-time high—this despite the murder of millions of unwanted babies."

Dr. Stillman, a tall woman with a coil of white hair on top of her head and bifocals perched on her nose, had a way of delivering her message that reminded Nora of someone. She couldn't remember who, only that the way she emphasized words by thrusting her head forward brought back to Nora, not a memory exactly, but the bad smell of one, like a food whose aftertaste comes up in an unpleasant burp. Nora felt the beginnings of a headache pressing against her temples. When Marty had heard she was going to a Coalition for Life meeting he'd thought she was out of her mind. Joanne had asked her if she believed in self-flagellation. Only Christine had been excited: "It's really interesting, Mom. It'll make you think about things." Which Nora might have laughed at if she'd been inclined toward amusement at her own dilemma, because she couldn't *stop* thinking and brooding and worrying. Was it a handicap to see every side of a question, she wondered, or was it a blessing? Was it a gift to be able to yield and bend or had she been stamped at birth with a tragic flaw? Was she wrong to desperately seek a middle ground between Marty and Christine? Or was she crazy to think it even existed?

"I'd like to tell you now about Celia, a woman I came to know through my work with the National Foundation for Life. Celia came to our attention through an emergency room physician who treated her second child for malnourishment and dehydration. Friends, this child, a two-year-old girl, was so badly neglected that she looked as if she had been born in some poor third world country instead of this land of plenty, our United States of America. Her limbs were thin and twisted, her hair was falling out, she had bleeding gums and a stomach that was bloated and grotesque. She was so far gone along the road of starvation that she no longer even had the energy to cry.

"Now, what makes Celia's case so interesting was that this

was the only one of her three children to have been so neglected. Both the oldest, a boy of four, and the baby, an infant girl of five months, were healthy and thriving. In between was little Paula— malnourished, apathetic, sickly and close to death. The question we had to ask ourselves is why one child out of three should suffer so, and what cruel and unusual punishment was this mother inflicting on this one innocent and helpless child?

"Will it surprise you, my friends, to discover that this woman had a history of abortion?"

Nora wasn't surprised one bit. Neither was the rest of the audience, but unlike her they didn't seem to mind that the plot line was so obvious. They were nodding and murmuring. Sylvia Allison, who was sitting up on the stage, looked smug, as if she'd engineered Celia's misery herself. As Nora closed her eyes and wished herself away, a name popped into her head. Moira Wilkes. Of course. The woman she'd met at the cocktail party in Washington. That's who Dr. Stillman reminded her of—Moira Wilkes. *Women must be taught to fantasize in a totally different way.* . . . Spoken with her jaw jutting forward and the same fever of righteousness burning in her eyes. Nora, who had suffered guilt and shame ever since that meeting, now got a spiteful pleasure in lumping Moira, who wanted to control her mind, together with Dr. Stillman, who wanted to control her body, into a pleasant revenge fantasy. She imagined putting them in the same jail cell and throwing away the key. How they would hate one another. How they would spit and screech and scratch.

"Let me tell you a bit about Celia's unhappy past. She became pregnant at eighteen and, at her parents' insistence, married the father, a nineteen-year-old garage mechanic. Although their life together wasn't luxurious, she appeared to have been an attentive and loving mother to her son. Unfortunately, she got pregnant again soon after his birth. Both her husband and her parents insisted that she abort the child. So much pressure was brought to bear on Celia that she yielded and had the abortion, although as she said, she didn't want to 'murder her baby.' Soon after that, she was pregnant again with little Paula. This time she was able to resist her parents and husband, but when the child was born she found that she could not take care of it. The guilt and the depression of that earlier abortion had taken its toll. 'I couldn't stop crying,' that's what she told us. 'I couldn't even look at Paula without thinking of the one that was dead.' "

The headache was now a sick, heavy pounding at her temples. Nora began to hate her chair, the auditorium, the rapt audience, Dr. Stillman at the podium, the whole damn pro-life movement. *Pound.* She hated Moira Wilkes for making her feel guilty over some innocent fantasies. *Pound.* She hated Marty and Christine for making her feel as if she were being split down the middle. *Pound.* But most of all, she hated herself for not having principles and standards. She didn't care if it would set a bad example to keep Christine and her baby. She didn't give a damn if Christine didn't deserve to be a mother. She'd let every banner droop if only things could go back to the way they were. *Pound. Pound.*

"Friends, there are thousands of Celias and thousands of small children abused because the insidious poison of a previous abortion has contaminated the very bond that exists between a mother and her child. It is our responsibility in the pro-life movement to confront the issues posed by the psychological aftermath of abortion. We cannot ignore these unhappy women. We cannot censure them for what they have done. That would be contrary to the philosophy of the National Foundation for Life. What we have to do is help these women. We have to be supportive, comforting and understanding. We must allow them to talk out their problems, because their families, their husbands and their friends often deny them that solace. We must remember that abortion is an act of expediency, undertaken because there seems to be no solution and no positive end to a pregnancy. It is, seemingly, an easy way out and—let's face it, friends—we live in a society that always seeks the easy way out."

It occurred to Nora between waves of pain that she had come to the Coalition in the hopes of having a sense of righteousness rub off on her. Not that she agreed with the pro-life dogma, in fact, she would have liked to stand up in front of all of them and ask why *her* life didn't have any value, why it was just fine for her to feel battered and abused and broken. No, she had come to the Coalition wanting to learn *how* to believe in something, anything. Wasn't that ridiculous? And no wonder she had a headache, sticking Dr. Stillman and Moira together in that jail cell in her mind. They were fighting it out between her temples. *Crash. Pound.* She opened the door and let them out. She brushed off their clothes and apologized profusely for inconveniencing them.

"And the psychological effects of abortion are not confined only to mothers. Fathers are often alienated by their wives' decisions, siblings often feel guilty that they are survivors, and society itself demonstrates a profound malaise at its very core when it kills the helpless, defenseless young. The trendy thing today is to marry and not have children, to join in a familial bond but have no family, to link together sexually without ever bearing the child that is the very reason for our sexuality. The pro-abortionists tell us that, with abortion on demand, every child is a wanted child. But I say to you that when people don't want children because they're expensive or the wrong sex or deformed, then children themselves have very little value in our society. And when children have little value, child battering becomes the norm instead of the unusual."

Nora tried to explain to Dr. Stillman and Moira, in halting words of shame, that she was terribly jealous of all the things she had despised them for: their rhetoric and their narrow convictions. "You see," she said, "I'd really like to be like you: so positive, so . . . sure of yourselves, so confident. But I just can't. . . . I don't know why. Is that silly? Is there something wrong with me? Sometimes I wonder if, historically speaking, I'd have been one of those people who would just keep shifting loyalties to save my skin. I don't think I'd have burned at the stake or been thrown to lions. I would have just gone with whatever side seemed to be winning at the moment. That isn't honorable, I know, but I'm afraid I'm just the kind of person that only knows how to . . . well, cope."

"So, friends," Dr. Stillman was saying, her head still thrust forward like a turtle's, her hands outstretched and emphatically chopping the air, "let us never forget one thing.

"Never let us forget this even when the good fight is hard and difficult!

"Never let us forget it when our enemies are *numerous* and our stalwart hearts *falter* in determination!

"Never let us forget"—her hands cleaved space—"that *abortion* is the *ultimate* in *child abuse!*"

Nora rose with the audience, wincing at the roar of their applause, her only thought to get home as fast as possible. But when she reached the foyer of the auditorium where the Coalition had set up a table with coffee and cookies, she saw Sylvia bearing down on her. There was no way of avoiding her. Sylvia was too big, her wings of silver hair like sails, her breasts a prow, her bulk and momentum carrying her like a large ship moving at a majestic pace through the crowd.

"Nora! Nora Beeme. What a surprise! I'm so delighted you could come." Nora felt her hand clasped and patted, and then she was being propelled toward the refreshment table. "You don't mind if I introduce you to some people, do you? Frances, come meet Christine Beeme's mother. Nora, Frances Hesselgrave. Frances is our scholar. She has a Ph.D. in medieval history."

Frances was a short thin woman with gold-rimmed spectacles and fine gray curls. "Don't let Sylvia intimidate you," she said as she shook Nora's hand. "There's nothing special about having a Ph.D."

"She's very modest," Sylvia confided to Nora. "Actually, she has a very important, definitive article appearing in the *Journal for Abortion Studies* on the relationship between abortion and Nazism."

"Looking at historical parallels," Frances said with enthusiasm. "A fascinating subject."

Nora felt the strain in her smile. "Yes," she said.

"And this is Jane Lovett. She's with 'Lawyers for Life.' And Father Bennett. Miriam Goldberg. Barbara Phillips. You know, Nora, we're all so pleased about Christine." The others nodded encouragingly. "She's gotten so mature."

One of them—Jane? the lawyer?—a tall blonde, elegantly dressed in a navy business suit, mauve blouse and long pearls, touched Nora on the hand (were they all hand-patters?) and said, "She's such a thoughtful girl."

They all chimed in:

"And so good at helping some of the other girls."

"Elly, for example."

"Oh, yes, Elly. She really needed support, didn't she?"

"And she helped the little Stewart girl, the one having so much trouble with her parents."

"Christine spent hours with her. Literally, hours."

"She's so devoted."

"And such a courageous person," Sylvia said. "We're very proud of her. You must feel the same."

Now they were all beaming at her—intensely, as if the wattage of lights in the room had suddenly gone up.

Like any parent, Nora had had an aspect of her children that she'd never seen before revealed to her by strangers. ("What lovely table manners," some mother had once said of Danny, who slurped and chewed loudly at all Beeme meals.) Although Nora felt only a jolt of irritation at this praise, she tried to look pleased. "Oh, yes," she said. "I do. Feel proud."

"And wasn't Dr. Stillman inspiring?" Frances Hesselgrave said to the group at large, all of whom nodded and gave enthusiastic murmurs of assent.

"A pillar of strength."

"A shining example of . . ."

". . . always goes right to the heart of the matter."

"And aren't we lucky she's joined the cause?"

"Oh, yes."

Sylvia leaned closer, so that Nora could see the powder line on her nose and tiny wrinkles in her jowls, and lowered her voice. "Dr. Stillman used to be an abortionist," she said in a low voice, "but then she saw the light."

"Really," Nora said. Her headache had retreated slightly after she'd left the auditorium, but now she felt it coming back in full force. Surreptitiously she glanced toward the exit and wondered how soon she could get away, but now Sylvia had put a hand firmly on her arm.

"And her message. So powerful."

Nora didn't actually hate Sylvia any more. The millstone had turned, and the fervent, convenient hatred was gone, washed over by the hundreds of other emotions that had followed—complex, awkward emotions concerning Marty, Christine and Danny. She had even passed Sylvia several times in the shopping mall and had seen her at a school concert, and had felt nothing left of that old anger except a residue of bone-deep weariness.

"That connection between abortion and child abuse," Sylvia went on, leaning closer and tightening her grip on Nora's arm. "It's even being documented in the scientific literature."

Nora's brain now felt like it was splitting, not down the middle, but across the circumference. A band of pain tightened across her brow and around to the back of her neck.

Frances Hesselgrave piped up, "And Dr. Stillman spoke about it so eloquently."

Nora's skin had started that hot, uncomfortable prickling again, and a drip of sweat made an agonizingly slow and ticklish journey down her side.

"A wonderful speaker," Sylvia said, her face now within inches of Nora's. "Wouldn't you agree?"

It was too much: the heat, her pounding head, their complacent smiles, her sense of not belonging, the whiff of stale breath coming from Sylvia's mouth. Nora had, with despair, believed herself to be an irresolute reed bending with every wind, but she now discovered in herself a profound distaste for Sylvia, her friends, and their self-indulgent, obnoxious need to proselytize.

The sensation was solid, satisfying, exhilarating. For a moment, Nora was even able to forget her headache.

"No," she said, yanking her arm out of Sylvia's grasp, "I don't."

Eyes blinked. Mouths dropped open. Sylvia frowned.

"As a matter of fact," Nora said, the words rolling off her tongue in pleasurable syllables, "I thought she was horrible. I thought she—*stank.*"

9

◇　◇　◇　"Oh, yes," Dr. Roya was saying. "There's an organization of Physicians for Life. They're very active."

"What gets me," Nora said, "is the rhetoric. It's so abusive."

"It's the thin edge of the wedge," Dr. Roya replied. "That's what each side is afraid of."

Nora was lying on the examining table, naked from the waist down. In mid-October she'd had a crazy menstrual cycle: bleeding, stopping and then bleeding again all month long. She'd thought that, like the headaches and the absentmindedness, the irregularity was related to stress, but it had scared her enough to make an appointment. Now she lay on the crinkly paper with her knees up, her eyes on the ceiling, while Dr. Roya probed her insides and poked her outsides. They hadn't yet discussed the state of her female organs, but had talked about Christine and Dr. Roya's other teenaged patients. ("She's not the only one who wants to keep her baby," Dr. Roya had said. "Unfortunately, it's the thing right now.") Then they had gone on to the Coalition.

"You see," Dr. Roya went on, "neither side will admit the

other has a legitimate argument. They're afraid to expose any weakness."

"But what annoys me the most, I suppose, is that the pro-life people seem to have seized the moral high ground. They refuse to leave space for anyone else."

"I still do abortions," Dr. Roya said, "and I don't want to see that becoming a criminal offense. I'm not planning to go back to the era of back-room surgery and perforated uteruses, thank you very much."

Nora raised her head and watched Dr. Roya do whatever it was that doctors did when they were about to take a pap smear. A drawer slammed, a glass slide appeared. It always surprised her that she now had a physician who was younger than she was. In her past experience, doctors were always older and therefore wiser. Dr. Roya was in her early thirties, a brisk woman with curly dark hair, glasses and sharp features. Her chin came to a point, her nose was thin and bony. She was unmarried but not unattached. Nora had seen her once in the supermarket, hand-in-hand and looking up adoringly at a man much younger than herself. So vulnerable had that sharp-featured face been that Nora had had the shameful feeling that she'd caught a glimpse of Dr. Roya naked.

("We don't like to think our doctors are human, do we?" she'd said to Marty afterward.

"It doesn't bother me to think Rustofson screws his wife." Dr. Rustofson was their internist.

"Maybe I feel that way," Nora said, "because I've had so many male doctors encouraging me to think they're gods."

"You know what a doctor is? A technician. That's all. You know what I said to Rustofson when he kept me waiting for forty-five minutes? I told him my time was valuable, too."

"What did he say to that?"

"He said he was sorry. He said he'd try not to do it again.")

Dr. Roya inserted a speculum, and Nora said, "The thing that gets me is that abortion is supposed to be murder, but when you think about it, people get away with all sorts of murders in our society. It all depends on the circumstances."

"Mmmm." Dr. Roya was sitting on a stool now, peering up Nora's vagina. "I think I see a cervical polyp."

"I had one of those when I was pregnant."

"It's tiny. Let's wait and see what happens with it. In the meantime, I'll do the pap." She inserted her hand into Nora, made a motion with it, and Nora felt something pinch deep inside. "The problem is," she went on, "that we can keep babies alive at much earlier stages of pregnancy. A lot of doctors can't stand saving a twenty-five-week fetus in one hospital room and killing another right next door." Her hand exited, and Nora heard the hiss of spray against the glass slide. "In Britain, the government is trying to limit the time an abortion can be performed to eighteen weeks. I don't think that'll work either. What are they going to do when a ten-week fetus becomes viable?"

"I don't know."

"It's messy," Dr. Roya said, removing the speculum. "Very messy. Well, there you are. Finished for the moment."

Nora sat up and reached for her panties. "What do you think?"

"I think you're getting to that stage."

"What stage?"

"A lot of women have strange periods as they approach menopause."

"Menopause?" The word conjured up a horrifying mixture of memories and images; her mother's hot flashes ("My God, but I wanted to strip right in public"), the disfiguring widow's hump, women with white-yellow hair and pink scalps, brittle bones, dry vaginas. "I'm only forty-three. My mother didn't go into menopause until she was in her mid-fifties."

"Your system is winding down. It's a long, slow process." Dr. Roya washed her hands in a small sink in the corner of the room.

Nora shook her head. "I'm not ready for this," she said with dismay.

"Think of women before modern medicine. Most of them didn't even make it to forty."

"Somehow that's not comforting."

Dr. Roya smiled as she dried her hands, and the smile almost made her pretty. "No, I don't suppose it is. But you'd be surprised how well some women weather menopause. And a lot of them get a second wind when they're post-menopausal. They've got energy to burn. Besides, we've got estrogen now to fight some of the symptoms." She gathered up Nora's file. "Now, I don't think we should do anything unless the problem persists. We can think about a D & C if it does, but let's give it some time. Okay?"

Nora nodded. "Okay."

She got dressed, drove to work, talked to customers, solved a scheduling problem, went home, made dinner, helped Danny with his spelling and watched television. On the exterior she was pleasant and smiling, but deep within, the knowledge of the end of her fertility weighed on her spirit. She could understand disliking the idea of getting old, but she was surprised at how sad she felt at the realization that she wouldn't have any more babies. Not that she actually could anyway, because of Marty's vasectomy. Not that she even wanted to. The very idea made her grimace. She remembered spit-up, the overpowering odor of ammonia in the diaper pail, nights of broken sleep, the irritations of toilet training. When Nora imagined herself pregnant, she caught a whiff of misery, panic, anger and frustration.

But a melancholy remained for all the pregnancies that would never be and the babies that wouldn't get born. Nora tried to shrug it off but it lingered, returning now and again, catching her while she was busy or occupied, when she was getting dressed, serving a customer, eating dinner. She would pause for a second, holding herself very still, and then go back to whatever it was she was doing. She told herself that this would pass, that one day she would realize that it was gone. She used medical terms to describe this to herself. She thought of "resistance" and "curing" as if she suffered from a viral infection, a persistent cold or a stubborn, annoying cough.

Not once did she ever call it grief.

* * *

Nora had had a terrible first pregnancy. Danny would prove to be a breeze, but Christine caused Nora more misery than she had ever thought possible. She began throwing up the day following conception and didn't stop for three months. She was continually nauseous and so exhausted that she had to go on sick leave. Staying home was supposed to give her a chance to nap during the day, but when she tried to sleep, she just couldn't. She would toss and turn and, in desperation, switch on the television. The result was a mild addiction to "As the World Turns" and a growing crankiness which by dinnertime, when Marty came home from work, also tired and wanting his meal, had blossomed into a full, strung-out bitchiness.

And that was just the first trimester.

Nora began to spot in the second trimester, red dots the size of quarters. Dr. Sullivan, worried about a miscarriage, ordered her to bed for a week and forbade sexual relations. The bleeding stopped, so Nora got up one morning, dusted the filthy apartment and made love with Marty that night. She immediately began spotting again. On-again, off-again bed-rest, sex and housecleaning continued until an exam revealed a bleeding and meaningless cervical polyp that had finally grown large enough to be seen. Nora's sense of relief was brought to an abrupt halt by a burning, painful and difficult-to-eradicate bladder infection. Back to bed, Dr. Sullivan said, and no more sex.

By the time the final trimester rolled around with its own quota of problems—itchy navel, constipation, swollen feet and heartburn—Nora hated being pregnant and hated those friends of hers who were sailing through their pregnancies, blooming with good health and optimism. She began to lose her hair and her face broke out. She had also put on far too much weight and waddled like a duck. By her ninth month, she and Marty had furnished the tiny second bedroom in their townhouse with a fluffy white carpet, a pastel-painted Port-A-Crib and a blue rocker. Nora spent hours in this rocker, wearing a pale pink bathrobe and tattered pink fluffy slippers. She rocked back and forth, back and forth, all the while rubbing her swollen abdomen and crying.

She cried because it wasn't fair.

She cried because she had wanted to be pregnant so badly and nobody had told her it was going to be like this.

She cried because she had pimples, thin wispy hair, a huge, veiny belly and a navel that stuck out like a pig's snout.

She cried because Marty was so good to her. He brought her books and flowers. He rubbed her back and massaged her calves when she had cramps. He helped make dinner and, for the only time in their married life, enthusiastically cleaned the toilet bowl and vacuumed the floors.

She cried because he still thought she was sexy.

("More than Gina Lollabrigida?"

"More," Marty said.

"Sophia Loren?"

"More."

"They're not available," Nora tearfully pointed out.

"You are," Marty said.

"I'm a lump."

He cupped her breasts in his hands. "Great lumps."

"Oh, Marty.")

And she cried because one night, finding her weeping in the rocking chair for the umpteenth time, he had stood in the doorway of the room, his shoulders slumped, and said wearily, "I wish you weren't pregnant any more. I'm *so* tired of you being pregnant."

Surprisingly, it was to her mother that Nora had then turned for solace when Marty's sympathies waned and ebbed, and she knew that she'd pushed her friends' tolerance to the limit. She found herself calling Esther twice a week, at night, when she knew her parents were finished in the bakery and in bed. Their telephone was by Leo's side of the bed, and he always answered first.

"Hello? Hello?"

"Daddy? It's me. Nora."

"So—how's the baby?"

"The doctor says it's fine."

"And Marty?"

"He's fine."

"And you?"

"Not so good."

"I'll put your mother on."

Nora had always known, even as a very young child, that the best way to get her mother's attention was to be sick or to provoke sickness. Esther believed that the head and the feet were the two great conduits of human illness and must be protected at all times. She had two axioms, one for summer and one for winter. In hot weather, the head should be covered against sunburn and sunstroke and the feet shod to prevent warts and lockjaw. In cold weather, a hat must cover the ears, while feet could be bare only in the bathtub and in bed. For many years, until Nora learned how germs are really carried and transferred, she was convinced that they entered the body either through the scalp or the soles of the feet. When prevention failed, Esther had several tried-and-true methods of medical care. Sunburn was always treated with a paste made of baking soda and water. Sore throats required either a lemon-honey or saltwater gargle. And not for Esther the theory that a cold must run its seven-day course. Colds were fought vigorously with steam heat. Every drippy nose found Nora sitting at the kitchen table, her head covered with a towel while her face hung above a saucepan of boiling water.

When Nora was a teenager she had hated the constant admonitions, the carping about hats and shoes, Esther's self-satisfaction when she could connect bronchitis to an act of disobedience. But none of this bothered Nora while she was pregnant. She had a voracious appetite for a sympathetic listener, and Esther not only listened, she also murmured, clucked and tut-tutted. She cast Nora's problems into an historic perspective, rehashing her own pregnancies and childbirths as well as Nora's grandmother's, Aunt Malka's and Muriel's, the wife of Albert, a second cousin. She was conversant with such subjects as varicose veins and stretch marks, and she said things like "a healthy apple doesn't drop from the tree," when Nora was afraid she might miscarry, and "a bun in the oven has to bake" and "with all this trouble, your coming-out party will probably be a snap."

Nora found an unexpected but oddly reassuring comfort in her mother's voice. It didn't last, of course. It ended precisely at that moment when she brought Christine home from the hospital. Esther had come up alone from the Bronx to Burtonville the day before Nora was to be released. She cleaned the entire apartment, including the woodwork and the oven, washed all the new diapers ("they were too stiff, and who knows what chemicals were inside") and made a huge pot of chicken soup, a brisket and sponge cake. She was in a housedress, slippers and an apron when Nora and Marty arrived, bustling forward as they came through the front door, her arms already outstretched for the baby, whose wails could be heard through layers of blankets.

"Oh, the cutie," she said, taking the baby and pushing aside the blankets so Christine's red, contorted face was visible. "There, there, Grandma's got you now. What's the matter? Are you hungry?"

Nora slipped off her coat and Marty hung it in the closet. "I just fed her," she said. All she wanted to do was crawl into her own bed. Her stitches were pulling and hurting, and she'd slept badly in the hospital.

"Look at her. She's starving."

"Mom, I think she's too hot."

"Gas. They kick like that when it's gas. You burp her?"

"Yes."

"Then it's the breast milk," Esther said smugly. "It probably doesn't agree with her."

All the old adolescent feelings washed over Nora, and with them went the gratitude she'd accumulated during her pregnancy. She couldn't stand the way Esther shuffled in her slippers or slurped her tea or fussed over the baby. She got sick of stories about her own and Ben's babyhoods, their croup and cradle cap and diarrhea. She wanted her mother out of her apartment and out of her life, and when Esther finally left, driven to the train station by Marty, Nora sat on the couch, sinking gratefully into the emptiness of the apartment. Not even Christine's thin wailing could dissipate her sudden happiness, her sensation of release. She closed her eyes, leaned her head against the back of the couch and smiled, while the crying rose and fell, rose and fell, surrounding her in bell curves of sound, encircling her in parabolas and flowing figures-of-eight.

One Saturday in October, Nora woke to the most vicious headache she'd ever had. It began the moment she tried to stand up, a crashing pain that hit her head, rocked her slightly and brought a bubble of bile to the back of her throat. She gagged and sat back down on the bed. Marty's side was rumpled and empty; he had already gone to the office. He hadn't been sleeping well, and he'd taken to rising earlier and earlier in the morning. Nora rarely saw him now until dinnertime or even later. His immediate boss, McAllister, had had a heart attack and was in the hospital, leaving Marty with a double work load. Devlin had already paid him a bonus and had promised another when the project was completed, but Nora didn't think the financial rewards were worth Marty's insomnia and anxiety. He'd developed a nervous habit of picking away at the dry skin on his lips, even to the point of sometimes drawing blood.

Nora's anxieties manifested themselves in increasingly frequent and ever more debilitating headaches. Sometimes she felt as if a sharp knife were being stabbed into her temple, other times as if her eye were being gouged out. Aspirin no longer did anything for her, so she'd gone to her internist and gotten painkillers. They worked, but only after drugging her into a deep sleep. She took them rarely, when the pain and nausea got so bad that she was afraid she'd vomit. On this particular morning she could hardly make it to the bathroom to get her pills, but staggered through the doorway, her hand pressed to her head. She couldn't lean over —that made the pounding worse—so she squatted down by the cupboard, opened the drawer and rummaged blindly through the vials of pills.

Danny showed up just as she located the codeine tablets.

"Mom, can I go over to Peter's this morning? And then to a movie with him at two o'clock? There's this great horror movie on in the mall with this really gross monster. I'll need six dollars though, for popcorn and stuff. I don't have any money left from my allowance. Mom, are you listening?"

"I have a terrible headache. Tell Christine I want her."

"Okay." He turned and hollered, "Christine! Christine, Mom wants you!"

Nora winced and swayed against the toilet. "Don't shout," she said.

"Sorry, Mom. So? Can I go?"

"What about lunch?"

"I'll eat at Peter's."

"Does his mother know about this?"

"Yeah, we told her. Mom, can I have some money?"

"In my purse."

"Where is it?"

Nora tried, through successive waves of pain, to remember where she'd put her purse. "On the kitchen counter," she finally said.

Danny took off, his "Thanks, Mom" drifting back to her.

Nora took two tablets with a glass of water, an effort that resulted in more gagging and retching. Her queasiness was so bad that she just sat on the floor by the toilet, leaning her aching head against the wall. Nora had realized a month ago that she should probably see a psychiatrist or a counselor about the headaches. Stacey Epstein had been going to a therapist for the past twenty years. She'd started with him when she was living in New York, and still commuted from Washington to see him when the need arose. In fact, when Nora had looked up Stacey, ten years after their high school graduation, it was one of the first things Stacey had brought up.

("Do you have a shrink?"

"No," Nora said, surprised. "Do you?"

"Oh, I couldn't live without him."

Nora couldn't help a look of disbelief. "Really?"

"Listen, Nora, you don't have to be mentally ill to see a shrink. Melvyn's like my eye, nose and throat man. When I feel a cold coming on I get some medicine. When I feel a problem coming on, I go and talk it out."

"And does it help?"

"Of course," Stacey had said. "Would I go otherwise? Melvyn costs me a *for*tune.")

Nora didn't have Marty's disdain for the psychology profession, but she had a reluctance to spilling her guts out to a stranger. She was, she'd discovered, her mother's daughter, which meant you kept things in the family, you didn't trust someone who wasn't a blood relation, and most of all, you didn't air dirty laundry for the entire world to see. It was the Jewish version of the stiff upper lip, and Nora had swallowed it whole. Now it sat uneasily in her stomach, and every once in a while she bent her head—the pounding!—over the toilet seat and stared blindly into the depths of the bowl.

"Mom? Are you okay?"

Nora lifted her head and waited while the sparks and flares faded from her vision. Christine was kneeling beside her, a worried look on her face.

"I have a headache."

"Again? You had one last week, too."

"I know. Listen, I want you to call Joanne and tell her I'm not coming in today. If she panics, tell her that I think—whatshername—Marion would come in for the afternoon. And take the spaghetti sauce out of the freezer for tonight."

Nora stood slowly upright and worked her way back to bed. Christine helped her, her hand firmly under Nora's elbow, matching her steps to Nora's shuffling motions.

"Boy, Mom, this one's really bad, isn't it?"

"Horrible," Nora said, sitting carefully down on the bed and then, with equally cautious motions, lying down and pulling the blankets up over her.

"Would you like a wet cloth for your head?"

"That would be nice. And would you get me my pills and a glass of water for my night table? Oh, and you better get a pail. I feel like I'm going to throw up."

"Sure, Mom."

As Nora lay there, waiting for the codeine to pull her into that dark and painless void, she contemplated the only pleasurable change in her life at the moment—the evolution of her daughter into a cooperative human being. This had come on so slowly that Nora hadn't been aware of it at first. The change was somehow connected, she knew, to the polished fingernails, the wholesome diet and the clean room. It had begun with a lack of complaining about emptying the dishwasher and had moved into a willingness to set the table without making the sort of face that let Nora know she'd just about pushed Christine beyond her level of endurance.

The next step in this alteration of personality had been really quite astonishing, now that Nora thought about it. Danny and two friends, Billy and Bruce, had sneaked into Christine's room one afternoon when she'd been out. There, Danny as impresario had given his friends a showing of her bras and a flamboyant demonstration of her cosmetics, squirting perfume around and leaving lipsticks and jars uncapped. In former times this behavior, admittedly wrong, would have driven Christine wild. She would have screamed at her brother and her parents. She would have demanded a punishment that far exceeded the crime. She would have stamped her feet and hollered throughout the house and made all of them miserable. This time she made an admirable attempt to restrain herself, asked Nora if a lock could be installed on her bedroom door and merely treated Danny like a leper for two weeks. Nora punished Danny herself, docking him an allowance and making him carry out the garbage by himself.

"Here, Mom."

Nora felt a coolness as Christine placed a wet washcloth on her forehead. She opened her eyes. "Thanks, dear."

Christine sat on the edge of the bed. "Here's your pills, the water and the pail. Do you want anything else?"

"Uh-uh. What are your plans for the day?"

"I've got some Math to do. Jay may come by."

"Well, I'm going to be out of it for hours. I probably won't wake up until after lunch. If your father calls, ask him what time he'll be home, okay?"

"Okay. I hope this makes you feel better, Mom."

"Me, too."

Nora closed her eyes and heard Christine tiptoe out of the bedroom and gently close the door. Even Marty was responding to this new Christine, she thought groggily. The atmosphere in the house was still tense, but they talked now and then, not about anything consequential, but politely about mundane subjects like the weather, or a television program or what was for dinner. Of course, neither had backed down from their respective positions. Christine insisted that she wanted to keep the baby; Marty refused to have it in the house. Nora had only been able to convince Christine not to move out before the baby was born, by emphasizing the importance of her diet and the expense of eating well enough to keep both her and the baby healthy. Christine had reluctantly agreed that she could eat better at home than anywhere else.

A minor victory in a major catastrophe.

One up for Nora Beeme.

Now if only she could get rid of her headaches, Nora thought sleepily. If only she could make sure that Danny's friend Peter wasn't a little shit who drank her whiskey. If only Danny could keep from getting into trouble. If only the world could slow down a little, please, so that she and Marty could step off for a moment and talk to each other again. Because they hadn't been. Not really. It was amazing that two people could live in the same house and sleep in the same bed, earn a living and pay the bills, see that the roof got repaired and summer clothes put away, and still act toward one another like acquaintances who meet in the grocery store and smile and nod before going on their respective ways. Nora turned over on her side and curled into the fetal position. No, it was worse than that. She and Marty didn't even smile any more. If only . . . But a numbness was setting in, emptying her head of pain and filling it with something heavy and thick and impenetrable. If only . . . And she slept.

When Nora awoke, it was late morning. She peered at her clock radio—11:21—earlier than she would have thought, considering that she'd taken two pills instead of one. She shifted gingerly, testing her pain threshold. Instead of the pounding and nausea she had a fragile, light-headed sensation, as if her skull were made of eggshell rather than bone. She sat up slowly and drank the entire glass of water on her night table. The pills always made her mouth so dry that her tongue and palate rubbed together like two pieces of flannel. Then she got up and went into the bathroom. The Nora that stared at her from the mirror looked like hell. Her hair was in tangles, the skin beneath her eyes was swollen, and she had a reddened crisscross pattern on one cheek from lying facedown on the fringed edge of the bedspread.

"God," she muttered, pulling a comb through her hair. "Where did the cat drag you in from?"

When she'd washed her face, she pulled a bathrobe over her nightgown and opened the door to the bedroom. It was silent in the house, and she guessed that Christine had gone out. As she made her way down the hallway, stopping now and then and putting her hand out to the wall for support because she still felt dizzy, Nora began to make plans. A cup of coffee and a piece of toast. A call to Joanne to see how business was going. Read the Saturday paper and, if she felt well when she was finished, get dressed and go to work. Don't forget to pick up the dry cleaning. Stop at the drug store. Pick up the fabric samples from the upholsterer.

Nora was almost at the door to the den, when she suddenly realized she was hearing sounds. She stopped and listened. Strange sounds: *shush-shush,* as if something were rubbing against something else, a faint *uhhh*—was that a groan?—and a breathy noise barely louder than the sound of the air coming through the vents in the heating system. With vague thoughts of Marzipan—could she be caught somewhere?—Nora stepped forward, looked into the den, and then faltered, catching her breath and holding it, feeling the blood drain from her face.

The *shush-shush* sound came from Christine's palms, which were moving rhythmically against the carpet. Naked, she was on her hands and knees, her head hanging down, her hair swaying against the floor. Jay was kneeling behind her, his fingers gripping her waist, his head thrown backwards, blond hair tumbled on his shoulders. He was moving back and forth, thrusting himself in and out of Christine, his angelic face strained with the effort, the eyes shut, jaw rigid. Nora, before she quickly stepped back out of sight, had the vision imprinted in her mind of pale, tightly clenched male buttocks, and Christine's breasts hanging loose and rocking against her large, blue-veined belly.

For a second she leaned against the wall, fighting dizziness. Then she turned and fled down the hallway, not stopping until she was safely in her bedroom, the door shut and locked behind her. Her heart was beating as if leaping around in her chest, and her breath came in ragged, ugly-sounding rasps. But Nora didn't hear her own sounds. She heard only the *shush-shush,* and she saw, not her bed and draperies and Chinese carpet, but Christine mounted by Jay, their joined bodies illuminated in a shaft of bright sunlight, their flesh transformed into slick and glistening whiteness.

10

◇　◇　◇　Nora didn't tell Marty.

What was the point? she asked herself, and then added with a heavy irony, Christine can't get pregnant, can she? But it had taken Nora a long time to distance herself enough from that act in the den to feel such an irony. The vision of copulation remained distinct on her retina, superimposing itself on reality. She might be talking to a customer in the store, only to find herself witnessing it all over again. She didn't sleep well either, but dreamed about Christine and Jay. In one dream she agreed to take Christine's baby into her own womb so that Jay could crawl into Christine's body and rest there, fully grown and blond, but shrunken to a homunculus. She cut herself open with a kitchen knife, a bloodless and painless operation, but when she looked down, she found that her own womb, caught in weed-like intestines, was full. Marzipan had had kittens there, small, hairless, blind kittens with tiny sharp claws. "I can't take him," she had cried to Christine, "there's no room." The baby floated in the air between them, not fully formed yet, but curled like a pale worm, its head square and blunt.

Nora didn't think that Marty could handle the dreams, the vision, the shock. The pressure at Devlin never let up, but seemed to increase in geometric proportion as the days went by. He was always tired and frequently short-tempered. His attention span for domestic details was limited, and Nora often found that she wasn't talking *to* him but *at* him. Conversation would begin with his full participation but would end with his mind in some other space, while Nora was still trying to discuss whether they should switch banks since the cost of checks had doubled at the First National, or did he think that the funny sound in the dryer meant that the belt was going again. Nora could always tell when Marty had drifted away. Although he seemed to be attentive, a rigid stillness came over him. It was as if all his muscles had locked into place, even those holding his eyes. He went from watching her to staring, his eyes fixed on her moving mouth, his fingers picking at his lips, and she knew that he no longer heard anything she was saying, but was listening intensely to his own thoughts.

During one of these conversations, when Nora was talking about windows that required caulking and Marty's spirit had clearly departed, she felt the now familiar goad of angry frustration.

"Do you ever wonder," she asked abruptly, "why we got married?"

Marty blinked. "What?"

They were sitting at the dining room table, having a coffee after a late dinner, a rare moment of peace and privacy. Both of them had gotten out of their work clothes, and Nora was in her bathrobe while Marty had put on a pair of jeans and a sweatshirt. The children were in their rooms, and the sound of rock music from one of their stereos could be heard faintly in the distance.

"I said—do you ever wonder why we got married?"

"Not particularly."

"I mean, why me? Why did you choose me?"

"It was mutual, wasn't it?"

"I don't know. You once told me that you could have had lots of potential mates."

"Did I?" Marty took a sip of coffee. "I talked a lot in those days, didn't I?"

"Well," she said sharply, "was it because you loved me?"

"Nora, what is this—an inquisition?"

"No. I just want to know."

Marty sighed. "What can I say? Christ, I was only twenty-five years old. I guess I wanted someone to sleep with and to share my life. I was tired of being by myself. I got really lonely. And you came along, and I liked you. And you seemed to like me. You seemed to like going to bed with me; you seemed to think I was special. I don't think I knew what love meant in those days, but," he shrugged, "sure—I loved you. If you want to call it that."

With a painful nostalgia, Nora remembered the romantic trappings of their courtship: the clasped hands and meaningful glances, the secret words and private jokes, the roses presented to her on Valentine's Day and the mutual exchanges of I-love-you's. They were a part and parcel of youth, of innocence, of ignorance. Like the delicate roses, they had all shriveled and crumbled with age, leaving behind the unadorned truth.

"It seems odd, doesn't it," she said sadly, "that two people should end up married for twenty years because they were both once lonely and horny?"

"It's probably more common than you think."

"Do you still? Love me, that is—if you want to use that word."

"Nora, what's going on?"

She took a sip of coffee and pulled the lapels of her bathrobe tight together. "I'm just wondering about things."

"Look, I know I've been really tied up at Devlin."

"I guess I'm just wondering why we stay together."

Marty closed his eyes and leaned back in his chair. "Do we have to talk about this now? Can't we wait until some other time when I'm feeling a little more prepared?"

"But don't you see?" Nora said stubbornly. "We each go our separate ways and do our own thing. We barely see each other anymore. We hardly talk. I can't remember the last time we slept together. What's the point of being married?"

Marty gave her a wary look. "Is this an intellectual discussion we're having or something deeply emotional?"

"Am I ranting and raving?"

"Then think about this," Marty said with a touch of anger. *"You're* busy, too. You're putting in a hundred hours a week at the store. And the last time I made a pass at you, you had a headache."

"Oh, I know," she said. "I'm not just blaming you."

There was a silence. Nora hunched her shoulders and contemplated her fingernails. Marty studied the small swirl of steam that came up from his coffee cup. An unhappy frown creased the skin between his eyebrows.

"I still don't know what love is," he finally said. "I mean, there's nothing you can measure."

Marty had always loved facts. He had gone into engineering because it was full of facts. Scientific facts. Facts with boundaries and dimensions. Facts whose clarity allowed them to be seen, measured, counted and defined. Nora understood that Marty found safety in facts. They were concrete and reliable, altered only by processes based on reason and logic. He was uncomfortable when faced with the amorphous, the ambiguous, the inexplicable.

"No," Nora said. "You can't."

"Look, we stay together for lots of reasons. Some good— like companionship and caring—others not so good—like the kids and the mortgage. Maybe that's what love is—that mixture of good and bad, all sort of muddled up together."

Nora felt incredibly weary, as if she'd just run up several flights of stairs. She hunched further over her coffee, breathing in its aroma. "Maybe."

"I don't suppose we're any different than anyone else."

"No."

Marty stood up and stretched. "I'm going to go work in the den. I've got a report due tomorrow. Don't bother waiting up for me."

He passed by her, patting her dismissively on the shoulder,

and Nora had one final burst of desperation. "Do we even *like* one another?" she cried. "Do we care?"

But Marty's mind was already on his report. "Take it easy," he said as he walked out of the dining room. "This will pass. You'll see. It'll pass and you won't even remember."

But Nora wasn't so sure. In the past when she'd felt too separate from Marty, too disconnected, she'd poked and prodded at him until whatever was causing the too-large emotional space between them was discussed and filled. Now, although their conversations began with the same needy energy, Nora soon found herself bogged down, as if she and Marty were traveling together through a heavy, dense fog. Sometimes in the middle of these discussions, Nora would look at Marty, at his thinning, curly hair, narrow shoulders, long, heavily knuckled fingers, and feel absolutely nothing. Not affection. Not attraction. Not a glimmer of sexuality. What she saw, objectively, as if Marty were someone she'd met at a party, another woman's husband, was a middle-aged man beyond his physical peak, limited in imagination and conventional in attitude. A nice man, though. Nonthreatening. Pleasant.

How odd it was to view Marty from that perspective. Nora felt like a stranger wandering around her own house, checking the furniture and appliances as if she were a potential buyer rather than the woman who lived there. *That lamp? Those cushions? I'm not sure about that couch.* What had once seemed to her harmonious now appeared drab or discordant, and it occurred to her for the first time that, if her marriage were to end, it would not come apart in some shocking or violent manner as she had always imagined in her worst moments, but with a slow, insidious dying.

Nora knew she should be terrified. A month ago she would have trembled at the very idea of her marriage falling apart. But the thickness of that fog seemed to muffle all her emotions. She envisioned her love for Marty fading—like a Polaroid photo in reverse. Instead of staying sharp and clear, the picture would dissolve, its color seeping away, the edges disappearing into the background, until nothing remained but a bland, yellow-white, glossy surface.

> *Orthodontist—10:00*
> *Dr. Roya—10:45*
> *dry-cleaning*
> *bank*
> *lip salve*
> *stockings*
> *haircut—11:30*
> *blouse*
> *milk, eggs*

"We mustn't forget the milk and eggs," Nora said. The list was scribbled in pencil on the back of a crumpled envelope that had once contained the Mastercard bill. The envelope looked quite incongruous next to the luncheon plate with its gold-and-pink rim, the fuschia linen napkin shaped into a miniature tent, the cut-glass goblet. She and Christine were celebrating her sixteenth birthday at Le Bistro, a new French restaurant in East Burtonville.

"This place is really nice," Christine said. She opened the leather-bound menu. "But expensive."

"Don't worry about it," Nora said. "It's a gift."

Christine leaned forward and rubbed the petals on a pink carnation in a bud base. "Real," she announced. "Not plastic. That would be pretty tacky in a place like this, wouldn't it?"

"I guess," Nora said, putting the envelope back in her purse, arranging one of the napkins over her skirt and trying not to notice the pointed gaze of a woman at a table near them. She'd spent the entire morning as the target for such looks. They came from the parking lot attendant, the teller in the bank, the nurse in the orthodontist's office, the other customers in the Stork Express Maternity Shop, and even casual passersby. Often, before she could slide her eyes away quickly enough, Nora caught the greedy curiosity in those looks. With her braces and bulge Christine was immediately identifiable: the quintessential unmarried, pregnant, adolescent girl. And Nora beside her—mother of the mother. Recipient of shocked expressions, embarrassed pity or, even worse, of a sly and smug satisfaction.

Christine hadn't noticed the other woman. She was still happily looking around the restaurant. "Wouldn't you like to eat like this every day?" she said. "I could handle it."

"Me too, except my bank manager and waistline wouldn't like it."

"Mom, you're not really fat."

"Thank you," Nora said dryly.

"But you could use some spot reduction. There are some great exercises in the November *Seventeen* for thigh-thinning."

Nora couldn't help laughing. "Christine, you're a great help and inspiration to me." She opened her menu. "Now, do you see anything you want?"

"Mom?"

"What?"

"You're not really angry with me anymore, are you?"

Christine, Nora thought, was looking exceptionally pretty today. Pregnancy suited her, bringing a pleasing fullness and higher color to her thin cheeks. Her dark hair had been cut to chin length again, and her bangs shortened so that her eyes were once again visible. They were Marty's eyes, hazel and flecked, and Christine had narrowed them to the same expression of shrewd assessment that Marty assumed when he was trying to get to the bottom of something. Seeing this, Nora considered how strangely children grew. In fits and starts. In steps backward and leaps forward. What was fifteen years old really, but the average of two and twenty-eight? The two-year-old held the stage most of the time, but occasionally the adult would make a startling appearance, full of maturity, insight and perception.

"No," she said, "I'm not angry any more."

This lunch, this shopping day, had been Nora's way of atoning for months of neglecting Christine. Oh, she had fed and housed her, had made sure she received an education of sorts and provided her with medical care, but she had withheld love by withholding money. Christine had asked for clothes and Nora had denied her. She'd wanted a haircut, and Nora had refused. Nora had heard herself sounding like Leo ("You think I have a printing press instead of a bakery? You think I'm making money down there?") and had cringed, but she hadn't been able to stop herself either. Shame (she'd anticipated those pitying looks) had kept her from being with Christine in public, and anger had made her stingy and sharp.

"I've been wondering about something," Christine said.

"Such as?"

"You know the money that you and Dad saved for my college education? Well, I was wondering if I could have it now. I mean, after the baby is born."

"Don't you think you might want to go someday?"

"Maybe, I don't know. But that's not as important as the baby, and it is my money, isn't it?"

Nora thought of years of scrimping and saving, at first only five dollars or ten, then more as Marty's income went up and the store became profitable. Years of a dream being deposited in the bank and recorded in a special account.

She sighed. "Technically, no, it isn't. It's money that Daddy and I made and put in the bank."

"But you saved it for *me,* didn't you? Don't you see what I mean? I know you put it away for my education, but I don't need it for that right now. Mom, the baby's going to need a crib and clothes and all kinds of stuff."

"I can't make the decision now," Nora said. "I'll have to discuss it with Daddy."

"But you think it's a good idea?" Christine said eagerly.

"I don't like it," Nora admitted, "but I know you're going to need help."

"What about Daddy? Do you think he'll agree?"

"I don't know."

"I guess . . . Well, I wish *he* wasn't still mad at me."

"He's not going to change," Nora said. "I hope you're not counting on that."

Christine gazed down at her fingers, which were twirling a

goblet around. "I think I am a little." She looked back up at Nora and her lips had that slight softening twist that often preceded tears. "I mean, usually he gets mad, but then once he's over being mad, he kind of gives in."

"Not this time," Nora said gently. "If you keep the baby, you're going to have to move out."

"That's sad, isn't it, Mom? That I have to leave?"

"I thought you wanted to be independent like Elly."

"Sometimes I do, but it's scary."

"I can see that."

"I just wish Daddy didn't have to be so angry about it."

"I'm afraid that comes with the territory."

Christine pressed her lips together, and then said in a quick flurry of words, "You know, sometimes, I think I must be crazy, like really crazy, to do this, and then other times, I know I'm doing the right thing."

The old parental urge to interfere and persuade washed over Nora in a powerful wave. It took everything she had not to yield to it. "It's your decision," she said as the waiter approached them. "Now, do you want the soup of the day? I think it's cream of cauliflower. Isn't that what *choufleur* is? You're the one taking French."

Opacity, Nora had learned, can have different textures and densities. The fog that lay over her marriage was heavy and smothering; what had stood between Christine and herself had been thick and folded, like a curtain before a stage. The curtain had separated spectator from actor, action from audience, adolescent daughter from mother. Like Marty protected in his cage of facts, Nora had felt safe on her side of the curtain. She had sat there all through Christine's childhood, administering justice, solace and nutrition in equal dollops and watching her daughter play out the games of pre-pubescence with dolls and skipping ropes and coloring books.

Not even Christine's pregnancy had budged the curtain. Nora had steadfastly ignored what had caused that pregnancy in the first place. Sex? Penetration? If such action had taken place, it was not only behind the closed curtain, but in some location so remote that it was beyond the reach of Nora's imagination. Instead, she preferred the images of babyhood. In a part of her mind Christine remained an infant, diaperless and bent over, peering at Nora from between her legs, her plump pink labia forming an upside-down heart.

The soup came with warm rolls, which were in a basket covered with a fuchsia napkin. Christine picked up a roll and held it in her hands as if to warm her palms. "You know something," she said. "I'm going to bring Jay here for *his* birthday. He'd really like this place."

"When is it?"

"Just before Christmas. He says it's a rotten time to have a birthday. Hardly anyone notices, because they're all busy baking and shopping for the holidays."

Nora buttered her roll. "How's his band doing?" Jay and three friends had organized a band called The Suicides. Nora had thought this name morbid and antisocial, but Christine had assured her that it was perfect, really *in*.

"Not terrific. You see, they really need another vocalist. Jay sings, but he isn't great. Another problem is that Brian isn't much of a drummer, and Nick . . . well, he's just in it for the girls. So it's not going too well at the moment."

"And are there a lot of girls?"

"Oh, sure. There's always girls who think it's neat to hang around musicians. Like maybe some of the glory will rub off."

"What about Jay?" Nora asked casually. "Is he in it for the girls?"

Christine took a sip of soup. "No, Jay's really dedicated. He's too serious for all that stuff."

Then the curtain had risen, and before Nora could avert her eyes, she had witnessed what she had not wanted to know. She still trembled when she thought of those two naked bodies, even though she wasn't a prude at all, even though she had knelt before Marty in the same position hundreds of times herself.

Mercifully, as the days passed, another curtain was slowly closing over that vision. It was lighter in weight and a smooth pale gray, sufficiently opaque so that the figure behind it remained blurred and just sheer enough so that Nora could see only an outline.

The outline of Christine.

The outline of a woman.

Separate, individual, sexual, distinct.

"Christine, can I ask you a question?" Nora said. "About Jay?"

"Sure, Mom."

"He isn't the father of the baby, is he?"

Christine had just taken a bite of bun, but now she began a laugh which turned into a choke. She coughed and tried to clear her throat until tears came into her eyes. Blinking them back, she took a sip of water from the glass that Nora was holding out to her. *"Jay!"* she finally exclaimed. "Of course not. He's my best friend. He's closer to me than almost anyone. Honestly, Mom, whatever made you think *that?"*

"Nothing," Nora said. "Nothing. I just wondered."

Nora had never been inside a police car before. It had a leathery smell mixed with the odor of cigarettes and aftershave. Nor had she ever been in such close proximity to a state trooper. He was tall, had pink cheeks and looked as if he'd just graduated from the Police Academy. Thirdly, she had never seen any child, much less her own, drunk. Danny giggled and snorted and couldn't put two words together. He wasn't a pretty sight.

The police car was parked in front of the Fairfax Drugstore. The store had recently been taken over by a Chinese family from Hong Kong who had moved into the area. They were sprucing up the look of the old store, getting rid of the dusty packets of Yardley soaps, the boxes of enema bags and the ancient counters. They'd put down a new linoleum floor over the scratched oak and installed new fixtures and lots of fluorescent lighting. Gone were the musty, shadowed corners where Dan Heaney, the former owner, had hidden the condoms, the menstrual pads and the

vaginal creams. Now, bright yellow signs with bold black letter-
ing told customers precisely where everything was.

"I'm so sorry," Mr. Liu had said. He'd had to call Nora at
The Kids' Place, and she in turn had had to call Joanne in to
replace her, because the store was so busy. "The police told me to
report any theft. So many of the children try to steal things."

Mr. Liu spoke passably good English and dressed in impeccably tailored suits. Nora had met him at a gathering of local
merchants and had noticed how westernized he seemed. But now
he kept bowing at her, hands clasped in front of him. Nora
realized that he was horribly embarrassed, maybe even more than
she was.

"Oh, I understand," she said hurriedly. "I know the problem. We get a lot of shoplifting, too."

Bow. "It's his first time. So sorry."

"You've done the right thing. Really."

Bow. Bow. "Sorry. Sorry."

Nora was so upset she could hardly breathe by the time she
got into the backseat of the trooper's car. Danny was in the
passenger seat in the front, huddled down against the door, gig-
gling to himself. Despite the chill outside and the fact that it was
snowing, he was only wearing his fall Little League jacket. No
hat. No mittens. Below his damp hair, his face was flushed an
unhealthy red.

The trooper had a clipboard on his knee. "Ma'am, I'm afraid
your son and another boy were caught stealing candy bars in the
drugstore."

Nora nodded.

"The other boy ran away, but Mr. Liu caught Danny and
held him until I arrived." The officer cleared his throat. "It would
also appear that Danny is under the influence of alcohol. Now,
we don't usually report a first-time petty theft for a minor, we
usually give a warning; but, ma'am, the drinking does add another element."

"Believe me, officer," Nora said. "I've never seen him drunk
before."

"Do you know who the other boy is?"

"I think so. Peter Meltzer."

"Where would they have gotten the liquor?"

Nora leaned over the seat. "Danny," she said. "Did you and Pete go into our liquor cabinet?"

"Mom," Danny said, his breath emitting such a strong smell of drink that Nora had to sit back, "Pete drank . . . uh, drank . . . you know, the tall bottle . . . hic . . . the funny little man."

"The Scotch," Nora said heavily. "Johnnie Walker."

"I would strongly suggest, ma'am, that you keep your liquor locked up in the future."

"Officer, I can promise you this isn't going to happen again."

"Well, ma'am . . ."

"I know this doesn't excuse him, but Danny's never stolen a thing before in his life."

The trooper pushed back his hat. "You know, ma'am, ever since Mr. Liu has taken over the drugstore, there've been problems. I hate to say it, but I think there's a racial issue here. The kids think it's a big joke to steal from a Chinaman."

"Oh dear," Nora said. "That's ugly."

"It certainly is. I hate hearing children talk that way, ma'am."

Nora caught the implication and wanted to protest: *We don't talk that way at home, officer. We're small "l" liberals. We grew up in the sixties. We're a mixed-faith marriage. We believe in democracy and equality and the American way of life.*

"I'm going to talk to him about this," she said vehemently. "He's not going to get off easy."

To her relief, the trooper put the clipboard on the seat beside him. "I'd like to come and talk to him after he sobers up."

"I think that would be a very good idea. I hope you scare the pants off him."

The trooper grinned. "That, ma'am, is the idea."

"Mom?"

"What?"

Danny's skin color had gone from red to a pale ash. "I think
. . . I'm going to . . . throw up."

Nora had no sooner gotten Danny out of the police cruiser
than he vomited explosively onto the road, great quantities of
liquid mixed with what looked like pizza. Nora held his head
and tried to keep from retching herself. She was feeling the beginnings of another headache, tiny jolts of pain in both temples.
When he was done, she put him in the car where he curled up
into a small, miserable ball, and she drove home. By the time they
reached the house he was nauseous again, and she had to rush
him up the stairs and position him over the toilet. Despite her
haste, he didn't quite make it but splattered the toilet, his jacket
and pants, his sneakers and Nora's shoes.

He began to cry in great, heaving sobs. "Mom, I'm sorry.
I'm sorry."

"You should be," Nora said grimly. "And you're going to be
sorrier, I can promise you that." She grabbed a washcloth and
dampened it. "Here, wipe your face."

"I'll never do it again."

Nora opened a drawer under the sink and pulled out a roll
of paper towel. "You're damned right you won't. Now, take off
those clothes."

"It was Pete's idea, Mom. Not mine."

"I don't care whose idea it was."

"Mom, please don't tell Daddy. Please?"

"Forget it, Danny," she said. "You're in big trouble. Don't
drop your clothes on the floor! Throw them in the bathtub. And
take some paper towel and wipe off your shoes."

"Please, Mom."

His face was smeared with tears and dirt. He'd taken off his
pants and shirt and was shivering in his underwear. Usually the
sight of that little-boy body with its toothpick legs and pale,
narrow chest made Nora soften, but not now. Her temples were
beginning that familiar throbbing, and a dizziness made her
sway. She steadied herself by putting one hand on the wall and
said, "I'm calling your father just as soon as we clean this up."

Christine had now arrived. She stood framed in the bathroom doorway, her face a grimace of distaste. "Oh my God, what an awful smell!"

"I threw up," Danny said. He was still crying.

"Oh, gross."

Nora was rinsing the clothes in the bathtub. She looked up. "Where were you when Danny and Peter got into the liquor?" she demanded.

"The liquor?"

"Where *were* you?"

"Mom, don't blame it on me. I wasn't home. I went for a walk. Remember? Dr. Roya told me I should be walking."

"Okay," Nora said wearily. "Just get me my headache pills."

"M-o-m, *please* don't tell Daddy."

The skin on Danny's legs and arms was covered with goose-bumps. "Go to your room and get some clothes on," Nora said. "And I don't want to see you for a while, you hear? Just go sit in your room and contemplate your sins."

"What're you going to do to me?"

"I haven't decided yet."

"I promise I won't do it again."

"Go!"

Having to shout made Nora's head feel worse. For a moment, she rested her brow against the cool porcelain of the bathtub. Then she finished rinsing the clothes, carried them downstairs to the basement and dumped them into the washer. The dizziness was now coming in waves that made her stop and lean against whatever wall was available until she could see straight again. By the time she got back upstairs to the kitchen phone, Christine had arrived with her pills and a glass of water. She swallowed them quickly, prayed that her stomach would hold steady, and called Marty.

"Mr. Beeme's office," his secretary answered.

"Marty, please."

"I'm sorry, but Mr. Beeme is in a meeting."

"Pat, this is Mrs. Beeme. I need to speak to him."

"Oh hello, Mrs. Beeme. Gee, Mr. Beeme asked not to be disturbed."

"This is important."

"Hold on a minute." Pat came back almost immediately. "Is it an emergency, Mrs. Beeme? He wanted to know."

Nora felt a bubble of nausea rising in her throat. "Not exactly an emergency," she said, "but I want to talk to him right now."

"Okay. Hold on, please."

Nora held through a series of clicks. Marty's voice came on. "Hello? Nora?"

"Marty, I'm sorry to—"

He interrupted her and spoke to someone else. "No, not that folder—the other file. Sorry, but we're having a meeting in my office. What's the matter?"

"It's . . ."

Nora was again interrupted, this time by a shrill buzzing. "I'm going to put you on hold," Marty said. "I'll be back in a sec."

Nora sat on a stool, put her elbow on the counter and let one hand bear the weight of her head. The other was tightly gripping the telephone receiver and pressing it against her ear. She closed her eyes and tried hard to ignore the nausea and the pain in her temples. She was concentrating so intensely that it was a while before she said "Hello?" and realized that she was no longer on hold, but in telephonic limbo.

"Marty?" she said helplessly into that void. "Marty?"

"Did I tell you the one about the National Association of Nymphomaniacs? Did I?"

Nora shook her head.

"Okay, now listen," Bernie said. "A guy is on the plane when this good-looking woman sits down next to him. She's wearing a T-shirt with the initials N.A.N. After a while, they strike up a conversation, and he asks what the initials stand for. 'The National Association of Nymphomaniacs,' she says. 'No kidding,' he says, 'I didn't know there'd be a national association of such people.' 'Oh, yes,' she says, 'we have state chapters and a national headquarters. I've just been to the annual convention.' 'Really,' he says in astonishment, 'so what do you do at such a convention?' So she explains that they have workshops on clothes and sexual positions and so on, and that this year they surveyed their membership to find out what kind of men make the best lovers. Now, he's really interested. 'What did the survey show?' he asks. 'That the best lovers are Red Indians and Jews,' she says. 'No kidding,' he says. Well, then, they talk some more, you know, airplane chitchat, and she finally says, 'Listen, we haven't even introduced ourselves. I'm Jane Sheridan, and you are . . . ?' And he replies, 'Tonto Ginsberg.' "

Bernie paused. "Cute, huh?"

Nora smiled weakly.

"Not the greatest," he admitted. "You still feeling dizzy?"

They were seated outside the shopping mall, on a bench in a glass-enclosed bus stop. The temperature had dropped the night before, and snow had started to fall right after breakfast. Gusts of wind carried the snow around the booth, blew it against the glass and whipped it through the cracks. Nora was bundled up in her coat, a fuzzy red hat and sheepskin-lined gloves. Bernie wore a lined raincoat and a fur fedora over his sandy curls. His ears were red, and he kept rubbing his hands together.

"I'm sorry," Nora said. "I should be fine in a minute. You don't have to stay."

Bernie had happened to be in the store at a moment when Nora had had a dizzy spell so severe that she'd been forced to lie down on the floor in the back room. Joanne had insisted that she go home no matter how busy they were ("Listen, Nora, do you have any idea what you look like? Death warmed over. It is not conducive to good sales."), and Bernie had offered to walk her to her car. Another spell had hit as they'd stepped out of the mall, and they'd been forced to take shelter in the bus stop.

"I don't have to stay?" Bernie asked. "You got a miracle recovery all of a sudden?"

"The cold air is making me feel better."

"You've seen a doctor for this?"

Nora nodded. She was now having dizzy spells with and

without the headaches. She'd gone to her internist and then a neurologist. Neither of them thought she had a brain tumor (Nora's self-diagnosis—she always diagnosed cancer; it seemed safer to do that right at the start), and both of them had said she was under terrific stress, should try to take more time off work and get some rest. The neurologist also suggested that she might have an inner-ear infection, which could not be treated with any medication but would slowly heal itself over time.

"And he said . . . ?"

"I shouldn't work so hard."

"This doctor know it's Christmas?"

"I think he thought I should postpone it."

"Oy, oy, oy." Bernie took one of her gloved hands and patted it.

Nora swayed against him as the world gave a sudden sickening spin, the snow and glass and cars whirling into a white, metallic kaleidoscope. "Oh, Bernie," she said. "I'm sorry."

"No problem." He sat closer so she could lean on him. "You have any medicine for this?"

Bernie felt big and solid and reassuring. "No," she said, "the doctor said I'll get over it."

"Well, maybe that's a blessing. My wife—they gave her new pills for her nerves—and the next thing you know, she's broken out in big hives. Boy, was she miserable, let me tell you. And boy, was I miserable. You ever sleep with someone with hives?"

"Uh-uh."

"It shouldn't happen to a dog. Now, listen, why don't I drive you home?"

The world settled into its normal patterns, and Nora sat up. "It's over," she said, taking a deep breath. "I'll be okay."

"You think I got no suave? You think I don't know when a lady is in distress?" He put a hand under her elbow, and they stood up. "Come on, I'll drive you. Is someone home?"

"My daughter."

And Jay, she suddenly realized, and God knows what they're doing. And a pile of laundry, and the store payroll, and a roast she'd taken out of the freezer for dinner.

"How is she?" Bernie asked as they stepped out of the booth and into the wind.

"Very pregnant. She's decided to keep the baby."

And her suit that needed to be taken to the cleaners, and bills to pay, and Danny's bad report card, and another night with Marty lying silently beside her.

"Oy, oy, oy. You know why the Polack put ice cubes in his condom?"

"No."

"To keep the swelling down."

And Nora started to laugh, and the laugh turned into something else, and suddenly she didn't think she could stand it anymore, none of it, not the house, her children, her husband, the cat, the laundry, the meals, the bills, the headaches, the dizziness, and she was choking and sobbing, her chest heaving, the cries tearing painfully out of her throat, the sounds coming from her mouth as harsh and raw as the wind that tore them from her lips.

Without thinking, Nora buried her face in the front of Bernie's coat.

Without hesitation his arms went around her, and his hands began to rub her back.

"It's okay," he said, softly. "There, there, it's okay. And I'll make like Speedy Gonzales. I'll have you home in no time."

"That's . . . the . . . problem," Nora cried, feeling her tears freeze on her face.

"What is?"

"Please . . . don't take me home."

The room at the Aurora Motel had a dark blue carpet, lamps with fringed turquoise shades, and twin double beds with pale blue spreads. It also had a dresser and desk with a cheap mahogany veneer and an electric heater that clicked and buzzed as it emitted a steady stream of hot air. Over the headboard of the bed that Nora and Bernie were in was an extremely green oil landscape with a clunky-looking cow and lopsided red barn. It wasn't a pretty room but it was warm, and Bernie's flesh against hers was solid and real and warm, and Nora desperately needed all those things. The inside of her had been so cold and empty for such a long time.

She pulled him closer, and his penis in its lubricated sheath slipped higher inside her. He had ejaculated already but was still erect. Nora felt his strangeness. He was bigger than Marty—all over. Bigger testicles sprinkled with short gray hairs. A wider chest and back so that it took the entire length of her arms to encircle him. Heavier buttocks and belly. Thicker calves and thighs. He didn't feel like Marty, but he was gently kneading the back of her thighs with his hands, and his mouth was nuzzling her neck. She sighed and he said, "You okay?"

"I'm fine."

"No dizzy spells?"

"Uh-uh."

"You didn't come."

"I couldn't."

"Did I do anything wrong?" he asked. "Or was it first-time nerves?"

"Nerves," she said. "It wasn't your fault."

Nora was well aware of why she had come to the Aurora, and it wasn't for an orgasm. She hadn't even tried to have one. She had let Bernie touch her clitoris, but she hadn't let herself feel anything. She supposed this had been her way of remaining loyal to Marty. (Was it really adultery when you didn't come?) No, Nora knew precisely why she was in bed with a toy salesman in the Aurora Motel. Because the fog had lifted. Because her marriage seemed to be dying. Because she couldn't seem to connect with her husband. Because she'd suddenly become very frightened, lonely and desperately hungry for affection.

None of which were good reasons for breaking a code of marital behavior in which Nora had firmly believed and to which she'd always adhered. She had thought that an act of adultery would be like a stone thrown through a window. The glass would shatter all around, in a cascade of shards and splinters. She had seen herself shattering, too, the bits and pieces painful and broken. Nora had a feeling that a time would come, when she was far away from this warm bedroom and comforting male body, that she would find herself picking up the pieces and crying. But right now, wrapped in the warmth of another's flesh (how needy she'd been for the sustenance of skin!), she felt nothing more than a light sorrow. It didn't weigh heavily but rested gently on her, tingeing the air with melancholy.

"Bernie?"

"Mmmm."

"Tell me a joke."

"A joke. Let's see." He slipped out of her, and with one deft motion rolled the condom off his penis, knotted it and threw it into a wastepaper basket. Then he lay back on the bed and tucked her next to him, pulling the blankets up over them. "You know something? I don't think I can remember a single joke. Me—the joke-teller of all times. That's funny, isn't it."

"You know something else that's funny? Your Jewish accent's almost gone."

"Yeah, well, I sell lots of toys being funny Bernie from the Bronx."

Nora propped herself up on her elbow and studied his features: the too-large, hooked nose, the too-short upper lip, the halo of sandy-red curls. He had a face, she thought, that made you smile, until you looked into his sad brown eyes.

"You're a nice man," she said.

He gave her a little smile. "You're a nice lady."

"I don't think this will ever happen again though."

"Sure, I know that. You got troubles right now."

"You, too."

"Yeah," he said with a sigh. "We all do."

"I've never done this before."

"Sure, I know that, too. You're one of those faithful ladies. Very married. Thinking all the time about your husband." He gave her an amused look. "Even when you're in bed with someone else."

Nora didn't deny it, but she said, "When I'm in bed with my husband, I have fantasies about strangers."

Bernie stretched and tucked one hand under his head. The

hair on his chest was completely gray, but in his armpit it was still flecked with red. "That makes you feel unfaithful?"

"Sometimes; well, maybe disloyal."

"Listen, as soon as my wife first started having her troubles, she lost interest in sex. Just like that." He snapped his fingers. "She used to lay there, and I had to do my own thing. So I had big, elaborate fantasies. Lots of ladies, lots of boobs, lots of kinky stuff. It was the only way I could stay faithful to her. Then even that didn't work anymore."

Was that why she was in the Aurora Motel, Nora wondered? Because her fantasies couldn't sustain her without the reality of Marty behind them?

"Besides," Bernie went on, "your fantasy is you, isn't it? I read that somewhere. See, when you're a traveling salesman, you spend a lot of time reading magazines and other garbage. Anyway, in this one article, it said that you have to own the people in your fantasies, because they're not really other people—they're figments of your imagination. So you're not really being disloyal, because those men must be you, or a part of you. See what I mean?"

Nora tried to understand this. She imagined her own face on the men in her fantasies, those who caressed and touched her, who tied her up, who ravished and raped her. If she put her features on them, then it was she touching herself, caressing, restraining, forcing, and filling. What did that mean? That she was giving herself pleasure? That wasn't disloyal or— But wait— what would Moira Wilkes have to say about it? *Fantasies are based on male images of pornography . . . Passive, submissive societal victims . . . Degrading to women.* Nora had accepted this when she'd heard it; she'd felt guilty for not being creative enough to come up with politically correct, feminist fantasies. Now suddenly Moira's words struck her as glib, too easy. She thought of the unknown man in black who appeared so often in her fantasies. If he was a part of her, then what part did he represent? The masculine side? The part of her that was powerful and strong? Was that what she was doing? Pulling that power into herself, matching the weak side of herself with the strong? Making herself whole?

If that was so, was it good or bad? Nora lay back on the bed and stared up at the cracked ceiling. Maybe there was no right or wrong. Maybe there were no answers. "That's confusing," she said. "Really confusing."

"Yeah, well, if I've learned anything after fifty-five years of living, it's that life is one big confusion. Hey, guess what, sweetheart? I've got two leper jokes for you."

"Oh no."

"What did the leper do at the poker game?"

Nora shook her head.

"Threw in his hand."

"Ugh."

"What did the leper say to the prostitute?"

"I don't know."

" 'Don't worry, I'll leave you a tip.' "

"That's awful."

"You're laughing, aren't you?"

11

◇   ◇   ◇   Nora had come to hate Christmas. Which wasn't right, because without Christmas, the store wouldn't survive. She and Joanne did more business in December than in all the other eleven months combined. The cash register rang continuously, the aisles were jammed with customers, and the merchandise moved. From Thanksgiving through until the first week in January, Nora was on her feet from eight-thirty in the morning until ten at night. She brought three pairs of shoes to work and rotated them every hour. Still, her feet ached by nighttime, as did her back and neck. She couldn't sleep at night unless she'd soaked in the hottest bath tolerable. The miracle of Christmas, Joanne often said, wasn't the birth of Jesus but the amazing stuff that people were willing to spend their hard-earned dollars to buy. Christmas Eve, especially, was an exercise in desperation. Items that hadn't moved all year flew off the shelves: dusty chemistry sets, overpriced Barbie furniture, toddler overalls in an ugly shade of green.

Nora had never had much attachment to any holiday—Jewish, Christian or otherwise. Leo, a self-proclaimed atheist, had said holidays were sops to the masses, and the Felshers had only celebrated Chanukah and Passover because Esther had insisted. For Nora, the paucity of spirit in their family celebrations had made her envious of everyone else's. What were the Maccabees and a menorah when compared to Santa Claus and a Christmas tree? Or Passover and the Hidden Matzo in the face of the Easter Bunny, the Macy's Thanksgiving Day parade and a new Easter bonnet? Nora could remember the swooning feeling that had come over her at eleven when a neighbor, a Catholic girl, had made her First Communion. She didn't think she'd ever seen anything quite so wonderful as the white dress decorated with little seed pearls, the misty veil, the gleaming white patent-leather shoes. And the stockings! Held up by a satin garter belt embroidered with tiny pink flowers. Nora, who wasn't allowed to wear stockings yet, had imagined herself in the white dress. She hadn't given much thought to the ceremony itself, what had interested her was the vision of herself floating down some aisle, a vision in beautiful, bridal white.

Marriage to Marty had given Nora a chance to have a Christmas tree and to bring up children who were allowed to believe in Santa Claus. For a long time she'd enjoyed it, hiding presents, singing carols, baking cookies, and hanging hand-knitted stockings on the mantelpiece. The menorah her mother had given her was lighted faithfully as well, but it lacked the enticing glitter of Christmas ornaments. Eventually it ended up on a shelf in the basement, gathering dust along with suitcases, an old doll house of Christine's, and garden equipment. As the children got older, even the appeal of Christmas began to pall. Nora cut the baking down to one batch of gingerbread men and shortbread stars, and she gave up the habit of elaborate gift-wrapping. By the time the store opened Nora had been ready to give up on Christmas altogether.

Of course, the children weren't as willing to forgo all the family traditions. This particular Christmas, with Marty and Nora working so hard, Christine stepped into the breach, dragging Danny along with her. They baked cookies, and decorated the picture window with white snowflakes made from stencils and spray-on snow. There were many whispered conversations, and shopping expeditions that required everyone else in the family to look the other way when the shopper came into the house, his or her arms laden with boxes. Danny was particularly excited this year, because he anticipated getting a new bike that he'd had his eye on all fall. Marty had first suggested that he not be given the bike as punishment for drinking and stealing, but Nora felt he'd already been punished enough. He'd been as sick as a dog for a day, had had to face the state trooper one more time, and his allowance had been docked for a month. Peter Meltzer was no longer a friend, and Danny'd been walking the straight line carefully ever since. ("You know something, Mom?" he'd confided. "The stuff is really gross-tasting anyway.") Nora didn't think he'd drink again for a long time.

Christine was now in her ninth month, and discomfort had set in. She napped in the afternoons and wandered the house at night, waddling from the kitchen to her bedroom and back, the weight of her abdomen swinging from side to side. Dr. Roya was predicting a baby over eight pounds, and Christine was carrying it high. She had heartburn, leg cramps, and a short bladder span, but she suffered most from a painful lower backache. Nora suggested hot baths and a heating pad and tried to help with massages, but nothing worked well and the pain made Christine irritable and snappish. When it was at its worst, even Danny knew enough to shut up and stay out of her way.

"Did you yell at people when you were pregnant with me?" Danny asked Nora one morning when Christine had screamed at him for walking into her room without knocking.

Nora was trying to get ready for work. "I don't remember," she said, applying pale blue eye shadow to one lid.

"When I'm a Daddy, I'm never going to yell at anyone."

"Daddy's don't have to have the babies. It's easier for them."

"That's not really fair, is it? That only girls get to have the babies?"

The eye shadow smudged. Nora sighed and began wiping her lid with a Kleenex. "It has nothing to do with being fair or not. It's nature."

"Well, I don't think Christine's going to be a very good mother."

"That's not a very nice thing to say."

"She yells too much."

"You're a brother. Don't forget that." Nora turned a pointed glance onto Danny. "And you can be a real pain."

"So is she, Mom!"

"It takes two to tango."

"What is a tango anyways?"

The eyeshadow smudged again. "Danny!"

"Now *you're* yelling, Mom."

Nora's temper frayed easily. She knew it, but she couldn't always help it. It was as if she had only a finite reservoir of smiles and pleasant cheer, and the store with its demanding and frustrated shoppers used up every drop. Her unfailing courtesy faded the minute she stepped into her own house. Small, innocuous things that she had previously ignored, like finding lights left on in empty rooms, now set her off. Larger events, like Esther's Chanukah phone call, left her steaming.

"Happy Holidays."

"The same to you, Mom."

"You celebrating this year?"

Nora lied. "Of course."

Esther wasn't deceived. "You're going to temple?"

Nora was surprised at this. Esther hadn't tried to talk her into joining a temple for years. Diplomatically, she tried to change the direction of the conversation to her mother's favorite subject. "How are you feeling? Any more back pain?"

Esther didn't bite. "Why do I even bother trying? In this respect, you're your father's daughter through and through. You and your brother. I brought up a bunch of atheists."

"Isn't Ben celebrating with you?"

"No, he's got his girlfriend to keep him warm. They're a sight, let me tell you, the two of them. Lovebirds. Cooing doves. Smooching like teenagers. A man of almost forty and a woman with three children."

"Mom, is there anyone to take you to temple?"

"Oh, he'll take me. I'll have to ask him three times, but he'll take me."

When Esther was feeling sorry for herself, Nora was always overcome with a painful sensation of helplessness. This helplessness did not translate itself into action. There was nothing she wanted to do or really could do without wrenching her own life completely out of whack, but a part of her was always full of remorse. This she manifested by making murmuring sounds that were supposed to soothe and calm. She also tried to change the subject.

"How's your bridge group?" she said.

"Your children are growing up, knowing from nothing."

"Mom . . ."

"They've got nothing, no traditions."

"They know what they are."

"And what's that?"

"They're half and half."

"Half and half," Esther echoed in disgust. "Half of zero makes nothing."

"They can make their own choice about what they want to be."

"What kind of choice is it when they don't even know their own people?"

"Mom, please."

"And you wonder why you have a pregnant daughter."

Guilt. Nora lived with the taste of it in her mouth, an acidic, coppery taste that made her back teeth ache. She had known that the sorrow she'd felt that afternoon with Bernie would deepen into something far worse, but she hadn't anticipated the way it would burn and cut. She couldn't look at Marty without thinking that she'd been unfaithful to him; when she lay down beside him in bed she felt an agony, compounded of remorse, sorrow, guilt, grief and panic. It didn't matter that she and Marty had become roommates, sharing nothing more than the same tube of toothpaste, the occasional meal, and a conversation now and then. The act of sleeping with Bernie had etched Marty in sharp relief. Nora saw him and everything he did with an unusual clarity, as if he were standing in a ray of very bright light.

She wondered how she could ever have thought that she might not love him any more. Unlike Marty, Nora did not question what love was. She didn't care that it was immeasurable and incalculable. If she tried to imagine what her love for Marty was like, she envisioned a curl of smoke or steam rising in the air, twisting in on itself, altering in shape. She couldn't hold that in her hand; she couldn't give it boundaries. What she had felt for Marty twenty years ago was different from what she felt today. What she had felt for him five minutes ago might be different from what she would feel for him five minutes in the future. Nora accepted this. What she could not accept was that it might have disappeared entirely, taking with it twenty years of emotions and memories.

This, Nora came to understand, was her religion. She didn't follow any political, social or cultural movement. She might agree with their ends and aims (who could argue with Peace, Ecology, Women's Rights?), but she wasn't a joiner or an adherent. If there was any spirituality in her life, it arose from the beliefs she held about her family—that it was all that really mattered, that without it she would be poorer in spirit, meaningless, lost. Nora didn't know if it was right for her to invest so much in three other people. They weren't like God or a church. Marty, Danny, Christine. Each was imperfect: selfish and needy, impermanent and fragile. They could all hurt her, leave her, abandon her.

Or she them. The hunger that had driven her into Bernie's arms could come back again. Nora saw herself visiting the Aurora Motel on a regular basis, dipping into that pool of anonymous affection offered by strange men. Was that what she'd be reduced to: sporadic adultery to hold her marriage together? Suppose it wasn't enough for her? Or suppose Marty felt the same hungers and started to look for sex and affection from other women? What had begun as a huge wide spiral seemed to be closing in on itself, the curves getting tighter, the angle steeper, and Nora felt herself spinning faster and faster, sliding precipitously toward a dark, frightening void.

The guilt. Its acid, cutting edge made her desperate. For all of their married life, Marty had been her confessor, her confidant, her closest friend. Who else could help her get rid of the pain and worry? Who else could stop that slide into nothingness? But Nora was terrified of what would happen if she told him. There was no guarantee of forgiveness, and she might be trading one pain for another even more agonizing. Marty might hate her; he might leave her. When she imagined him packing his clothes and walking out of the house, Nora felt something inside of her wrench and snap.

She turned to magazines for help, and pored over articles like "Ten Steps to a Better Marriage" and "What Men Want Most from Women." She took a self-help book out of the library entitled *The Guide to Marital Survival.* She broached the subject, very obliquely, to Joanne.

"How're things with Grant?" she asked one morning before the store had opened. They were in the back room, sorting boxes of merchandise and checking items against the invoices. Joanne was unwrapping games by a company that advertised non-aggressive toys; Nora was releasing small stuffed animals from piles of shredded newspaper.

"I've been meaning to tell you about that," Joanne said. "Grant and I had a long talk about a week ago. About why he's never home and how little I get to see him. You know, there were a lot of things bothering him."

"Like what?"

"That he'd come home from work and every appliance with a speaker would be blaring: the TV, the stereo, three radios. He said the noise level in our house was driving him crazy. He said he stayed at the office to get a little peace and quiet." Joanne held up a small checkerboard set. "This was advertised as 'Checkers without opponents.' How do you suppose that's going to work?"

"Is it the kids that are bothering him?"

"Not our kids. Everyone else's. Matthew always has one friend and Nina about three. Patrick seems to belong to a gang of boys. No, I take that back. A *horde* of twelve-year-olds with big, loud feet and an irresistible attraction to the refrigerator. Nora, you wouldn't believe the food we go through. Anyway, he was also feeling unappreciated, and I have to admit that he doesn't get a lot of strokes. I can't remember the last time anyone thanked him for bringing home the bacon and keeping the cars running and making sure the roof wasn't leaking."

"So you think Grant wasn't having an affair after all?"

Joanne rocked back on her heels. "I didn't actually ask him. I have a philosophy about these things: that they're not matters that require sharing to ensure marital happiness. In fact, I think I'm better off not knowing. Just the way he's been better off not knowing about me. Ignorance *is* bliss, that's what I decided."

Nora held a soft white unicorn in her hands. "Didn't you ever feel so much guilt that you wanted to confess?"

"That's the worst reason," Joanne said. "Or so they say. You're unloading your guilt at your spouse's expense. Anyway, I realized that I'd forgotten how much I like Grant. I tend to do that, you know—lose sight of the forest for the trees. I mean, we fight a lot, we can't seem to help that. Then he says something sweet or funny or terribly logical, and I remember why I married him. Because he can be sweet and he has such a wry sense of humor. And God knows I can use the logic."

Nora was surprised at this recital of Grant's good points, then thought how odd it was that she should be surprised. Hadn't Joanne ever mentioned them before? Or did Nora filter through her friends' marital confidences, saving only the unhappy morsels, the stories of grouchiness, selfishness and irritability? Perhaps this was her subconscious way of making sure that she never got too interested in the most available men around. No matter how sexy her friends' husbands might be, Nora never found any of them appealing. She thought of Grant, whom she'd recently seen at a community meeting on sewage disposal. He'd grown a mustache, a gray-blond mustache of handsome proportions, and had spoken with that calm and assurance that Nora had always admired. No, perhaps it was the other way around. She didn't edit her friends' confessions; they all edited themselves, entering into an unspoken agreement never to discuss their husbands in other than slightly disparaging tones. A method of wifely survival—keeping predators at bay.

"So things are okay then?"

Joanne threw up her hands. "It's all relative, isn't it? Good today; a disaster tomorrow. What I promised to do is tone the kids down to a dull roar. And I offered to treat him to dinner out every Friday night, as soon as Christmas is over. Just the two of us. No one else. That'll make him feel special." She glanced at her watch. "Christ. It's almost ten o'clock. Ready for another profitable day?"

"I'm trying."

"How're the headaches?"

"Still hanging around."

"I'll bet they disappear when the baby is born."

Nora gave her a disbelieving look. "Sympathetic labor headaches?"

"I mean, maybe they're a metaphor. I don't know. Maybe you're giving birth to something."

"They don't feel like a metaphor. They hurt."

Joanne shrugged as her watch beeped ten. "Just my deep and heavy thought for the day. Okay, you ready?"

Nora nodded, standing up and brushing shredded newspaper off her skirt.

"Set. And let's go."

As she unlocked the door and let in a crowd of shoppers, Nora wasn't thinking about all the items she would sell that day and the shelves she would have to restock and how her feet would hurt at the end of it all. She was contemplating the famous and often-quoted opening of *Anna Karenina*: "Happy families are all alike: every unhappy family is unhappy in its own way." Untrue, she thought, absolutely untrue. Why is it I believe everything I read or that people tell me? Joanne would never consider her marriage as an unhappy one, merely turbulent—the adultery, anger and confrontations just drops in an already rolling, heaving sea. Nora's marriage, on the other hand, had been a calm pool in which one thrown stone had created disturbance, ripples upon ripples agitating the surface.

What did Tolstoy know?

Nothing.

Who else could tell her what was the right thing to do?

No one.

Where else could she turn?

Nowhere.

"I wonder if you could help me? I'm looking for a gift for a baby that has absolutely everything."

An older woman was standing next to her. She was bulky, in a sweater and overcoat, her face already flushed with the exertion of shopping, her arms filled with toys.

"Everything?" Nora said.

"Rattles, teething rings, stuffed animals, cloth books, sleepers, a jolly jumper, mobiles. Everything. I'm going absolutely crazy over this baby."

"Not to worry," Nora said soothingly, leading her down an aisle. "I'm sure we can find something."

Christine gave birth the day after Christmas: a day marked by gloomy skies and intermittent snow flurries.

Nora and Joanne had ordered posters announcing that everything in the store was twenty percent off that day. They were expecting huge crowds at the shopping mall, and Nora had planned to go into work an hour early. Marty's office was closed between Christmas and New Year's. He'd brought home a briefcase full of work, but had set the day aside to take Danny skiing, having agreed with Nora after the drinking episode that what Danny really needed was some attention.

It was a day that Nora would recall in bits and pieces, memory chopped up and returned to her in snapshots or short clips of film.

Waking up at five o'clock in the morning and seeing Christine standing at the foot of the bed, looking as pale and frightened as the five-year-old she'd once been, who had scary dreams and was afraid to sleep alone.

* * *

Sitting in the back seat of the car while Marty drove, holding hands with Christine and reminiscing. "Remember, Marty? Remember going to the hospital when Christine was born?"

"The weather was lousy," he said. "That's what I remember."

"No, that's not what I mean. It was when we got to the hospital and got in that elevator. You were looking so grim, and I was as white as a sheet and out to here." She made a wide arc with her free hand in front of her abdomen. "This doctor got on the elevator with us and stared at the both of us and then said, 'Someday, you're going to laugh about this.'"

"And did you?" Christine asked.

"Many times."

In the dim light of a street lamp, Christine's eyes were dark smudges in a wan face. "I'm never going to laugh about this," she said. "Never."

Marty embracing Christine after they'd gone through the admissions procedure and a nurse was about to take her to a labor room. He patted her awkwardly on the shoulder, hesitated and then gave her a quick hug.

"Take it easy," he said.

Christine threw her arms around his neck. "I love you, Daddy."

"There, there," he said. "I love you, too."

Looking at Marty as he watched Christine walk down the hall and feeling as if she'd been away for a long time and come back to find that he'd aged badly. His face was etched with new lines beneath the shadow of unshaven beard; his hair was grayer and thinner at the forehead.

Feeling the soft tugs of pity and affection, Nora stepped forward and said, "Marty . . ."

But his hands came up quickly, warding her off. "I'll be home," he said.

"You're not going skiing?"

"No, no, I'll be home." He had also turned his head so that he wasn't facing Nora and their eyes could not meet. "You'll call?"

So this is how far we've gone, Nora thought, from touching to not touching, from looking to not looking. Despair draped itself over her, a heavy black weight that made her feel small and shrunken.

"I'll call," she said.

Marty nodded and walked away. It wasn't until then that Nora noticed that he carried the burden, too. His shoulders were slumped beneath the gray wool of his winter coat, his head angled forward, his hands made into fists and jammed into his pockets.

Never feeling comfortable in the labor room, with its odd choice of wallpaper: girls in pastel gowns carrying parasols and strolling beneath the overhanging branches of willow trees. Nora couldn't seem to adjust to the incongruities that the wallpaper presented: that Victorian delicacy next to the squat presence of the fetal monitor machine with its bright green heart blips. That blithe, maidenly ignorance. The feral sounds of Christine in labor.

"That was . . . so . . . horrible."

"You're doing wonderfully, honey."

"At least I didn't scream."

Next door, a woman had been screaming on and off for the past two hours. "No, you didn't," Nora said, wiping Christine's forehead with a damp cloth. Her hair was lank with sweat. "You're not the screaming type."

"I used to be. When I was little and fell off my bike, I used to start screaming even if nothing hurt—just to get your attention."

"I never knew that."

"I was so jealous of Danny, especially when he was a baby. Everybody thought he was so cute."

"You were cute, too."

"I always wanted to be an only child."

Mother-guilt: not paying enough attention, having more than one child, cutting the pie into unequal portions, punishing unfairly, dominating, controlling—all in the name of doing one's best. There was no end to the ways in which a mother could be wrong, Nora thought. Her crimes began in the womb and lasted a lifetime.

"Oh, no . . . Here comes another one. Mom!"

"I'm right here. Hold on now. A big breath now."

Holding onto Marty while she was in labor with Christine. Not his hand. Not when the contractions got so bad that she didn't think she could bear it. But holding onto him with her arms, gripping him around the waist, her face pressed into the sweat-shirt he was wearing, the fabric absorbing her tears.

Going to the bathroom while Christine was being examined by Dr. Roya and finding that the maternity ward was so full that there was now a bed in the hallway, holding a girl no older than Christine, who was moaning and crying. The husband, equally young and spotted with acne, was leaning over her, his back in a seemingly solicitous curve, but as Nora passed by she heard him saying in a low, intense voice, "Shut up. Shut up! Goddamn it. Would you please shut up?"

Watching Dr. Roya strip off the examination glove and seeing not her hand emerging from the thin latex, but that of the resident sixteen years ago. Lying flat on a hard bed, the back of her knees chilled by the cold metal of the stirrups.

"A breech presentation," the resident said to a nurse.

"What?" Nora said.

He turned to her. "Your baby's coming feet first."

"Oh, I don't think so," she said emphatically. "The baby was head down when I saw Dr. Sullivan last week."

"I'm sorry, lady, but I can feel a foot."

That foot. Danny would arrive head first, almost leaping out of her, but Christine took her sweet time. Her foot appeared first, the five toes peeking out of Nora and then retreating, peeking and retreating over and over again. Nora watched them in a mirror that a nurse held between her parted legs. Tiny, white, round toes that looked like pearls.

"Why did you have Danny anyway?"

Dampening Christine's dry lips with a cloth wrapped around an ice cube. "Because Daddy and I wanted another baby."

"Why would anyone want to go through this twice?"

"The pain isn't important."

Tears filling the hazel eyes. "Nobody told me it was going to be this awful."

"Women are like cats," Nora said. "They forget."

Sitting on a bench in the corridor, leaning her head tiredly against the wall, and overhearing a fragment of conversation between two young doctors who were passing by.

Doctor One: "I still tell them to wait six weeks."

Doctor Two: "Shit, they know it's the party line."

Doctor One: "Yours don't wait?"

Doctor Two: "Yours don't either. They're just too afraid to tell you."

Remembering the night Marty had persuaded her to sleep with him again, only four weeks after Christine was born. Remembering that it hadn't required much persuasion. Remembering, and feeling the ponderous weight of despair fall over her again.

Noticing that Dr. Roya, gowned and masked in pale hospital green, no longer looked like a real doctor but like an actress in a medical drama on television. Having the same sense of unreality about the delivery room with its huge, round light and gleaming apparatus. Feeling as if the volume had been turned down as the nurses bustled silently about on their rubber-soled shoes, putting paper booties on Christine's feet and draping her abdomen with cloths. Feeling the volume rising, as Christine began to pant and her own breathing rustled the mask on her nose. Matching the hoarse pants, breath by breath.

That foot . . . Straining to get it out, concentrating on it, hearing nothing, seeing nothing but those toes in the mirror. Nora missed everything else: the pediatrician who stopped in to see how close she was to delivering, the medical student who couldn't figure out how the forceps worked, the episiotomy ("I thought he'd use a scalpel," Marty would say later, "but he just picked up a pair of scissors and went snip, snip.") and the hot scent of blood that fell to a basin on the floor.

"Mom?"

"I'm right here."

"Okay," Dr. Roya said. "I can see the baby's crown now. You push when you're ready."

"Mom!"

Holding tight to Christine's hand. "Go ahead, honey. You're almost there."

The wedge that was the front of the foot finally yielding to a puckered heel which in turn yielded to a thin, bluish leg and a wrinkled knee.

"I see the scrotum," Dr. Sullivan said.

Nora felt Marty's hands tighten on her shoulders.

Then Dr. Sullivan said, "I take that back. That's not the scrotum. It's the other foot."

"Now. Push. That's right. Thatsa girl."

"It hurts!"

"That means it's almost over. Take a big breath now and push. Push, Christine. . . . Push . . . *harder.*"

"M-o-m!"

Both legs were out, the hips following quickly, the body of an infant girl slipping swiftly out of her. A thin, scrawny girl with dark strands of hair wet on her scalp, with blue eyes wide open, with her mouth already emitting a thin, wailing cry.

"A boy!" Dr. Roya exclaimed, holding him up by the heels, up-side-down, for all of them to see. A blood-streaked body, plum-colored hands tightened into fists, eyes squeezed shut. "And isn't he just *lovely.*"

Nora stood in the doorway to the den. Marty was sitting on the couch with newspapers strewn around him, but he wasn't read-ing. Instead, he was staring out the window into the darkness of the night. Although it was close to two o'clock in the morning, he was still dressed, wearing jeans and a sweater. Nora had gone to bed earlier, fallen asleep and then woken up. She'd tried to read, clicking on the light and picking up *Kristin Lavransdatter,* which she had put aside months ago. Kristin now had seven difficult sons, her knight husband had died, the black plague had struck. Nora usually found some consolation in knowing that the hardship and miseries of the fourteenth century were worse than anything she'd been forced to bear in the twentieth, but lately the solace was wearing thin. She hadn't been able to concentrate and had finally gotten out of bed, pulling on her bathrobe and think-ing that she'd make herself a piece of toast.

"Marty?" she said.

"What?"

"It's late."

"I'm not tired."

Nora walked into the room and sat down in the armchair, tucking her feet beneath her. "It's cold in here." She wrapped her bathrobe around her. "Are you going to see the baby tomorrow?"

"I thought I'd take Danny."

"He's beautiful."

"So you said."

"Marty . . ."

"Don't start," he said impatiently.

"Start what?"

"The usual. The fixing and arranging. The trying to put everyone into their proper places."

Nora felt a familiar spurt of anger. "I'm not."

"Oh, yes you are. The baby's birth was a big sentimental moment, and you want to cash in on it."

"It was so amazing," Nora said. "Watching that baby being born. I can't get it out of my mind."

"You're hoping I'll go soft and cave in."

There was enough truth in his statement to make it sting. Nora had had pleasant visions of Marty holding Christine's baby in his arms, staring in wonder down at its face, and confessing that he was won over. Well, so much for wishful thinking. She tucked her hands inside the sleeves of her bathrobe and clasped her forearms. "Christine needs you," she said.

"She and I are going to have to make our peace. In our own way—not yours."

"Oh, Marty," she said wearily. "Is there *going* to be a peace?"

The lamplight formed a pool of illumination in Marty's lap, where his hands restlessly moved, one against the other. "I don't know," he said.

"I can't believe that this is happening to us," she said.

"We're just going through a bad time."

"It's worse than that," Nora said vehemently. "A lot worse."

"Okay. I admit I was surprised about Danny. We're just going to have to spend more time with him." Marty corrected himself. *"I'm* going to have to spend more time with him. I've been overdoing it at work. I admit it. But Bariskofsky—"

Another spurt of anger. "I don't want to hear about god-damned Bariskofsky," Nora said.

"Christ, Nora, what do you want me to do? Divide myself in half? Leave the office and forget it exists?"

"There's a lot more at stake here! Our family is falling apart!"

"Stop being melodramatic."

"I'm not. Can't you see what you're doing?"

"Oh, now it's *my* fault."

Nora felt her jaw tighten. "A hell of a lot of it is."

"Now, wait a minute. *I* didn't get pregnant, *I* didn't decide not to have an abortion, *I* didn't decide to keep the baby."

"Your pride is tearing us apart."

"It's not just pride."

"Well, what else is it? Love? Concern? Caring?"

"It's the principle that—"

Fury filled her. *"The principle?* This is our daughter and grandson! Who gives a fuck about *principles?"*

Marty's voice rose in pitch to match hers. "I do, damn it!" He paused. "I didn't become a parent to bring up children who'd have no standards, no way of judging what's right and what's wrong. You might not care, but I do. And you think it's been easy? Do you think I like it? I haven't slept one night through for a month."

"Then why not give in, Marty? Why not just . . . *give . . . in?"*

"That's your solution. Not mine."

Nora felt the fury draining out of her. What was the point of it all, anyway? What was the point in getting upset? They talked and talked and talked, the emotions flaring and sputtering like the flames of old candles, and they got nowhere. "God," she said, "there's no end to this, is there?"

Marty said nothing, and Nora saw her marriage stretching out before her, a bleak moonscape: miles of grayness, broken rock and dust. She saw herself running, stumbling, tripping, falling. She saw herself gashing her hands on the sharp edges and bruising her knees on the stone. When she looked ahead, she saw that there was no horizon to this wasteland. It would have an infinite capacity to inflict pain.

During the past months, Nora had hit emotional lows, but nothing matched her sense now that she'd come to the very end of her capacity to endure. There was nowhere else she could go; nowhere else she could turn.

"You want to know how bad things are?" she said in despair.

He gave her a wary, tired look. "Not really."

"I . . ." Without being conscious of what she was doing, Nora curled up in a defensive position, bringing her knees up to her chin, tucking her nightgown under her toes, and wrapping her arms tight around her legs. "I . . . slept . . . with someone else."

In all the scenarios of confession that Nora had enacted in her head an explosion had occurred, the stone thrown through glass. Marty would stand up, yell, smash one hand violently against the other, walk out, turn on her, berate her, hate her—on and on and on. She had never expected this silence. He didn't say anything; he didn't move. When Nora finally got the courage to look at him, he was sitting in exactly the same position, his eyes on the window, his expression reflective. The only difference was his hands. They were no longer moving, but lay very still in his lap, one curled in the other.

"I didn't mean to. . . . I didn't even want to . . . but I couldn't help it. I was so unhappy that . . ." Nora felt herself running on like a wound-up toy, but she couldn't stop. "I didn't do it because I wanted someone else. That wasn't why. I did it because . . . because I was so lonely."

The hands in his lap now rose upward toward his face. They hovered before his eyes, trembling slightly, and then the tips of the fingers met. Very slowly, the hands sank and moved under his chin, the fingers pressing upward against the skin. Very slowly, the professorial wrinkle appeared in his flesh.

Nora hugged her legs tighter. "Aren't you going to say anything?"

"Who was it?"

"No one special. Just one of the toy salesmen."

"When?"

"A few weeks ago."

Another silence.

"I'm not telling you this because I need a place to dump my guilt," Nora said quickly. "That's not why. I wanted you to see how bad things were . . . how desperate I was feeling."

The third silence. It stretched and stretched, like a rubber band being pulled in opposite directions. It grew taut and narrow, thinning, attenuating, until it was nothing but a thread between them. Nora felt its fragility, the sudden brittleness, the imminent danger of snapping.

"Please. Marty . . ."

"I went to bed with another woman once."

The fourth silence had a different quality. It was empty, dark, void (was this the end of the spiral?) and airless. The sound that forced its way out of Nora's mouth was not a cough exactly, but a choking, strangling sound.

"That February after you first opened the store," he said. "When business was so bad, and you were working so hard. I had that trip to Boston for a conference and met a woman there."

That February: Nora remembered a gray, worrying time, hours of lost sleep, long intense conversations with Joanne, longer and even more intense conversations with their accountant. What she remembered of Marty was a shadowy figure in the background, hovering at the edge of her peripheral vision.

"I don't mean you have to worry about it now," Marty went on. "I've never seen her again. It was just a one-night thing."

The shock in her throat was clearing. "Well," Nora said shakily, "I expected all kinds of reactions from you. But not this. I have to admit it—not this."

Marty didn't say anything. Nor did he look at her. His fingers just pressed deeper into his chin.

"I never guessed. . . . It never even crossed my mind."

"You were pretty taken up with the store."

Nora thought of the enormous load of guilt she'd carried ever since sleeping with Bernie. "Five years," she said. "Didn't you want to tell me? How could you bear it?"

"I felt bad, but I was . . . scared you'd leave me." He took off his glasses and rubbed his eyes as he turned toward her. Without them, without the protective barrier they provided, his face looked softer and less defined. Nora saw that the skin had crumpled around his eyes, that tears glistened in his lashes. "Christ, Nora, I can't stand this. I'm crying again."

She would never remember getting up out of her chair and

crossing over to him. What she would remember was holding him as tightly as she could, gripping onto the coarse weave of his sweater, and feeling his arms around her. His face was pressed against her shoulder, and the dampness of his tears spread through the fabric of her bathrobe until Nora felt it on her skin.

"Oh, Marty," she said, her own voice cracking. "I don't believe this. It's like a nightmare."

He lifted his head. Wetness gleamed in the folds beneath his eyes and his lids were red. "You know what I thought when you told me you'd slept with someone else? That you were going to leave me. And then when I realized you weren't, I thought, shit, she'd not even scared that I might leave her."

"I was. Oh, Marty, you'll never know how much."

His lips trembled. "Yeah, but you told me."

"I had to. I thought our marriage was dying."

"Christ, Nora. What have we done?"

Nora sat in the chair by Christine's hospital bed with the baby in her lap. He seemed to be a good baby. He slept most of the time, wrapped up papoose-style in the blanket, only his face visible. His skin was fine and mottled, and he had a faint red streak between his feathery eyebrows. ("A flame mark," the pediatrician had said. "It'll fade.") His hair was almost black, and where it was longer in the back it showed promise of curling. Nora searched for a resemblance to her family in his small, round face, but there was nothing in it yet that spoke of the Beemes. He had that anonymous beauty of the healthy newborn, the faint tracery of veins beneath the skin, the wide bridge of nose, the tiny, soft mouth. As she watched him a grimace rippled over his features, and she felt his legs push against the blanket.

"I think he's having a dream," she said. "I wonder what he's dreaming about."

Christine was sitting up, leaning against several pillows. Although she'd washed her hair earlier and put on her prettiest nightgown, the one that had blue ribbons threaded through lace on the neckline, she looked tired, a soft mauve color staining the skin under her eyes. Nor did she speak very much. Since Nora's arrival, she had sat there and played with the ribbons, wrapping them around her fingers, unwrapping them and then starting all over again.

"What does Daddy think of him?" she said.

Nora gave her a look of surprise. "Didn't he say when he was here?"

Christine shook her head. "He didn't even want to hold him. Danny did—he thought the baby was neat."

Nora thought of Marty, whom she'd left that morning, still sleeping, exhaustion creasing his face. For the third night in a row they'd lain naked in one another's arms, making love, and talking. The nights had grown dark and then lightened around them, the digital clock on the night table clicking away the minutes and the hours, a steady counterpoint to the rise and fall of their voices.

Marty had talked of work.

"It's real stressful. It hasn't helped."

"Could you ease up a bit? Refuse to take on anymore?"

"You know what I'm beginning to understand—that I let it take over. You see, I could throw myself in it. I could drown in it. That helped me avoid everything that was happening at home."

They talked about love.

"I don't want to be married to anyone else," Marty said. "Maybe that's what love is—that knowing."

"I don't worry about definitions."

"I like things cut and dried."

"I know. That's the way you are."

"Is that bad?"

"Well, life isn't cut and dried."

"Why do you find that easier than I do?"

"I don't," Nora said. "I keep trying to fix things. I keep trying to make things whole. I guess that's my version of love."

And they spoke of danger and edges, of how close they had come to the precipice, as if their marriage was not round like the earth, but a flat surface that they could fall from into the emptiness of space.

"The idea of divorce is so scary," Nora said. "It would be like someone cutting me in half. How do people do it?"

"They have to hate each other or just not care anymore."

"I thought I'd stopped caring, but I hadn't. Not really."

"You want to hear something ridiculous, Nora? I'm afraid to get out of this bed. It's the only place I feel safe at the moment."

Nora had known just what Marty meant, but Danny was there and they couldn't stay permanently in the bedroom. During the day, they got on with the mundane business of life. Marty, being home for the week, made meals and did laundries. Nora went to the store and visited the hospital. They took Danny to a movie, read the newspaper, and bought Marty a new winter coat during the sales. But when both of them were in the house they couldn't stay apart for long, and sought each other out, touching when they met. Only hands if Danny was there, but fleeting, reassuring touches.

"It's going to take a while for Daddy to get used to him," Nora said. "He's trying though. Believe me, he's trying."

Christine wound a ribbon around her pinky. "But he still won't let me live at home?"

"No, only for the first three months." This was the compromise she and Marty had agreed to: that Christine could live with them for those first difficult weeks, when the baby's eating and sleeping patterns would be erratic and Christine would most need their support. Nora couldn't help nursing a secret hope that Marty would change his mind when that time was over, but she wasn't counting on it.

The ribbon was rapidly unwound from Christine's pinky and then spiraled on her ring finger. "I've been doing a lot of thinking."

In his sleep, the baby made sucking motions with his mouth. Of course, Nora thought, he dreams of the pleasures of eating. What else would a baby dream about but a hard nipple and warm milk?

"Thinking about what?" she said.

"About giving him up for adoption."

Startled, Nora looked up at Christine. The ribbon was wildly flying around her fingers. "Because of Daddy?" she said.

"No, not just because of him. For lots of reasons. You know, Mom, I thought I was going to have a girl. Someone just like me. I'd know how to take care of a girl. I'd know the right things to do with her. I . . . I don't know how to bring up a boy. And he wouldn't have a father. Fathers are important."

"Fathers are important to girls, too."

"I know that, but a boy . . . Well, it seems different. And then, when I think about living by myself, I get really scared. I know I thought Elly had a wonderful life, but I never told you how ugly her apartment is or that she has cockroaches. When I was babysitting Melissa, I went into the kitchen late one night and switched on the light. There were hundreds of them. Mom, it was awful. They were running all over the place." Christine gave a small shudder and took a deep, shaky breath. "And then Dr. Roya came in this morning and mentioned this couple that can't have any children of their own. He's an engineer like Daddy, and she's a nurse. If they had a baby, she would quit working for a while. They sound nice, don't they?"

Nora didn't say anything, but looked down at the baby in her arms. He had no name, and she'd wondered why it was taking Christine so long to choose one.

"I think I had sort of a fantasy," Christine went on, "about what it was going to be like. Having a baby and taking care of her and dressing her. And she would love me, because I loved her. And everything would be really wonderful. I really liked that fantasy. It made me happy."

Nora understood perfectly. She was just beginning to comprehend how much of her own life had been fueled by fantasies. Not just sexual fantasies, that was only a small part of it. Family fantasies. Marital fantasies. Dreams of the way things should be and the way people should act. Socially acceptable fantasies which she'd swallowed intact and projected onto her family. She'd dreamed of the Beemes as a happy, loving and devoted foursome —which, when Christine had gotten pregnant, she'd extended to a fivesome.

Then there was the fantasy of Marty and Nora. That was even more fantastical than her family dream. That fantasy was about the ideal husband. It allowed Nora to believe that Marty would always protect her, that he loved her too much to hurt her, that he was the infallible spouse who would never stray. She knew where this fantasy came from. Leo had never been father enough; Marty was the father she'd chosen. He was also a lover and a friend and the father of her children, but she'd clung to a childish belief in his ever-present, all-forgiving, never-hurting paternal affection. Of course, the trouble with such a belief was that she'd never been able to acknowledge that Marty might have an emotional life of his own, separate from hers, with different goals, with secrets she might never know.

What had Joanne said? *Maybe you're giving birth to something.* Nora studied her grandson's face. As part of growing up, a baby had to learn that its mother was not an extension of itself. Well, that's what she'd had to learn, too, wasn't it? That her family was not just an extension of her wishes and desires, but that each member was a distinct individual. Was that what she'd given birth to: a finally grown-up Nora? Or did it never end, the baby within so powerful that it never easily relinquished its dreams and fantasies?

"I decided last night, and I cried and cried," Christine said, her face twisting. "I promised myself I wouldn't cry today."

Nora should have been happy. She should have been jumping for joy. Christine had just given her what she'd wanted most: the possibility of having everything go back to the way it was. Well, not precisely the way it was, she acknowledged. Danny required a lot of guidance. Christine would never be the carefree teenager she'd been. Her marriage would never be the same. But the externals would be the same: the foursome, the house at 172 Cedarview Crescent, the two cars in the garage and the bicycle lying in the driveway. The Beeme family would be close, wouldn't it? To what it had once been?

So why wasn't she happier?

The baby opened his eyes and stared quizzically at Nora. The irises were a deep blue, the color of Danny's. She thought of the times she'd tried to convince Christine to put the baby up for adoption. She'd acknowledged a possible attachment between mother and baby, but only in an abstract, intellectual way. She'd talked of "giving the baby away," throwing the phrase around with a careless abandon. And she'd not once given thought to a connection between grandmother and baby. That had never crossed her mind. All she had contemplated was the overwhelming sense of relief she would feel if Christine's baby could be handed over to someone else and disappear forever from their lives.

It had never occurred to her that a part of herself would also disappear—that her grandchild would be somebody's baby, cradled in arms other than hers. It had never occurred to her that this knowledge would be so painful.

"You're sure about this? You're not just doing it because of Daddy and me?" she said. "I don't want you to blame us later."

"No, Mom. I'm doing it for me. I want to have my old life back. . . . My friends and school and . . . and I'm doing it for him. He needs real parents." Christine's features finally crumpled, and she buried her face in her hands.

Slowly, Nora put the baby back in his cot. His eyes, slightly crossed, watched her and then closed in sleep. She lightly touched the flame streak on his forehead. *Good-bye, baby.* Then she turned her back to him and sat down on the edge of the bed. She took Christine in her arms and held her tightly, feeling the new thinness of her, the delicate ridge of her spine, the softness of her hair.

"Cry," Nora said. "It's okay to cry."

About the Author

Claire Harrison has written stories, articles, and book reviews for such publications as the *Washington Post*, the *Detroit Free Press*, the *Toronto Globe and Mail*, and *Ladies' Home Journal*. She is the author of fifteen books of romantic fiction and has written an award-winning radio documentary on the romance novel for the Canadian Broadcasting Corporation. Raised on Long Island in New York, she now lives with her husband and two daughters in Ottawa, Ontario.